The Dawn at Dusk

The Dawn at Dusk

Sandeep Nayyar

Ocean Paperbacks
A Division of Ocean Books Pvt. Ltd.
ISO 9001:2008 Publishers

Published by
Ocean Paperbacks
A Division of Ocean Books Pvt. Ltd.
4/19 Asaf Ali Road,
New Delhi-110 002 (INDIA)
e-mail: info@oceanbooks.in

ISBN 978-81-8430-402-2
THE DAWN AT DUSK
by Sandeep Nayyar

Edition
First, 2016

Price
₹ 200.00 (Rupees Two Hundred only)

Printed at
R-Tech Offset Printers, Delhi

Dedicated to
My Mother and the Motherland

Acknowledgements

'The Dawn at Dusk' is not written by me alone. It is a collective work. And in this collective work have contributed many experts and talents, from my father to my eleven year old son, from my local friends in the UK to the friends living across the seas in India and in the US.

The dear friend Harshit Bhardwaj, almost worked as co-author and author assistant. Harshit's ample assistance in the story narration and ornamentation of the style and language is paramount in this endeavour. Without Harshit, the book would have been a distant dream.

Dear friends Imran Bootwala and Minnie Singh also played vital roles in polishing the narration and embellishing the style further. And finally my father Mr. Ramesh Nayyar brought together all individual efforts and gave the book its final shape.

I am grateful to my friend and a former colleague Steve Spruce who took constant interest in this endeavour and always nourished my day-dream of becoming rich and famous through writing.

I cannot thank enough my publisher for showing confidence in a first time author like me and my work.

I am also grateful to my friends Vandana Vishwas and Vishwas Thoke for not only composing, singing and producing the theme song of the book but also for promoting the book through their musical performances and media interactions.

And above all, to my dear sons Udayan and Utkarsh and my beloved wife Yamini whose love and inspirations have been constant source of the drive and energy I needed to write this long saga of magical realism.

Chapter 1

Frustrated once again with another failure in her spiritual pursuit, Shatvari slowly opened her heavy eyes. Coming out of her trance, she instantly locked stares with a jackal. Its eyes were two hot embers like the burning pyres around in the crematorium. Shatvari looked deep into those amber eyes as if seeing there a reflection of the fury that was smoldering inside her. Suddenly, her attention turned to the sound of footsteps beside her. A group of people was going back from the crematorium, obviously after performing last rites of someone. Seeing the people approaching nearer, the jackal jumped to run away. Shatvari remained disinterested.

Shatvari was middle-aged woman of average height and build. Her sun burnt fair complexion, bright bluish eyes and sharp features were indicative of her high caste origin. Extra layers of fat were deposited around her waist. A single garb made of lion-skin covered her breasts and lower body. Tangled grey black hair were tied in a lock at the top of her head as if a constant reminder to avenge the cruelty and inhuman injustice done to her. She had anointed her body with ash from the burnt pyres and a rosary of Rudraksha beads dangled freely on her neck.

A nimble feet young man of about 20 walked up to her. The young man of average build and height had a simple personality. He could have looked attractive had he been well fed. An animal skin was draped around his thin waist. He had tied a worn-out piece of cloth to cover the lower part of his body.

Shatvari looked sharply at the young man. *'Seems like another futile day'*, she thought observing the disappointment written large over the face of her son.

However, she asked him while fiercely probing his eyes, "Did you find out anything about the 'Yantra' (Magic wand)?"

He simply nodded in negative and kept looking down with his bowed head.

"Do you have the faintest of idea how important it is for us to find that Yantra?" Her voice turned a bit harsh.

"Yes, I know that Yantra can bestow upon you extraordinary powers", replied the young man mustering all the courage to raise his head to face her.

"The word extraordinary pales in comparison to what that Yantra can enable me to attain. Its miraculous powers are beyond human perception. It can empower us to avenge all the miseries heaped upon us by the wily coterie of priests, men of riches and the ruling class."

The young man remained silent, but a little agitated. He clenched his fists to express his resolve to fight the wily coterie, which according to his mother, had driven them to this sordid state.

Shatvari closed her eyes and tried to calm down. She remained silent for a few minutes. After regaining her composure, she looked at him affectionately. She spotted a small bundle of cloth tightly kept by him under his left armpit.

"What are you holding there?" asked Shatvari looking at the bundle.

The young man showed her a neatly folded sheet of raw silk and a blanket.

"Where from have you brought them?" She asked again, sternly.

"These were removed from the dead body before putting that on the pyre." The youth meekly replied.

Her eyes moistened and asked softly, "No, my son! You should not have even touched these clothes."

"But, Maa! All Chandaals and Doms do it."

She opened her lips to say something but preferred to keep silent, as she heard footsteps of someone approaching them.

An old man with snow white hair appeared before them. His face was glowing with a saintly aura. Shatvari was mesmerized by the piousness of the old man. She took him to be tranquility personified. She bowed to touch his feet. In a soft voice, the old man stopped her from doing so. He sweetly said, "My child, we don't allow our daughters to touch our feet. Rather we bow before them in reverence. You too must have heard the ancient saying that gods dwell there, where the women are worshipped". He stopped for a minute and then said, "Forgive me for overhearing your conversation. I didn't do it intently. I was just passing through this area, when you were talking to your son. A small row of wild bushes were between you and me. Probably because of them you could not notice my presence."

Shatvari folded her hands to greet the saintly old man. Meekly, she requested, "Being a holy saint you must have been gifted with the heavenly bliss to see through the past, the present and perceive the future. Kindly, tell me when and from where I could get the magic wand, for which I have been observing very difficult Tantrik rituals and worshipping goddess Kaali, the mightiest destroyer of the demons".

"I can realise the agony suffered by you at the hands of the inhumanly cruel ruling class. I can also see the turmoil boiling in your heart and mind. But I am not a soothsayer, so can't tell the destiny of you and your son. But can assure you that you are not alone in this war between the oppressed and the oppressors. In fact, it has already started. Backward classes have joined hands under the leadership of an intelligent young Nishaad king to fight the tyrannical emperor, who has usurped large territories of small rulers. Right now I can't tell the eventuality of the Great War. A disastrous storm is gathering all around. Be brave my child to face that. None, but you alone, can chisel out your destiny. In fact, every person makes or unmakes his or her destiny," told the saintly old man.

Turning towards the young man, he said, "Listen! Neither you, nor your parents are Chandaals. How your most beautiful and gifted mother was excommunicated from the high caste by the ruthless ruling class is a long story to tell. Have patience. It would gradually unfold. Also, muster all the courage to join the war that would be long drawn. Your mother had lost the battle, that is a reality. Don't lose patience. Gird up to face and fight the war ahead."

The young man kneeled before him. Spreading his palm, he said, "I am sure you are a great sage. Kindly, tell me my future."

The old man lifted him. Putting his affectionate hand over his head, he said, "Even gods can't foretell anybody's future. You yourself write your future by your present *karma*. Whatever you sow in the wide arable land of events today, you will have to reap their harvest tomorrow. Gird up to stand firm and fight the enemies of society. My blessings will always remain with you."

After showering blessings on Shatvari and her son, the old man slowly walked towards the bushes and disappeared.

The young man felt a stream of great strength flowing from his heart and soul. Politely, but firmly, he asked his mother, "Why don't you tell me the truth about my caste? The sage has told that neither I, nor my parents are Chandaals. Then why we are doomed to live in the *shamshan* (crematorium) along with a few families of untouchable outcastes?"

Shatvari's eyes moistened. Trying to hold in her tears, she said, "My son, the sage is right that you are not born of untouchable parents. By birth I was a Brahmin. So was your father. The mighty schemers of the ruling clique excommunicated me from the upper-caste society and forced me to live here among the dead bodies. To avenge that humiliation and injustice, I have been in pursuit of the Yantra. Armed with that Yantra, I would liquidate those demons."

"Oh! my unfortunate mother, now stop worrying. The sage has already bestowed the source of strength to us. He has also told that a large number of oppressed and exploited people from the backward castes have got up in rebellion against the tyrannical Emperor and his wily coterie. Let us have patience and wait for the right time to give a deadly blow to them."

□

Chapter 2

Neel knelt down to greet and to feel the pure silken water of Narmada revered as the only virgin river in India. Using both his palms, he drew a handful of water to soothe his parched lips. In the calm water of the Narmdakund, he could clearly see a reflection of himself. An unkempt and tired looking sullen face, tresses of overgrown hair tangled loosely on the shoulders, lines of stress drawn on the forehead and estranged eyes looking blank and nervous. A spate of unfortunate events over the past year had transformed this tall and handsome twenty-one year-old youth who could mesmerise any Mekal girl with no effort, into a distrait man, unaware of the impact of the stress and anxiety having left on his attractive persona. It had been fading the gleam of his eyes, snatching the charm from his face and taking away the spring from his strides.

Bringing palms closer to his lips, he took a sip, feeling the soothing effect of the cold water in his lungs. A current of freshness ran through his body. The cold and fresh water did not just quench his thirst, but also helped to calm down his raging nerves. Getting back on his feet, he again bowed down to pay his thanks to Narmada. Looking at the serene stillness of the water, he only wished if his disturbing thoughts could be stilled even for a few moments.

Neel started walking towards the east. The picturesque valley of Amarkantak was endowed with flowering shrubs of most beautiful colours and kind. Herbs of miraculous medicinal value were blooming there in abundance. Hovering over the flowers were countless butterflies appearing as if to be treated to every nip of nectar until the last ray of the sun fades away into the dark night sky. Soaring from within the shrubs were towering Sal trees eagerly waiting to bid good night to the sun sinking into the lap of the Vindhya. Envying the tall Sal trees stood mango trees of average height unaware of the fact that their own fruits' sweetness was envy of every other being. Melodious singing of birds returning to their nests was adding new tunes to gamut of the evening.

But Neel's heart wasn't in harmony with such surreal surroundings. He restlessly glanced at the backdrop. Amarkantak was a major town of the tribal kingdom of Mekal, nearly as important as a state capital. He had spent all the 21 years of his life in these mountains and the valley. Playing in the mango orchards; learning to hunt with other boys of the Nishaad community; running around in the thick but familiar jungle valley marked the happy days of his childhood and adolescence. The flora and fauna of this valley had nourished him into a strong and shapely youth. His father was the king of this tribal kingdom of Mekal and also the chief of Nishaad tribe. After his father's untimely demise, Neel had been made to shoulder his father's responsibilities.

Walking through the valley, Neel found himself lost in the beauty of Amarkantak. On one side, Narmada moved towards the north-west caressing the bosom of the Vindhya; on the other from Sonmuda, Sone River leaped north-east to fall into the arms of Riksh Mountains; down in the far south spread as far as the horizon, the defiant dark forests of Dandkaranya were daring the champions and warriors of Aryavart to a combat. In the southeast beyond the wild valleys, the lowlands of Mekal were kissing the borders of the large and mighty kingdom of South Kosala—the birthplace of Kausalya, daughter of Emperor Bhanumant and mother of Raghukul's emperor Rama. Rama was an epitome of human dignity and a sea of compassion. One who taught the lessons of highest empathy towards one and all. He embraced Nishaads and other downtrodden communities to fight against the tyrannical rulers. His elder son Kusha had expanded the kingdom of South Kosala, and established a mighty empire. The descendants of Raja Rama and Kusha had given new dimensions to the empire's opulence and might. South Kosala's capital Shripur's splendor and glory were the envy of the several kings of the Aryavart. The same South Kosala was now under siege of Yaduvanshis. They had captured the villages of the lowland areas of the Mekal. Mekal's youth were made their captives; Mekal's maidens were their valets.

A flurry of disturbing thoughts crossed Neel's mind: *How would they were being treated there? Would they be demeaned to the level of animals? Would they be still alive?* The thought of the plight of young girls made him tremble with alarm and determination. His fists tightened, arms strained and a stream of perspiration flowed enormously.

Neel took a deep breath to regain his composure. He took off the white cloth wrapped around his neck and wiped the back of his neck and shoulders. Putting it back around his shoulders, he again drifted into the stream of his thoughts: *Has that time arrived where loss of righteousness was presaged? Are virtues really failing in Bharatvarsh? What is happening to Aryans nobility? Do Aryans care anything about the Nishaads anymore? It is thanks to the dense forests and vicious valleys of Mekal that our kingdom is not under the possession of Yaduvanshis. Would Mekal too eventually meet this fate? What's my responsibility being a king? Is it not my duty to protect my populace? Is it not my utmost responsibility to free my villages and people from the clutches of Yaduvanshis? But, are we ready to face the mighty Kosala? Do we have a trained army that can stand face-to-face with Yaduvanshis in a dire battle and defeat them?*

The sun had set. Calls of birds were nowhere to be heard. Moths and bees were making their humming dance around the flowering shrubs. The buzz of butterflies had taken a pause until the next morning. Glimmering fireflies flickered from far away. Neel decided to call it a day. His small strides moved west-way to take him back home.

Neel's house stood not far from Narmada's furrow. It was fifty yards away from the western main entrance of town. Supported by wooden pillars, the brick walls of the house met the roof made of wooden beams and bamboos. Dried twigs and reeds filled the rooftop to make it impregnable from sun and rain. A wide wooden double-door made of Sal tree stood at the entrance of the house. The door had a triangular top. Both parts of the door had fantastic fine engravings.

The night was almost over but it wasn't dawn yet. The moist breeze was cold and spread the Tuberose fragrance around. The crescent moon was waxing towards the first quarter. With drowsy eyes, guards greeted Dhananjay with a bow. Dhananjay accepted the greeting with a courteous smile and a little bow. The guards were tall and broad chested and holding big spears in their hands. Hanging from the leather belts tied over their *dhotis* were long iron swords, sheathed in carved wood. One guard immediately opened the left door of the gates to let Dhananjay in. The respect that Dhananjay got from the guards suggested that he enjoyed a high status and was pretty close to Neel.

Dhananjay went in and made his way towards a large room on the right. He tapped gently on the wooden door and waited a few moments. There was no reply from inside. He tapped again, this time a little more intensely. There was no response yet. He wondered if Neel was fast asleep. But he needed to wake him up for the worship of the Sun god. The whole town would gather for the occasion soon. He knocked again with intent. Neel opened the door rubbing his eyes.

"What is it Dhananjay that you had to wake me up so early?" asked Neel while still rubbing sleep off his eyes.

"This is what I want to know your Highness—what's troubling you so much?"

"You are one strange man, you woke me up at the break of dawn and you ask me what's the problem?" Neel got a little irritated.

"Your Highness, you obviously seem to be in some grief. Sleeping late at nights and forgetting important state business. All this generally points to a man bitten by love bug", said Dhananjay with a mischievous smile.

"Yeah, whatever you can think my friend", Neel tried to avoid his mischief.

"Really! I am sure these are sure shot symptoms of cupid's touch." Dhananjay still had the same impish smile on his face.

"There are other serious emotions than love, such as, hatred, anger and malice."

"But hatred...that can really poison the breath of the beholder, can it not?"

"Those who know how to handle poison can consume it like a potion", said Neel in a measured tone, "well, leave it and tell me what made you knock on my door at this hour?"

"Oh, so I have to remind you that today's the day for Sun worship." Dhananjay said as if he opened a secret on Neel.

"Aah right, I remember now. What a sin! Anyway you get in and sit while I quickly dress up."

Neel walked hurried to dress up. Dhananjay went in and leaned back on his couch. He looked around the large royal chamber and noticed deerskin rugs and stag's horns put on one of the walls as a prized hunter's trophy. The sight carried him to the past when he and Neel used to enjoy the stress-free days of game hunting in the Mekal's forests.

Away from this environ restless, Shatvari was resolving to calm down. She remembered how her father had trained her for practicing meditation. She closed her eyes. A light kindled in her bosom.

□

Chapter 3

"How long will you take to dress up Shatvari? Adit has been waiting for you outside", Gautami, the mother of Shatvari shouted towards the room where Shatvari was busy dressing up.

"Just the last bit of *kaajal* left to put on Ma."

Shatvari pried upon her appearance in the mirror while dabbing extra bit of kohl from under her eyes. She blinked a few times to let it set in. Newborn youth spends more attention in beholding the beauty than embellishing it further. Slight dash of kohl on two starry eyes set perfectly within the round full-moon face; bright red *bindi* sitting right in the centre of converging eyebrows; slightly moist and tender rosy lips; open dangling hair braided with fresh jasmine flowers; earrings of shining gold, and a pendant round the neck studded with rubies—she felt as if some vagrant clouds had descended upon two lakes in a valley of flowers.

Shatvari was barely of eighteen years, wheatish complexion, average height, and of slender build. Giving final touches to her make-up, she slightly adjusted the silver chain worn round her thin waist below her navel. She smiled at her beautiful self in the mirror and ran outside.

"Oh, Aditi must have been waiting for long now. We have to get going for our music lesson from Pandit Achyut Acharya. He is very punctual and expects discipline", thought Shatvari while running out to Aditi, who was waiting in a bullock cart all set to go.

"You took so long to dress up Shatvari, as if you are going to learn music from a Gandharva and not from our Acharya ji", teased Aditi.

"You never know, we might come across a Gandharva on our way", laughed Shatvari enjoying her own comment.

The bullock cart made of wood and metal was designed like a carriage. The cart had two large wooden wheels and a back seat wide enough for three people. At the front was a seat for the coachman and two more seats behind that. All the seats had cotton cushion covered with a red-coloured cloth. A roof made of dry twigs covered with a brown cloth was there to save passengers from the sun. Two white oxen tied together and restrained with a rope that went through their nostrils was in the left hand of the coachman. He had a wooden stick for a whip in his right hand.

Shatvari motioned the coachman to move as soon as she took her seat beside Aditi.

"To Pandit Achyut Acharya's house?" asked the coachman while moving on.

"Yes, he teaches us music", Shatvari replied while trying to hold her pink *dupatta* slipping off her slender shoulders. In her quest to look beautiful, she had even forgotten to cover her arms in *choli* (a sort of blouse).

"You are really fortunate that you have got Acharya ji as your teacher. There is nobody as good as him when it comes to classical music in the entire state", said the coachman whilst pulling the reins of bullocks.

"Yes, it's a matter of pride for us that we are Acharya ji's disciples. He is a good friend of my father Pandit Aditya Shastri and that's why he accepted us as his students, otherwise it's very difficult to gain his blessings," covering her arms with the *dupatta*, Shatvari adjusted her silken blouse pulling it a little down.

"Shastri ji himself has earned great respect of every villager. His mastery of Vedas and Shastras is matched by none."

Shatvari felt good to hear praise of her father. A tinge of brightness lit up her face with pride.

"Listen..." Shatvari called out but was interrupted by the coachman even before she could finish, "My name is Gunjan."

Gunjan was a dusky young boy of barely twenty years. His build was slight but muscular. A light beard on his long face looked very attractive. Shoulder-length hair were tied together behind his neck, making his high forehead look bright and lustrous. A white loincloth covered his waist and legs and one part of the cloth rested on his left shoulder. He wore a black thread with a silver coin threaded in it around his neck. His ear lobes were pierced with small silver earrings that dangled as he talked.

"Gunjan! Your name itself is so lyrical," Shatvari said and smiled. "My name is Shatvari and she is Aditi, my friend."

"Do you know any music?" Shatvari asked after a small pause.

"Our music falls into the tradition of holy Vedas. I am a Shudra from a lower caste. How will I learn music? Where from?" asked Gunjan. An element of sadness surfaced on his face.

"Music doesn't follow any tradition, if at all it's bound to the breath of every living being. Knowing Vedas can be helpful in understanding music but is not a requirement for sure. Music is also in the calls of cuckoos and in the humming of bees."

"You are right in a way. I might not know the correct notes and *ragas* but I do enjoy singing folk songs with my friends. I have learnt some music that way over the years. Also, the priest of Sheetala Mata mandir in our locality plays beautiful flute and he has taught me too to play it." Gunjan recounted his interest of music. A sweet smile had replaced the poignant look on his face.

"Very nice, then let's hear your song and see how good you are at music. Moreover, the passage will go by swiftly," said Aditi jumping into the conversation.

Gunjan was taken aback by this abrupt request from Aditi and embarrassingly said "You both are Acharya ji's students and must know the nuances of music very well. You will make fun of me."

"Don't say that, music should come from the heart and nobody should laugh upon a true heart's song", said Shatvari to encourage him.

Gunjan felt at ease by Shatvari's comment. A smile passed upon his lips feeling lighter at the intimacy shown by Shatvari.

'What's the harm in singing anyway, Shatvari might like it and get impressed,' thought Gunjan.

Gunjan struck up a tune in high note and started a folk song appropriate for the wet season. Listening to the first few notes emanating from his throat, both Shatvari and Aditi realised his superb voice quality and mastery over the musical notes. Gunjan soon got lost in the tempo and music of the song like a bee sipping nectar from a lotus filament. Shatvari tapped her feet and the tiny tinkle bells from her silver anklets added to the beat. The intoxicating moist monsoon breeze, earthen fragrance spreading out from the freshly-ploughed fields added to the melody of Gunjan's song-mesmerized Shatvari and Aditi. By the time the song concluded, they had arrived at Acharya ji's house.

"Wow! Gunjan, you sing so melodious and you have a great voice. I am sure if you learn classical music, you will become a renowned singer," Shatvari exclaimed as she seemed overjoyed, rather than surprised.

"You are joking, aren't you? Who would teach classical music to a Shudra like me!"

"Will you like to learn from me, if I were to teach you music?" asked Shatvari leaning forward and soon Gunjan was besotted by a scent of jasmine emanating from Shatvari's silken hair. Gunjan was engrossed in the sweet aroma when he was suddenly interrupted by the same voice of Shatvari. He turned around to see both Shatvari and Aditi walk towards Acharya ji's house. He couldn't help but notice Shatvari's seductive gait and lost himself in thoughts. No girl as beautiful as Shatvari had come so close to him and talked to him the way she did. An unknown incense effused from Gunjan as if flowing forth from moist soil after the first showers of monsoon.

"Is Shatvari impressed by me? Does she like me?" thought Gunjan.

Gunjan's heart fluttered with emotions. He wanted not to let the waves eroding inside him run amuck.

"Is it proper for a Shudra like me to have amorous feelings for a Brahmin girl like Shatvari? My mother who was a Brahmin herself had to break ties with her relatives for loving my father who was a

Shudra. A relationship between a Brahmin girl and a Shudra boy will never be tolerated by this society. This is the time to clip the wings of this bemused dream. Right thing would be to politely decline Shatvari's proposal."

Shatvari and Aditi entered Acharya ji's house and went straight to the study on the left. It was a three-room modest house made up of earthen bricks. Acharya ji sat there in his usual poise. Both the girls bowed and greeted their teacher. He accepted the greetings and smiled in reply. He was a medium built man in his fifties. Fair complexion and a certain aura on his face marked his personality. Long wavy hair rested peacefully on his shoulders. He was wearing a white loincloth and white body corset.

"Meet my son Damodar," Acharya ji introduced his son, who was standing on his left. Damodar looked barely of twenty-two years and a tall young man. "He has returned from Shripur today only after finishing his studies. He has been learning music since an early age and he is now no less than a master musician himself. He will assist you in learning as well."

Damodar joined his palms to greet both the girls. He looked at Shatvari's beautiful face and couldn't resist himself saying, "You are Shastri ji's daughter Shatvari, if I am not mistaken? One could tell that you would turn out to be a pretty lady when you were just a little girl."

Shatvari smirked at Damodar's comment. She wondered how a young man can start a conversation with a stranger girl in this manner. She replied, "Thank you. You really are an expert in judging young beauty. This art definitely comes from long practice."

Damodar almost blushed at Shatvari's retort.

Acharya ji was visibly unhappy at the dialogues between Damodar and Shatvari. He took charge and said, "Today we will talk about Rasas used in classical music and dance forms. Please all of you take your places."

Acharya ji took his place on a small cushion over a cotton sheet spread on the ground. Shatvari, Aditi and Damodar waited until Acharya ji was seated comfortably. They also sat down.

Shatvari realised that Damodar sat rather closely beside her. She elbowed Aditi, who was sitting on the other side, to move further so that she could move away from Damodar.

Acharya ji raised his face to grab everyone's attention. He started by saying, "Rasa, in artistic context, means quintessence—the absolute fundamental essence of an entity. Similar to essence of flowers, the essence of life is also contained in some Rasas."

"But what does that have anything to do with music?" asked Aditi.

"Well, it has direct relation with life itself and music is an important part of life. Rasa and music have a deep bond. We can say that Rasas define finer emotions of human beings. Music too does that. Music preceded the creation of Vedas and *ragas*. Music was born as soon as God thought about the creation. The world itself came forth from *naad*, a sound. The whole creation reflects the presence of music everywhere; it's in the flowing streams of rivers; it's in the wildness of storms; in the drizzling of monsoon; and the roar of pregnant clouds. Different styles of music depict different aspects of life, and also different Rasas, with which these emotions are attached. It's paramount for a musician to have the understanding of these Rasas, in order to be able to portray these emotions in the music. If music is played without the inherent understanding of these Rasas, it will be dull and lifeless. Just like a human being without emotions and sensitivity."

"Rasa can be classified in eight categories. Most vital and popularly known is Shringaar Rasa. It entails adornment, love and softer emotions. Rati, the Goddess of love, symbolises all that Shringaar Rasa means. In simpler words, Shringaar can mean enjoyment of love between couples of opposite sex in a sensual environment. This might make it sound simply erotic and confined only to sensual pleasures. That is not so. Love encompasses a lot more beyond the sexual feelings. To understand this deeply, we must know that nature is the master creation of Brahma in the dichotomy of male and female, spirit and nature, Shiva and Shakti. The present universe as we know it is a result of the spiritual play, *leela* of these opposites immersing themselves in Shringaar. Shiva is the supreme consciousness and Shakti is its driving force. When they come together, creation begins. When a man and a woman come close in love and they become one in unison, they create a cosmos within themselves akin to Shiva and Shakti. The lovemaking that brings the two together remains not simply an act of erotic nature but becomes an exercise of surrender to Brahma."

Meanwhile, Shatvari realised that Damodar had been looking at her throughout the whole lecture from Acharya ji. She could feel his eyes literally caressing her body. She adjusted her *dupatta* and moved slightly farther away from Damodar.

"But the meaning of Shringaar as we know is to embellish our appearance and beauty," asked Aditi.

"That's true. Beauty is adorable. Love and beauty have this amazing relation. Whatever that is beautiful becomes adorable. On the other hand, whatever that is dear becomes beautiful. For a mother, her son is the most beautiful creature alive. A father thinks his daughter is most pretty," replied Acharya ji.

Acharya ji suddenly realized that Damodar was paying more attention to Shatvari than the lecture. He thought it best to stop the day's session right there. Damodar must be made aware of his thoughts before the next class. He announced, "So that's it for today. How Rasas are employed in music, how they can enhance the reach and popularity of music—all this we'll discuss tomorrow."

Shatvari and Aditi got up and bowed to Acharya ji. They walked out of the house. Damodar quickly followed them to the front of the house and said, "I have brought a new horse cab from Shripur. If you don't mind, I can drop you home."

Shatvari looked at Aditi, who smiled back.

"No, thank you, we have brought our own cart today. Maybe some other day." Shatvari said with a sharpness steeped in her smile.

Damodar was a tall and attractive young man. He had an irresistible charm enough to impress any young lady.

Shatvari carefully judged Damodar's antics. She knew what he was up to. She preferred to sit on the fence to see what to make of him as the times passed.

Sitting at the back seat of Gunjan's bullock cart, Shatvari asked him, "So what have you decided, will you learn music from me?"

"You are a Brahmin girl and I am a Shudra. Will it be proper for me to learn from you? Will the society tolerate it?" replied Gunjan.

"This is the same society where Shudras like Valmiki and Vedvyas became great saints. So, don't worry about all that."

"That was long ago. Now society has changed. The caste system is much deeper. I doubt people would like it."

"Society is always changing. If it changed from that time to this, why can't we change it for the better again? Don't worry too much about all this, you just tell me if you want to learn music or not?" replied Shatvari with the tone and authority that partly came from her own judgement but also from the broad-minded teachings of her father.

"Okay, if I say I am willing, will your father be ready to let you do it?" asked Gunjan.

"My father is not a hypocrite. He is a learned man with true understanding of religious texts. Unlike other Brahmins, he does not interpret holy texts as per his convenience. I am sure of him."

"By the way, what's the harm in learning music and after all Shatvari would be my teacher. A teacher should be respected and revered. I was unnecessarily getting carried away by emotions". Gunjan thought and confirmed his willingness to Shatvari.

"Then it's final. I am now your guru and you are my disciple. Remember you have to give guru's fee sooner or later." said Shatvari.

"Yeah, and that would include touching her feet every day," teased Aditi and glanced at Shatvari and they both laughed together.

"I heard that you are going to teach Gunjan?" asked Shastri ji.

"Yes father, that's right. I hoped you have no issues with that. I believe you are not concerned that he is a male and a

Shudra?" Shatvari replied back trying to assess what her father was thinking at that moment.

"No, I am not concerned. I am happy that you are sharing your art. What I must tell you, though, is that one must judge whether the disciple is able enough to receive the gift of knowledge from an able teacher."

"Father I have heard him. His voice is melodious. He sings well. All he needs is some knowledge of classical music."

"Well, if you have judged his abilities, fine." He stopped for a pause as if looking for right words to continue.

Shatvari guessed her father's dilemma and asked, "Father you look unusually worried, what it is, please tell me?"

"No, nothing like that. I just hope you understand that a teacher-student relation is considered very holy in our tradition. It is similar to a father-daughter, or a mother-son relation. It is important that the decorum of such a relation is maintained at all times. Can you promise me that you will take care of this?"

"Do you not trust your daughter, father?"

"I trust you Shatvari that's why I am asking for the promise. No point getting a promise from a person who can't keep it."

"If it comforts your mind, I promise you that I will respect that tradition and decorum of teacher-disciple relation."

"I am sure you will my dear," replied Shastri ji and walked out of the room.

Pandit Aditya Shastri had an indomitable personality—both in his physical form and in his spiritual prowess. He was tall, fair, wide chested, and glowed with an aura of a yogi. He was a renowned expert of Vedic texts and hence the title of 'Shastri'. He had complete command over the whole canon of Hindu holy texts—both under *Shruti* and *Smriti* categories. Apart from that he was well versed with the day's religious rituals and state traditions of the present.

Although Shastri ji reflected broad mindedness in his interpretation of ancient Vedic text, on certain topics, he liked to agree with the conservatives. Caste-wise classification in the society was one such topic. He believed that this system was necessary to bestow a balance to the society. Still he was against all forms of discrimination based on the caste system. For him caste system should be based only on a man's profession and it should be confined to that. But it was a tight rope to walk. He would oppose the atrocities done in the name of caste, but he never revolted against the tradition wholeheartedly. He was well respected not only in the village but all around the state. People from all over the state would come to take advice on matters—religious, political, social, spiritual. His financial state was not sound. The major source of income was the alms and donations he received in return of performing Vedic discourses at people's houses.

He was always aware and steadfast about his reputation. He allowed Shatvari to teach Gunjan because he was liberal in his thoughts about caste system, but somewhere deep down he wasn't really sure. Shatvari's promise, however, relieved him from his worries.

□

Chapter 4

"Wake up mate. You pushed me out of bed and now snoozing away yourself." Neel said tapping lightly on Dhananjay's right shoulder. By his tone it was evident that his mood had improved.

"Excuse me, your Highness! The moments of wait are felt longer than the moments of toil", said Dhananjay waking up from his slumber.

"Yeah, you can blame me. Maybe you think I take longer than young women in dressing up. And why do you keep calling me 'your Highness', you are my childhood friend and have always been calling me Neel."

"That was a different time. Now you are our king and the chief of our tribe." Dhananjay tried to make his point clear.

"Change in rank should not change personal relations. Better you call me Neel now on." Neel insisted. But his tone lacked command.

"As you wish your Highness", Dhananjay said with a cheeky smile.

Neel glanced at him and soon a natural smile appeared upon his face.

Neel adorned special attire for this year's Sun worship festival. A white loincloth with a thin black border, sturdy pair of black shoes, deer skin cloth covering his wide chest and a sidelong white cockade turban. A white pearl and silver necklace round the neck gleamed with sunlight. Both arms had beautifully engraved silver armlets that made his biceps look robust and strong. The man who walked back home last night under the spells of gloom was nowhere to be seen now. Neel portrayed a leader with poise and command.

Both friends walked out to proceed to the festival ground. Neel himself took the reins of the horse cart waiting outside. It wasn't unusual for Mekal leaders to do their own chores wherever possible. Neel held a rein made of strong jute rope to control the lone horse pulling the cart. In his other hand, he held a leather whip to guide and control the muscular beast.

The dawn was broken. Sky mellowed with orange sun rays. Birds were starting to leave their nests to begin another bright and breezy day. Butterflies emerged out from their night shelters to hover around the fresh morning flowers. Neel and Dhananjay's carriage galloped towards the east part of the town.

The thirty feet wide main passage built of sand and stones divided the town in roughly two parts. The town of Amarkantak was not designed to be a state capital. It was almost an afterthought. No architect or Vastu expert was probably consulted. Most of the houses were modest huts at best. The bigger and brick houses were also there scattered amidst the wooden huts and cottages. The town wasn't planned to segregate people in terms of their caste, creed, or financial status.

The carriage stopped at Narmadakund ground, which was the designated venue for this year's Sun worship. Neel felt a sense of pride at seeing the enormous crowd congregated for the event. He felt satisfied to see that the Nishaad people still valued and respected such religious and cultural events. He looked around to quickly assess the arrangements made at the ground. Even though it was a religious ceremony to worship Sun God, the whole event was planned to celebrate the beauty of human life and nature as a festival. A huge idol of Sun God was placed on one side of the ground in a large carriage. A large area was cleaned and rolled out flat and painted with cow dung and yellow earth paste. It was barricaded using a rope leaving only some space for the entry. Outside this perimeter, there were some marked places to seat the special guests. The rest of the crowd stood around.

Neel and Dhananjay arrived with some other important town members. They first came and bowed to the Sun idol. Then

Neel grabbed a bow and an arrow placed at the feet of Sun idol. He placed one of the arrows on the string, flexed it backwards, pointed to the sky and let go of the arrow. It pierced up into the sky and disappeared. The ritual was to pay tribute to Sun as the source of all energy and strength to mortals on earth. As soon as the arrow was shot, the crowd burst into the sound of 'Jai Suryadev'. Everybody joined in and then saluted the Sun God once again. Neel and his accomplice took their seats. The festival was about to begin.

A group of young men and women dressed in special attires came to the ground. Some of the men carried a percussion drum called *Mardal*. Some had cymbals—a round small cymbal in each hand. The drums and cymbals started to play a rhythm and the rest of them throbbed into dancing to the beats. The folk music and dance created an amazing atmosphere. The steps of the dancers complimented the beats of the percussion. The whole crowd was engulfed by the musical melody. Neel and Dhananjay were enjoying and swaying with the folk beats.

The festival was at its peak when two armed soldiers suddenly appeared on their horses. They pierced the crowd and came straight to Neel.

"What's the urgency? Any trouble?" asked Neel standing up from his seat.

"Yes, your Highness! Our south-east camp has been attacked by an infantry from Kosala," replied a soldier nearly out of breath.

"So the evil demons have reached this far!" Neel clenched his fists and turned to face the two soldiers. "These Yaduvanshis have flayed all the rules and ethics of war. They knew we will be occupied here in the festival today, so they took the opportunity to sneak in like the cowards they are."

"Yes, my lord, we were taken by surprise. Some of our soldiers have already died and the rest are losing courage," the second soldier added.

"Don't insult the martyrs by using such expressions, my dear soldier", retorted Neel.

"My apologies, your Highness," replied the soldier keeping his head down realizing that the new ideals put forward by Neel as a forward-thinking king must be respected.

"We will give a befitting reply to this cowardly trickery of Yaduvanshis. I call upon all young men present here, who are trained in warfare, to join me to teach them a lesson."

Realizing that the festival might get disrupted by this sudden unfolding, Neel announced to the organisers to keep the festival going unhindered. Nobody needed to know what was happening out there on the periphery of their state. Neel subscribed to the idea that the warfare should be limited to the army and its soldiers and the general populace should remain unaffected by it.

Around two hundred armed men were ready to join Neel for the attack. Dhananjay was on his horseback waiting for instructions from Neel. Neel knew that their number wasn't enough to beat the Kosala army.

He thought for a moment and addressed a soldier, "We are going to support the camp that has been attacked. You go to our north-east command camp and pass my orders to move towards the south-east."

Neel kicked his horse and quickly galloped towards the battlefield, followed by two hundred brave Nishaad warriors.

Neel slowed down after a few minutes. He stalled his horse and turned around to address his cavalry.

"We will have to accept that we are not enough in numbers to face them in a man-to-man battle. We will have to plan smartly. I have an idea I just conceived. We will split in two units. One group will go ahead and reinforce our battalion fighting the Kosala army. You will join them and keep attacking the Kosalas from the north. After some time, you'll withdraw so that they will think that you are running away. They will chase you and you will draw them towards the dense forest. As you know the forests terrain would confuse the enemy then you can spread out and make their composition haphazard. The second unit headed by me will be waiting for you there and we will strike them from south taking them by surprise. With no exit option and no knowledge of the forest, they will be baffled and we can easily overcome."

Dhananjay was listening keenly to Neel's plan. As soon as Neel finished speaking, he asked, "Your Highness do you think this plan aligns with the ethics of war that we Nishaads have pledged to stand by under your leadership at all times? Is it right to attack from behind?"

"Dhananjay I can see your point. But we did not strike first. We are simply responding to their shrewdness and trickery in their own unethical way," replied Neel.

Dhananjay as well as all the soldiers present nodded in affirmation. They realized that their king was not simply an idealist talking of ethics and morals. He knew the war games and also how to use tact and plans.

As per the plan, they split into two units. Dhananjay was leading one of the units and Neel the other. All the soldiers galloped towards the battle zone. They knew the importance of reaching as soon as possible to help their dwindling battalion. Dhananjay led the unit that were to go and assist the fighting soldiers. Neel took his soldiers towards the forest and settled in camouflage waiting for the right moment.

Dhananjay's unit stormed with the passionate slogans of 'Jai Suryadev' and 'Jai Mekal'. The soldiers who faced an enormous Kosala army were losing hope with every passing minute. As soon as they noticed the rising dust and slogans coming to aid them, a newfound wave of energy infused their bodies and weapons.

Dhananjay sprang forth and struck a Kosala soldier on his right shoulder taking him by surprise. As he turned around to assess his attacker, the Mekal soldier who was fighting with him attacked him on his chest. This toppled him over his horse onto the ground. Soon as the Kosala soldier fell on the ground, a foot soldier pierced his heart with a sharp unforgiving spear. It was clear the traditional ethics of war were not being followed here.

Dhananjay rode around the battle zone with a surprising agility and purpose. Rather than meeting any Kosala soldier for a face to face duel, he sneaked around here and there and attacked them from behind or just by rushing past. Slicing one here, gashing one there, piercing a chest of a horseback soldier running towards him, darting a spear from behind, drilling daggers into foot soldiers obstructing his path. It took Kosala soldiers by surprise who were still engaged in man-to-man duels.

Soon one of the Kosala soldiers took the initiative to try and stop Dhananjay's mayhem. He challenged Dhananjay for a duel by coming right in front of him purposefully stopping him. Dhananjay took the challenge. He knew this was inevitable. He struck first blow on the left shoulder of the soldier. The blow was skillfully tackled and a counter attack off balanced Dhananjay. A few swings of swords exchanged between them. Dhananjay moved and fought like a champion warrior. Soon he deliberately took one of the blows on his left shoulder. It looked like he was slashed by his opponent's sword. Dhananjay looked back at one of his soldiers and winked. It was time to make the tactical move. Dhananjay took another body blow and made it look more severe than it actually was. He had to appear defeated and scared enough to run for his life. He quickly kicked his horse around and ran in the opposite direction. Kosala soldiers realised this. They also noticed that all the Mekal soldiers were withdrawing from the fight. An order was shouted around Kosala soldiers to chase the cowardly Nishaads running away from the battle ground.

The plan was working. Dhananjay lead the tactical withdrawal. His horse galloped on wind towards the trap that was waiting for the Kosalas in the dense and dark forests in the south. Two armies raced towards one destination. The web was already cast and spiders waiting.

□

Chapter 5

Gunjan arrived at Shatvari's house at the prescribed time. It was his first day as her student. It was a small room. Veena, Mridangam and other musical instruments sat in one corner. An idol of Goddess Saraswati was placed higher up. A fresco on the adjoining wall depicted a dance move of a Gandharv and Apsara. A mat was placed on the ground for sitting. Shatvari sat right in front of him. It was a comfortable distance. He tried not to look nervous but he found himself fiddling with the silver coin pierced in a black thread that he wore round his neck. As soon as he saw Shatvari noticing it, he abruptly stopped. She wore a sky blue silk sari. One corner end of the sari was draped casually on and over her bosom. The slender waist and navel still were clearly visible. Gunjan tried to look away and focus on the fact that he had come to learn music. He also remembered his vow not to get enamoured with his teacher.

"Gunjan I have heard your song that day. You said you also play flute. Let's hear how well you play your flute", said Shatvari.

"But I have come here to learn music, not to play."

"Sure, but I need to see how good you are with the understanding of musical notes and grasp on your breathing. I need to assess you before I can start teaching you."

"Okay if you say so, but please don't make fun of me."

"A teacher will never make fun of a student; it'll be akin to flaying her own teachings. Come on don't be ashamed or worry about anything."

Shatvari's soft words mixed with her intoxicating smile roused an ache in Gunjan's heart. But he quickly got hold of himself and recalled the fact that she was his teacher. He refocused and grabbed a bamboo flute tucked in his loin cloth. He positioned it across his lips, put his fingers on the flute holes and blew into it to play a devotional song based on a folk tune.

Shatvari noticed how his fingers and breaths were playing in tandem to produce beautiful music. She realised that he knew how to correctly access sharp and flat notes. His style of holding the instrument was proper. The combination of melody mixed with devotional tune immersed Shatvari in the moment.

As soon Gunjan stopped, Shatvari exclaimed, "Gunjan you play fantastic flute. If you pay good attention to your music, you will be a great musician one day, no doubt."

She noticed how his face erupted with astonishment. He felt at ease and now was totally comfortable with her. She added, "Okay, tell me what you would do once you are a great musician?"

"I will continue to play as I do. Sing and play to entertain myself and others."

"Why? You can become a renowned teacher of music just like Acharya ji. You can become a reputed social personality."

"Don't drive me to these dreams, which can't be fulfilled. My father saw a similar dream when being a Shudra he married a Brahmin girl. He was not accepted by the society. He and my mother had to leave the town and come to live here in the village."

"But that should make you even more resolved to do something about attaining justice that was denied to your parents. Don't you think so?"

"Who are we to make decision on right and wrong? We should leave that on the pundits of religion and ethics."

"I don't feel whatever happened with your parents was right. Acharya ji says that the whole universe was created out of love and for love. Then how can phony rules of a society put two lovers in such misery and outcast them. Do you not feel angry about this? Do you not feel angry at the injustice done to your parents and to yourself? Despite being a Brahmin woman's son, you have to drive a bullockcart to make your living?"

"I don't have any problems with the bullockcart. I feel free and happy roaming in the fresh air, singing folklore to my passengers and even my oxen, enjoying the tolling of bells as they move on, I enjoy all this, really. But I also want to learn the Shastras—all the Vedic holy texts, but being a Shudra I don't even know the language to read them."

Shatvari watched him grow more disappointed and hapless as he spoke. She witnessed a caged parrot that got so used to the captivity that even if somebody let the parrot free, it wouldn't fly away. Freedom ceased to exist for Gunjan. This perturbed Shatvari.

"Why doesn't our society allow Shudras to study Holy Scriptures, father?" Shatvari asked.

"Who gave you the reason to believe that?"

"Nobody! But why is it that only Brahmins get to study the texts?"

"Simply because that's the tradition. To study and to teach holy books is Brahmin's duty."

"What if a Shudra wants to study them?"

"If he is capable and willing, yes, why not!" responded Shastri ji to the volley of questions from his daughter. He knew where this conversation was headed and this worried him.

"Who decides the ability of a Shudra for studying holy texts?"

"A guru or an acharya, most of the times. But why all these concerns, my child?"

"If Gunjan is capable and willing, will you be ready to give him the education of Vedic texts?" Shatvari quashed all the arising concerns in her father's head regarding Gunjan's name.

"Can I ask why have you become so interested in Gunjan lately?"

"I am not interested, just sympathetic. I totally believe that it's not right to keep him away from the texts and learning he deserves. He was born of a Brahmin mother from a reputed family. He has to work and live like a Shudra, just like his father."

"No work is small. Each of us has a place in society. A cartman is needed by a society as much as a learned scholar. If he is content doing what he does, why should you be worried?"

"It's not about what he does to earn a living. It's about his feelings and ambitions. If he yearns to study and be learned like a Brahmin boy, why can't he be allowed to do that? You yourself say that will is a form of energy, hence the term willpower. So it's clear that if you kill a man's will and desires, you kill the man."

"Yes, you are right and I agree with you. But we have infinite desires and wishes. It's our duty to restrain the ones that aren't practical."

"You mean to say that it's not practical thinking for a Shudra to fancy thought of becoming a Vedic scholar. You think it's a wild whim?"

"Not entirely, it will purely depend upon his abilities and skills. On the other hand, if all Shudras harnessed the desires of doing a Brahmin's work, who will do the job assigned to them. Our social system will simply collapse."

"I am not talking about all Shudras. I am only concerned about Gunjan. Will you be willing to assess his ability? Will you impart the knowledge he seeks if he qualifies to be your student?"

"I will have to think over on this." Shastri ji knew it wasn't an easy decision.

Shastri ji often pondered over the social problems of his times. He was a strong believer that religion and occupation should be an individual choice. There were many examples in Vedic tradition where the great sages belonged to non-Brahmin and at times lower castes. Valmiki, Vedavyas, and Vishvamitra became one of the greatest sages not because of their lineage but their ability and wisdom. The caste system had its own challenges. Some crony Brahmin priests commanded favours from the state and they flexed their influence over the lower castes. Plenty of discriminatory offences were on a rise. Though despite all this, the system was working and still in place. There had been no imminent threats of revolutions from the suppressed classes.

But that didn't mean there would be no threat in future. No way to guess if the society was actually running smoothly or sitting on a dormant volcano filled with inequity, discrimination, and anger and suppressed fury.

He forced his mind to think over why Gunjan can't access the Vedic texts being a Shudra? Traditionally, only Brahmins and people from royal lineage could study the scriptures. Tradition had also proved that it could be modified and changed keeping with the times. Shudras also worship the same gods. They build temples and they appoint priests adept at religious rituals. So why couldn't Gunjan be educated?

Shastri ji felt at ease at his newfound conclusion. He made up his mind to assess Gunjan for his abilities to be his student.

Shastri ji scanned Gunjan's face who sat in front of him. Shastri ji wasn't prepared to be lenient with Gunjan.

"Shatvari told me about your interest in Vedas and Vedic scriptures. Is that correct?"

"Yes, that's right I told her so."

"Why will that be? Why do you want to study the holy texts?"

Gunjan felt the razor sharp attention of Shastri ji's eyes on his face. He replied, "Because I want to understand life."

"Life...it's inside of you. Why do you wish to seek it in scriptures?" Shastri ji's forehead suddenly became a holy ground of many furrows as he continued to probe Gunjan.

"My life is only finite. Its experiences are limited. I want to study the experiences of the great saints and sages who understood life more than me through years of spiritual pursuits and devotion."

Shastri ji looked at ease by Gujnaj's increasingly evident self-confidence. It was clear that his personality didn't scare Gunjan. He asked, "How would you know if their experiences are relevant for you or not? If they are true or fake, if they'll be of any use to you at all?"

"That's why I am seeking a teacher. Only a guru can enlighten me."

Shastri ji's forehead furrows eased and a smile descended upon his lips. He sat observing Gunjan for a few moments to make sure his replies were genuine and if he actually felt that way. He finally spoke, "Gunjan, I am convinced that you are fit to be my student and study the holy texts of our civilisation."

Gunjan almost jumped with happiness. He got up and bowed down to touch Shastri ji's feet. Shastri ji touched his head and blessed him by saying, "We will start from tomorrow morning. Come before sunrise in *Brahma-muhurta*. I expect my students to be punctual."

Worried from not finding Gunjan's cart outside Acharya ji's house, Shatvari looked around confused. She felt a bit puzzled but realised there must be something with Gunjan that stopped him coming. Maybe the oxen got sick or something. They never get to rest. Yoked in carts, oil mills, or ploughing in the fields. We exploit these animals so much and on the other hand they were also worshipped in temples.

"Seems like your cart man is nowhere in sight today, so would you give me the pleasure of dropping you home Shatvari? I also want to seek Shastri ji's blessings." Shatvari found Damodar standing at the door looking at her.

"Thanks, but I am sure Gunjan is on his way here," replied Shatvari and turned back towards the road.

Damodar was adamant, he added, "Why not just try my carriage today. It goes like wind, by the time your Gunjan will come here, you'll be home."

"I am sure your carriage is fast and comfortable. It looks real nice. But I am sure he is coming here and he'll be disappointed not to find us here."

"Aah, so you are concerned about the feelings of that cartman, but have no idea that your friend might feel worse." Damodar stepped back, sighed, and looked disappointed.

Shatvari noticed Damodar's body language. She looked straight into his eyes and said, "Are we friends already you think? I think you are getting too excited."

Shatvari took pleasure in how Damodar blushed and looked down to hide it? He seemed to gain more courage from it and spoke again, "That's what I am saying, I'll drop you to your house and we'll get chance to speak and be friends."

"But as you said your carriage goes like wind, we'll hardly have time to know each other. Your habit of rushing things may get you in trouble, again."

Damodar knew what she meant. He kept quiet.

Soon a slow moving cart came in sight. It was Gunjan.

Gunjan was soaked in perspiration. "Please accept my apologies for being late. One of the wheels got stuck in mud. As you know it is rainy season and it was hard to get around all the muddy roads."

Shatvari quickly glanced at Damodar and spoke with a playful tone, "It's okay Gunjan it's only a modest bullockcart and not a bullet carriage that goes like wind."

Damodar knew what was happening. He noticed Shatvari quickly jumping to be seated in the cart. She looked back at him one final time. She had one corner of her lower lip pursed between her teeth. Damodar wasn't sure what to make of the entire conversation. On one hand, he was glad of the playful sarcasm that was exchanged between the two. But he was also worried if Shatvari took him to be a vagrant flirt who tried his hand at every passing beautiful girl. He knew he always liked her from childhood. As she had been younger than him, there never was a chance to be friends. Now they were both adults and can be friends and lot more. He was only a few years older than her.

"So how's your study going on Gunjan?" Shatvari asked as soon as the cart moved.

"Very good. Shastri ji has been telling me so many new things which I never knew about," replied Gunjan while tending the oxen.

"Really! What kind of new things? Let me too hear them."

"I am sure you already know this. Shastri ji told me that the whole universe is comprised of Brahma. Every living or non-living thing comes from the same source. Our soul is just a fragment of the divine universal soul. So when the source is the same, we all are same. There is no inequality."

"Yes, very true, even Acharya ji says something similar. He says that the universe is the divine play of Shiva and Shakti. So, yes, as you say, we are all equals, as if coming from same parents."

"If we are actually same and have a same divine source, why are we divided in the social system of caste and creed? Why a Brahmin doesn't willfully embraces a Shudra in our society? Why the society doesn't approve relationship between a Shudra and a Brahmin. You are right when you say that the society stands opposite to what religion says."

"Gunjan the problem is not in the entire society. People interpret religion and traditions as per their understanding and convenience. Not everyone thinks like Acharya ji or my father."

Shatvari felt that this topic is again prodding Gunjan's soft spot. She tried to change the topic. She asked, "Okay, tell me what you would do if you fell in love with a Brahmin girl?"

Gunjan was visibly blushing. He looked away and replied, "I will try not to let this happen."

"You don't do love, my dear, you fall in love. It's not in your hands." Shatvari was enjoying this now.

Gunjan wasn't sure what Shatvari was pointing at. Could she feel the way his heart fluttered at her sight? Was she hinting at something she couldn't utter in words? Gunjan regrouped his thoughts and replied confidently, "Yes, I know love can't be controlled but one must always control his *karma*. Shastri ji says that a man must never act out of selfishness. Every man's *karma* should be to enrich the society and people around him. Love that hurts your society and your own family can't be any good and it should be controlled and shunned as soon as possible."

"I disagree with you Gunjan. By doing what you are saying you are feeding the ego of society and not serving your religion and humanity. Your *karma* should align with your religion or *dharma*. And all scriptures prove that love is supreme. There is nothing beyond or above love. I can't agree with any argument otherwise."

"Okay well, you are engaging me in an argument that I can't win. Not yet."

Gunjan kicked one of his oxen and whipped his lash in air. He was unconsciously thinking about him and Shatvari. He felt worried.

□

Chapter 6

Neel was shocked to see that against his plan only half of the Kosala soldiers went after Dhanajay's battalion. The rest of them stayed there and hoisted South Kosala's flag as if they had won the battle. Many of them had opened bottles of wine to celebrate the perceived victory. The message was clear, they had won the battle and they would wait there until a message comes from the other half of the army.

Disappointed to see his plan failing, Neel gathered his thoughts. He believed that this was not a simple attack on Mekal state but a raid on the fundamental identity of the people. The loss would mean giving up on the ultimate hope.

He could sense that his wide forehead was shrinking with deepening of lines of worry. His eyes, so filled with hope and excitement just a while ago, now showed growing pain of despair. He quickly recollected himself. He knew this wasn't the time to behave like a spineless leader. His whole army was looking at him for inspiration. He couldn't allow them to see a weak and nervous leader. He took a couple of deep breaths and addressed his soldiers, "My dear friends, as you can see our plan hasn't fared as per our expectations. It can be slightly difficult for us to defeat them. But as we know we cannot allow them under any circumstance to defeat us. They are fighting for their ambitious intention of expanding their state. They have nothing to lose, they will simply go back to their state. We, on the other hand, have everything to fight for. Our pride, our history, our identity, our culture, and our role in consolidation of foundation stones of Aryavart. If we are defeated, we will be wiped out from the pages of history. We will be made an undignified part of Kosala. Do not forget that a lot of our men are still captive in Kosala prisons. So many of our women are in their captivity and we don't know how many of them have been pushed to prostitution. This moment, my brave soldiers, is the moment to write destiny of ourselves and our future generations. We owe our existence to our ancestors who fought and laid their lives to give us the freedom that we have enjoyed so far. Now, the time has come for us to stand up and defend our own freedom. Are you ready to stand up and reclaim your freedom from the enemy?"

The army erupted with the deafening shouts of "Jai Mekal" and "Jai Suryadev".

All the soldiers became one single unit. Now they got a reason to stride forward and fight out the enemy at every cost. Their king's ideals struck a chord with each and every one of them; they could now see that it's their own battle. It's the battle for their identity and future and not just warfare between two states. They had to win this battle.

Neel led the strike on approaching Kosala soldiers. Loud echoes of 'Jai Suryadev' could be heard all around. The enemy soldiers were taken aback by this wave of passion. They felt that the Mekal king had given his soldiers some secret strategy to defeat the enemy. Neel moved his horse around with lightning speed. He pulled one of his daggers and threw it at one Kosala soldier. The dagger darted into the soldier's right shoulder. He nearly fell off from his horse. Neel raised his sword and slashed an agile blow on the soldier's shoulder again. This toppled him off the horse and he dropped his sword. As the soldier was leaning backwards and trying to get hold of his horse's rein, Neel sprung forth onto him slicing the air around his body so fiercely it took the soldier's head away from his body. The lifeless head fell on the ground and a jet of fresh blood gushed. Neel looked at his blood stained sword and raised it to dedicate his first kill to the Sun God. He tightened his grip and moved on again onto another enemy soldier.

Soon it was evident that Mekal's hundred soldiers would thrash Kosala's five hundred in a matter of time. Riding on the wave of motivational echoes of their king's speech, they stormed the war zone with spectacular agility and prowess. Kosala's army was taken by surprise. The celebrations of a victory that they anticipated to fall into their lap without any struggle, now seemed a distant dream. It was fading fast. They had to run to save their lives. They started to flee towards their state's territory in south-west. Neel stopped his soldiers to follow them. This would not achieve the desired result they were looking for. He instructed half of the soldiers to stay there to guard the camp and rest would follow him to the forest where Dhananjay was fighting as per the plan.

On the other front, a battalion of Kosala army was chasing Dhananjay and his soldiers deep into the forests, completely unaware of the trap they were being led into. They also had no idea of what had befallen their mates on the other front. Ambling down unknown rocky terrains and diminishing light they kept moving with a single intent to hunt down the Mekal men. They had already killed and injured a few and the rest seemed like a simple formality to them.

Dhananjay and his soldiers had different ideas. Deep into the forest, the paths diverged into four directions. He stalled his horse and looked at the one in front of him going straight up north towards the hills, another one turned a corner to move towards north-west; another descended down the valley; and a fourth path towards the south-west valley. The neigh of his horse seemed to instruct rest of the horses to stop and respond back. Dhananjay turned round to address his soldiers, "The path diverges into four directions. We should also split into four groups. We will move ahead on our respective paths and suitably choose a spot to hide ourselves. Kosala men do not have any idea about these terrains. As they are following our footsteps and will be here soon, they will soon be confused. So we move ahead now and find a place not far from here so that we can keep an eye on this crossroad. Let's hope that our other battalion comes and finds us. In the meantime, we can wage a gorilla war on the Kosala men." All the men heard the instructions and split in four groups. They took their positions and waited for the enemy to appear.

Kosala's men chased Mekal soldiers into the forest. They now stood at the crossroads where paths diverged in different directions. They looked for signs to figure out where their enemy might have gone. Nothing conclusive could be found and they stood clueless and disappointed.

One of the horsemen, who stood taller and more composed than the rest took a semicircle with his horse to face his fellow men. He addressed them saying, "As you can all see it's difficult to assess where the Mekal soldiers have disappeared. I assume they have moved north-west towards their state capital. But I might be wrong as this is only an assumption and we cannot plan to fight a battle based on assumptions alone. We have no idea of their might in their territory. Best not to go to attack the enemy in its backyard. I suggest that we should retreat and go back."

This seemed to perturb a few Kosala men who had enemy bounty in their sights. One of the soldiers said, "But commander we are all here and their capital is not far off, why not intensify attack and win it today itself? We have already captured one of their camps and their soldiers are running for their life. All this points at the fact that they have already given up and do not have any will to fight back."

"Don't be an excited fool! Battles are fought on the basis of pre-planned strategies and strategy needs certain information, which we don't have. We are standing in the middle of a forest within enemy territory. We have no idea what lies ahead. I order all men to retreat", said the commander.

The commander turned his horse around and started to make his way towards the Mekal camp that they had captured earlier. The rest of the soldiers followed him. Sooner than they could get out of the darker part of the forest, they were showered with lethal arrows from all the four sides.

"Take guard," shouted the commander, "The cowards have attacked us from behind. They couldn't face us directly so are stooping low to these tactics. What else can be expected from these lowly people? Find them and thrash them to pieces." He took guard himself and looked around to assess the situation.

He noticed that many arrows were coming from bushes from the east of where they stood. He pounced towards that direction.

The soldier behind the bushes was none other than Dhananjay. Kosala's commander quickly found him and pounced upon him with supreme agility and vigour. Dhananjay responded with same alertness. He turned around and quickly drew his sword and attacked the commander.

A duel was on between the two warriors of opposite armies. Kosala's commander was a tall and sturdy young man of about 35 years of age. The way he moved and struck blows at Dhananjay proved his muscular strength and years of training in arms and weapons. His wide chest and bulging biceps were fearsome enough to force adversaries into submission. In comparison, Dhananjay looked smaller. But Dhananjay made up with his fierce agility what he lacked in size. One couldn't tell who was weaker in the duel. The overall sight of the two fearless warriors swaying and moving on the cackling of swords was so emotive that it was impossible to imagine that the logical conclusion of this fight would be a sudden death of one of them. Just like life itself they would roll and sway and continue to fight and thwart deadly blows just to meet the eventual moment.

They matched each other blow by blow. Dhananjay's swift movements made the commander move around faster than he would normally do. Not able to pierce the commander's guard, Dhananjay stumbled upon a quick trick. He drew a small dagger tucked in his waist belt and aimed at his rival's right shoulder. He let go of the dagger with full might intending to slash the captain's stronger arm. It missed its aim and struck his shield on the chest. The shield moved down exposing the wide chest of the captain.

Mekal's soldiers continued to shoot arrows at Kosala men from behind the bushes. Kosala's soldiers were literally running and hiding to save their life. They stooped low to duck the barrage of arrows aimed to take their life. Suddenly, one such arrow missed its intended target and hit a flying bird on its way. The injured bird plummeted down towards ground and landed on Dhananjay's right shoulder. This disrupted his concentration and for a split of moment he took his eyes off his enemy's sword and looked at the bloodied bird now lying at his feet. The commander smelled the opportunity and moved his sword so fast that Dhananjay only realized its impact when his sword fell on the ground. He was now armless. He looked ahead at the tall man pointing his sword on Dhananjay's chest. Dhananjay stood baffled; scared for his life and confused at the sudden turn of the events.

Dhananjay looked up at the man who could easily behead him a moment ago but was still standing with his sword on his chest. Maybe he wanted to give Dhananjay another valiant chance to pick up his sword and to fight him man-to-man. The ethics of war required such behaviour on the battlefield.

Dhananjay stood bewildered looking at his rival standing victorious and yet vulnerable in front of him. Something was going to give. Suddenly, a blood-soiled tip of a sword emerged out of the middle of the commander's chest. Dhananjay saw Neel standing behind the commander who collapsed in front of him as if lightning had hit him. Neel sliced his sword out of the captain's body and looked down at the fallen captain with disdain.

"You slayers of *dharma*! You have proved that regardless of how much wars you fight, a Shudra remains a lowly disgraceful Shudra," cried the fallen commander at the top of his waning voice.

"*Adharma*! You talk about the ethics and morals. You people, who deprive others of the right to live peacefully in their own land. We have to fight our battle of survival, even if we have to defy the so-called rules of wars and ethics, this is our *dharma*" shouted Neel.

"The talk of morals does not suit your tongue young man," said the commander lying in the pool of fresh blood still spurting out of his wounded chest. "Those who kill their opponents from behind like a coward don't have a right to talk of such things. You'll gain no respect this way—not from your own people, from history, or even from your own self."

"Yes, everybody knows who has enslaved history and society. You people make your own definition of justice and ethics as per your convenience. Even a Nishaad king is simply a Shudra for you. In a civilization where *dharma* has been distorted by the rulers to suit their needs, we have to fight a battle for our existence and we cannot care more for just or fair in the war to win it."

But the commander wasn't alive to hear Neel's reply. He lay with his eyes wide open as if still looking for a justification for the betrayal that led to his fall.

The fall of their commander and incessant strikes from Mekal men devastated the remaining Kosala soldiers. To add to their agony, another battalion of Mekal stormed its way to them. That proved to be the final nail in their coffins. They were comprehensibly beaten and those remained alive haplessly surrendered on by bowing to their knees.

Neel glanced at Dhananjay with a proud smile and they both shared the joy of victory without uttering a single word. He raised both his hands and waived at his soldiers and acknowledged their bravery. He looked at the enemy soldiers down on their knees and said, "We have nothing personal against you. We, in fact, have no real enmity against Kosala and its people. Our battle aims only to salvage our pride and identity. We only want the same respect back from you and your people. If you want to expand and spread on the expense of our identity, we will never allow that to happen. Now it's up to the Yaduvanshis whether they want progress or destruction. You are soldiers too, and we respect you. You will not be treated as war-prisoners but only as our guests. We are forced to imprison you because some of our men and women are in captivity in your prisons. We will negotiate their freedom in exchange of your return."

□

Chapter 7

It was a damp monsoon morning. The wet monsoon days were almost over. Nights were getting longer with every passing day. Sun slumbered longer than usual to shine upon the hazy mornings.

Gunjan looked up at the morning sky still filled with stars. It seemed like a farm filled with millions of paddy crop shining through. It was an auspicious day. It was the Pola festival of the farmers. It marked an end to a long and laborious *Kharif* season. Farmers celebrated this as a thanks giving for their oxen tilled their farms all these months. Gunjan's oxen helped him earn his livelihood by carting his carriage. He had named them Shambhu and Nandu. On the Pola day, he always paid his gratitude by washing and decorating them. Later he would take them to the festival with the hope that they would win the race.

"Aditi, look who is here! Damodar how come you are here in this cattle festival? We thought you'd be roaming in your horse carriage that 'runs like the wind'", said Shatvari and she looked at Aditi with the usual sparkle. Aditi elbowed her from inside her scarf and laughed.

Damodar promptly responded, "Seems your indifference has affected my horse also. Poor beast is not well today."

"Thank God that you are well. Shatvari has driven a lot of boys crazy in our village," said Aditi.

"Nothing surprising in that. Shatvari is indeed so beautiful that anybody would become crazy and fall in love. But I just want to be friends. Our families are already in good terms and we are co-students of music. So, why not know each other better?" said Damodar.

Aditi looked at Shatvari who blushed at Damodar's remark. Aditi said, "A young boy and a girl cannot remain just friends for long. Either they develop fancy for each other or fall apart".

Shatvari heard Aditi's remark and it made her think. She looked away and got lost. Suddenly, she found herself pondering upon a seemingly useless thought. She shook her head and started to fiddle with a lock of her hair. Twisting and turning it around her index finger.

Aditi knew she had made an impact on both Damodar and Shatvari. But before she could assess the situation any further, she noticed a pair of beautifully decorated oxen coming forward with Gunjan. The sight of Shambhu and Nandu with Gunjan gave her an excuse to change the topic. Gunjan walked on with an unusual playfulness. He was whistling and walking slowly, enjoying his own self. The oxen echoed Gunjan's tipsy mood. Maybe because today they were walking like two free animals devoid of any cart to pull.

"Hello Gunjan, your companions today looking more attractive than you!" said Aditi as Gunjan came by their side.

"Of course, it's their day. That's the whole point, isn't it?" replied Gunjan. He bowed and greeted Shatvari and Damodar.

Shatvari was still trying to come out of the previous round of thoughts. She knew it's becoming obvious. She asked, "There is a race as well today Gunjan. Your oxen going to compete?"

"Yes, why not! My Shambhu won the race last year and I am looking forward to this year's race for sure," replied Gunjan.

"You must be proud. Are you confident for this year?"

"Of course. No point in competing if you don't want to win."

"They have become lazy and weak by carrying light weight women all day. My ox Bhima toils in farms all day, he is the real contender. He is going to win," a voice came from behind them. It was Veera. Tall, strongly-built, clad in a red stripes loin cloth.

Veera was the son of a rich farmer. His father had hundreds of acres of land in and around the village. He was a respectable man and many small farmers worked for him.

Veera was a good friend of Damodar. His physical build clearly reflected that he was as fond of physical exercises as he was of working in the farm. He loved wrestling and other physical sports. His ox Bheema was of a different breed than rest of the oxen in the village. Strong, sturdy and with an arrogant vitality in the eyes made Bheema look like a raging bull rather than a meek farm cattle. Veera decorated his body with colors and painted images of swords, daggers and javelins. Its two rounded horns were painted red.

Gunjan felt uneasy at Veera's words and his presence. It wasn't sensible to argue with him. He had a reputation of picking up quarrels. He was both physically and financially a strongman.

Shatvari felt awful at the way Veera spoke. She also felt that Gunjan should have given befitting reply. However, she moved forward and stroked the head of Shambhu and Nandu and said, "We'll see what wins—masculine ego, or, feminine love."

Veera looked at Shatvari, he pursed his lips to say something but stopped. He simply moved on looking at Gunjan, Shatvari and Aditi and patted Damodar on his shoulder and said, "Let's go my friend and enjoy the event rather than waste our time here amongst the women."

Then he gave Gunjan a taunting look as if he was counting him also among women.

Gunjan couldn't stand Veera insulting him in such a way.

"Insulting others is not manliness either", he said.

"If you care so much about your pride then do something worthy of respect. Gossiping with women doesn't help garnering any respect." Veera taunted him again.

"So is picking fights for no reason helps gaining respect?"

"You'd only fight with someone if you yourself knew any tricks of wrestling, you weakling!"

"Yeah, you think I know nothing about fighting. Fact is that I do not believe in picking fights without any reason."

"Really! You know wresting then prove it. Let's have a bout. Why are you standing cosy, holding onto a girl's hands for comfort."

Veera was clearly excited and pumped up now. Although Gunjan was trying his best to remain calm, Shatvari knew sooner or later his masculine ego would come into play. She held his hand more strongly and pressed hard as if to suggest him not to pay attention to Veera's threats. She knew Gunjan had no chance if a duel between the two happened.

Veera sensed that Shatvari was trying to protect Gunjan. "You know fighting and wrestling is for real men and not for people like you who hide behind a girl's scarf."

"What do you know about a woman's love, attention and support? Seems like nothing. Maybe you never got to feel even your mother's lap," interrupted Aditi now.

Veera seemed visibly upset by that remark. He had lost his mother when he was a little boy. He really had no motherly love as his stepmother never treated him well. He tried to look not affected at all by her remark and said to Gunjan, "Will you just let the women speak for you all your life, or say something yourself?"

"Say what? There is no court here that I should defend and argue for myself. You are unnecessarily stretching the matter," replied Gunjan.

"Why don't you accept that you can't even argue to defend yourself? Why not go to one corner and double-check yourself whether you are a man at all!" Veera laughed aloud like a jinn released from captivity.

It was evident that Veera was desperate and helpless at the same time.

Gunjan's patience was running out. He couldn't keep hold of himself under continuous insults from Veera. Every time he tried to lunge forward Shatvari would hold his hand even tighter.

Damodar was upset at the way Shatvari protected and held Gunjan's hand. Out of fury, he wished that it would be a good lesson for Gunjan if Veera thrashed him in a duel. He said, "What's the problem Gunjan? Maybe you are not an expert wrestler but you are adept at kabaddi. Coming from behind to topple your opponent is your trick."

That was the final to fan Gunjan's patience. He stepped forward and said, "So be it, Veera, if that's what you want let's see how much of a man you are!"

Shatvari ran after him as he let go of her hand. She could see he had made up his mind. She stepped back and crossed her heart with her hands and folded them to pray.

Gunjan and Veera tightened up their loincloths and now stood in front of each other for a duel. Veera's towering figure, wide chest, and solid shoulders made Gunjan look like a limp collection of flesh and bones. Even though Veera was muscular and big, his bulging tummy pointed towards his liking for food and wine. In contrast, Gunjan was lanky but athletic with not an ounce of extra bulge anywhere.

Shatvari stood hapless looking at them. She knew that even though Gunjan was courageous and wiry, yet the contest was surely uneven.

Veera was looking at Gunjan just like a hunter enjoying the sight of a trapped deer in his trap. He was going to tear Gunjan apart.

Gunjan stood silent and composed. He had no plans, whatsoever except to face whatever was coming his way.

Both bowed down to lock their heads and hands in a combat position. Veera pushed with both his hands and threw Gunjan off balance. Sensing the opportunity, he quickly tackled Gunjan's right foot, curled his arm round his neck and lifted up and dropped him on ground with a thud. Gunjan fell on his right arm and got up sooner. He saw the gap between Veera's legs, he thought of trying the kabaddi trick of shoving his head between Veera's legs and lift him up and throw down. As soon he rushed to attempt his trick, Veera guessed his intentions and quickly tripped a step aside and grabbing Gunjan's waist threw him in air. Gunjan was flat back bumped on the ground. A slight moan of anguish passed his lips. It seemed his back was seriously hurt. Veera sensed this opportunity and pounced upon Gunjan but he was surprised to see that his rival had quickly rolled over and sprung up.

Both fighters again regained their stance and locked fists and were trying their strength. Veera knew that Gunjan's back was hurt in the previous fall. One more descend to the ground would be enough for Gunjan. He quickly pulled Gunjan towards him, bent down grabbed both his feet from behind and lifted him upon his shoulders and plummeted down on the ground. This time around Gunjan couldn't get up and simply lay on the ground in visible pain. Veera quickly jumped upon Gunjan and sat on his chest. Gunjan tried with all his strength to push him back but Veera was almost double his body weight. Veera took Gunjan's right arm and twisted it around his neck. Gunjan cried in agony but Veera continued to twist it further.

Shatvari couldn't continue to watch hapless Gunjan's state. It was evident that Gunjan was totally subdued and Veera was not going to give his stance away. He was enjoying Gunjan's pain. She shouted at the top of her voice, "You have already won the bout, now leave him alone. Are you going to kill him?"

Shatvari's plea fell on Veera's deaf ears. He wasn't in a mood to give up. He continued to hold Gunjan's arm and now entwined his right arm around Gunjan's neck as if he was now hell bent to kill him. Shatvari looked at Damodar who was now a bit stunned at the unfolding events in front of him. He went forward towards Veera and said, "Leave him now Veera, you are going beyond all rules and ethics of wrestling."

Veera looked at Damodar and said, "Now you too want to come in support of him together with the girls. I am going to make sure I make him bleed today."

"Stop it Veera, you are not going to do anything violent. Leave him, else I will have to intervene."

"Really! Who is scared of you? See, how you changed sides for a girl."

Damodar said nothing but moved ahead and grabbed Veera's arm that held Gunjan's neck. Veera let go of Gunjan and wanted to grab Damodar's waist but Damodar quickly turned around and grasped Veera's hands. Damodar tried to tackle and throw Veera off balance. But in the effort they both fell to the ground together. Damodar fell on his belly and Veera snapped back to jump up on Damodar's back. Veera took Damodar's right arm and twisted it backwards. Lying on his belly with face down and one arm being twisted by Veera, Damodar was helpless and in pain.

Shatvari was sitting on the ground with Gunjan, now looked up to find Damodar in the same agonising state. She rushed to her feet and looked around at the crowd of young men gathered to watch the fight. She said, "Is there not a single real man amongst you here? Are you simply enjoying the beastly violence of this man here?"

Normally, nobody would have interfered in Veera's business but Shatvari's call motivated a few young men to move on and control Veera. They grabbed him and set Damodar free from his clutches. While still fending these men off, Veera said to Damodar, "So you showed your true self and broke our friendship for a girl. People forget their families for them, what of mere friends!"

Damodar kept quiet. He rubbed his elbows and knees, dusted his clothes and got up from the ground.

Shatvari suddenly realised that Gunjan was still lying on the ground and moaning slowly with his eyes closed. His right arm was swollen and he couldn't even move it an inch. His eyes were moist with tears of pain and embarrassment. Shatvari tried to lift his head up but he couldn't move. She lifted his head and put it in her lap as she sat down beside him on the ground. She was softly fondling his right injured arm and his forehead. Some drops of perspiration fell on Gunjan's cheeks as she was bent over him. Gunjan felt at ease as a result of Shatvari's touch and tenderness. Her presence shrouded him in soft light and made him feel better. He felt no pain, only the caring breath of Shatvari touching his skin. He wouldn't care if he had to go through this pain again to feel this soft touch and tender love. Suddenly, it dawned upon him and he opened his eyes to see the crowd watching them intently. He could feel the peering eyes of the people brimmed with many questions. Maybe they were right. He shook the aura away and tried to get up. But he couldn't and pain forced him to lie back down again.

As Gunjan moaned again, Shatvari too felt the physical world around her. She looked around to see the gathered crowd looking down at her and Gunjan. She looked down again and tried to help Gunjan to get up. Watching her attempts, some people came forward and helped Gunjan onto a nearby cart. One of the boys volunteered to take him to a vaidya nearby. Shatvari couldn't muster any more courage to walk up to him to say good bye. She stood there like an idol while Gunjan was carted away slowly.

While she was engulfed in her own thoughts, she realised Damodar was standing in front of her. She tried to smile at him. She wanted to say something but she kept quiet for a few moments and then said, "Are you hurt badly?"

"No, not much. Maybe some old wounds have surfaced."

"You have to admit that you encouraged Gunjan for the fight knowing well the outcome. At that moment I was really aghast and angry at you."

"I admit my mistake but I really had no idea that Veera would go to this extent."

"He was your friend, and you couldn't understand him?"

"Only if we could understand people that easily. Sometimes it takes a lifetime to know people." Damodar smiled and now Shatvari smiled back at him. They were looking into each other's eyes.

Shatvari was looking for answers in his eyes. On one hand, he excited and initiated Gunjan into a fight knowing the result and then he went to save him and got beaten himself. He wasn't simply trying all that to impress her.

While they were lost in their train of thoughts, somebody patted Shatvari's shoulder and said, "It's getting dark, let's go home." It was Aditi.

"Okay Damodar we shall take leave now," said Shatvari.

Damodar nodded and kept looking at her.

Shatvari walked away with Aditi. She wasn't the same Shatvari that walked to the festival that morning. Something had changed.

□

Chapter 8

Neel and Dhananjay stood on a Sone river cliff erected over Sonmuda. Neel pointed in south-east direction across the cliff and said, "Do you see these valleys spread all over there?"

"Yes, your Highness. I have known these since childhood. Anything special about them?"

"Special is what lies beyond them—the Aryan Civilization. A civilization that teaches its citizens to carve their destiny as per their skills and nature. It defines a role for every individual within the society. Also teaches the importance of sacrificing for the welfare of the society."

"Yes, your Highness. But is man's destiny to only live according to his nature? Just to be confined in the perimeter of his society? How come you are wondering about the Aryan Civilization?"

Still looking far into the south-eastern valley, Neel said, "A man's destiny is defined by his essential nature."

"But a man's nature can never be the same or constant, your Highness. Life expands itself by design or by default. New nature forms itself and new skills are learnt every day, don't you think!"

"Yes, you may be right but every unified society stands on the individuals and the nature of those individuals must play within the perimeter of that society. Else the foundation will never stand. Individual egos will clash; ambitions will collide and the society will disintegrate for sure." Neel turned around to his left to look directly at Dhananjay's face.

"So do you envisage such an issue can befall Aryans? Do you see clash of egos within Aryans to be the start of its downfall?"

Neel raised his right hand and slowly caressed his chin and said, "Not definitely sure but every society goes through this phase. And I suspect Yaduvanshis cannot remain unaffected of this for long. We must be watchful if we have to fight and defeat Yaduvanshis. We must know them better. We must know their friends and enemies closely."

"I agree. But how is that possible. We do not have any spy there who can keep us updated."

"We will have ourselves to become spies to go and seek first-hand information."

"What do you mean?"

"I have decided that both of us should go to Shripur—the capital of South Kosala. We will study their culture and society in totality. We will assess their strength and weakness from within. It's imperative that we know as much about our enemy as we can."

"But your Highness who will look after Mekal if we leave it like this. We do need a leader to be present in Mekal for day-to-day situations. What if they attack us again in your absence?"

"I don't think they'll be able to pull themselves together for another combat soon. They will take their time to plan that. We will be there to find out what they are up to anyway. I have decided that I will delegate my responsibilities to our commander-in-chief and we both will leave soon for South Kosala."

"If you want and you find me capable, I can stay back to look after the security of Mekal during your absence?"

"Dhananjay, of course, I trust you. But there is a purpose for which I am taking you with me. You are needed for this mission. I will feel very lonely without you."

Dhananjay nodded in acceptance and said, "Sure, as you command your Highness."

Arriving at Shripur's main entrance, Neel and Dhananjay scanned around the enormous fortification of the city. A sturdy stone wall of about hundred and fifty feet high and fifty feet thick enclosed the city. At the top of the wall, a flat road was built for armed soldiers to keep vigil. On top of the perimeter wall, a thirty feet high barricado of red stone was erected to strategically place vigilant soldiers to keep an eye on approaching enemies round the clock. At every six hundred feet, there was a fifty feet high watch-tower. Set of stairs from the barricado went up to the watch towers, which had round windows as the surveillance points. Those points could easily look up to two kilometers. The fort had four main entrances in each direction with armed brigades guarding all the time. At a distance of about thirty feet, a hundred feet wide deep trench encircled the fort. It was about fifty feet deep and its inner walls were lined with earthen bricks. The trench was connected via a tunnel that pumped water from river Mahanadi. The water flew in clockwise direction. The water level was controlled by a machine. The trench was populated with crocodiles to stop anybody from trying to swim through to reach the fort. The distance between the fort wall and the trench was covered by toxic and thorny shrubs.

Neel and Dhananjay looked at each other. They realised that the fort could never be breached in a direct attack. They would have to think of alternative plans and make a rational assessment. That's why they were there.

They had changed their appearance and disguised as two Brahmin students. They had shaved their beards off and trimmed their hair leaving behind only a pony tail typical of a Brahmin scholar. They wore plain white loin cloth instead of the striped one they wore in Mekal. The upper corset was also of simple cotton cloth rather than the usual leather one. Wooden pattern slippers covered their feet instead of leather.

Arriving at the main entrance, which was also called the 'Brahmdwaar', they greeted the armed guards by respectfully bowing their heads. One of the guards who was taller and looked enormous with his loathsome persona asked Neel, "Where have you come from? What do you want?"

"Sir, we have come from north-west state of Takshkhand's capital Takshashila. We are students of sociology at the university there. We are doing research on the social, economical, political, cultural and philosophical aspects of Aryan Civilization. Shripur being one of the largest cultural centres of Aryan culture, we have come here to seek more information to aid our research," replied Neel.

The guard spoke even before Neel had finished, "You are coming here for education. Do you have identity card of any sort."

Neel nodded in negative looking up at the guard.

"So your school never told you that you need papers to enter a state capital. What have you been studying?"

"Sir, our school...in fact university taught us about knowledge and not much about what you are asking. Besides, we have been to many other states and nobody demanded any papers?"

"Whatever…you might have gone to Raghuvanshi states, they generally trust anybody. This is a Yaduvanshi capital and we have strict rules and tight security. We cannot just let any stranger to walk through into our capital." The guard stepped back and took his usual guarding stance with head high-up and spear in front of him clutched tightly in front of his wide chest.

Realising that the guard wasn't showing any interest, Neel tried again. "Sir we have come from far. We are simple students. We only want to study about your culture. Our study will have profitable effect on you and your people. We will share whatever we have."

The mention of profit and share made another guard to take interest in Neel. He nudged him aside and whispered in his ears, "I can help you by making you meet our security officer. If he allows then you can enter. That's the best I can do for you."

Neel's eyes lit up and he knew that the guard took his bait. He said, "That will be very kind of you sir."

The guard went away inside and soon came back with a stout man of average height, dark complexion, and long face. His hair were tied back in a ponytail on his back. Glancing at Neel and Dhananjay he asked, "So you have come to study?"

"Yes sir. We have heard a lot of great things about Shripur," replied Neel.

"You have heard it right but this will cost you my friends four hundred gages."

"One has to pay four hundred to enter the capital? Are you asking for bribe" replied Neel.

"Not bribe, a simple entry fee. Two hundred each."

"Do we have to pay anything else beside this?"

"No. But you will have to arrange and pay for your boarding, lodging and food. I will introduce you to teachers from our university employed here. They can help you in your research. You can pay them something as a gesture of goodwill if you feel."

Neel knew where the entry fee was going to end up. That guard's intent to help and this officer's over generousness gave some glimpse of how the system in Shripur worked. They paid the required amount.

The officer took them inside and on the left towards a big official building adjacent to the inside of the perimeter wall. The building was clearly marked as 'Security Office'. A large *chakra* was drawn underneath the label. They went up the stairs and through a large wooden door entered a big hall. A table with a large seat on one side and four ordinary wooden chairs were placed on the other side. They all took their seats and the officer addressed the duo.

"So, what did you say your names were?"

"I am Badrinath and this is my friend Kedarnath, " replied Neel.

"How long will you stay?"

"As long as it takes for us to finish our research. Maybe a few months."

"Okay. As soon as you get a place to stay you have to come back here and report your address. You will have to come here every Monday each month to inform us of your presence as long as you are staying here. In case you are unable to come due to sickness, you will have to intimate us by some other means. Failure to do so can result in your expulsion and maybe imprisonment. You understand?"

"No problem sir. We understand everything."

The officer noted all the details on a thin bronze leaf. He stood up and motioned them both to follow him, "Okay then let me introduce you to a teacher who will help you in your research."

They all went outside the building where a four-wheeled carriage was waiting for them. The officer sat at the front and instructed both of them to sit behind him.

It was a two-horse driven carriage. Neel was astonished to see the carriage as it was roughly double the size of his own carriage in Mekal. If an ordinary security officer had this kind of carriage, it was impossible for Neel to visualise what would the royal chariot of South Kosala look like. That thought forced him to draw comparison between the two states and Mekal's modest resources made him ponder.

□

Chapter 9

All three arrived at the nearby university where the officer took Neel and Dhananjay to a history scholar.

"Meet Shri Itivrat. He teaches history here. And these two boys—Badrinath and Kedarnath are students from Takshashila. They are studying sociology and they are doing some research on Aryan Civilization. They would appreciate your help," said the officer.

Itivrat was a short and plump man with round face. Shaved head with only a customary Brahmin ponytail emerging from the top of the scalp. He wore a plain white loincloth and a simple shirt.

Neel joined hands to greet him and said, "History teacher? But we are looking to know more about the present civilisation not the ancient."

"History creates the present young man. To understand the present, you must know the past," emphasised Itivrat addressing both the newfound students. His cheeks expanded even further when he smiled.

"But who will give us the knowledge of the present society then?" asked Neel.

The officer moved up and patted Neel's shoulder and added, "First understand the history then we'll arrange for the present as well, don't worry." He left the two with the history professor.

Itivrat motioned both of them to sit at two wooden chairs placed opposite him and started his lecture.

"We will start from the Rig Vedic era of the Aryan Civilization. The word 'rig' is a corrupted derivation of an ancient Sanskrit word 'rik', which means 'praise'. The Rig Veda culture was based on paying gratitude and expressing praise and devotion to divine powers with the ritual of sacrificial fires and auspicious mantras. Politically and socially, it was a tribal culture system. The fundamental entity of that society was joint-family. It was a patriarchal society with men as the heads of families and a king as the head of the tribe. The king was supposed to be the guardian of the tribe and was referred to as 'gopa', literally meaning the saviour. Since that era our society has been divided into four categories—Brahmin, Kshatriya, Vaishya, and Shudra. This is mentioned in Rig Veda's *Purusha* hymn in the tenth chapter, where it's said that *Purusha,* the cosmic being created Brahmin from his mouth and head, Kshatriya from his arms, Vaishya from his thighs, and Shudra from his feet. This signified that their work in the society was as follows—Brahmin to educate and be involved in scholarly pursuits; Kshatriya to act as warriors and protect the society; Vaishya to produce resources for the society with agriculture and trade; and Shudra was to serve all the other three. The system gave Brahmins a top-most place in the society and Shudra was put at the bottom. The economy was based on animal husbandry and agriculture."

The professor of history went on about the Rig Vedic culture for some time that made Neel and Dhananjay squirm in their seats and yawn. Suddenly, the professor stopped and said, "Okay then I have to stop here and would go to teach my other students. We will discuss the rest later when I am back. You can wait here for me."

"Sure, but as we are tired due to a long journey, we will rather have the rest of the lecture tomorrow. We also have to arrange for our accommodation," replied Neel and both stood up with folded hands.

"As you wish," replied the professor with a smile.

While moving out, Neel and Dhananjay looked at the professor who stood smiling. Neel asked, "Do you want to say something?"

"Well...only if you could settle today's fees?" The professor's smile widened.

"Oh yes, why not? How much would that be?" asked Neel.

"Only twenty."

Neel took out twenty gages from his pouch and handed over to the professor. He realised this would be a costly affair. They would have to find some alternative way. Anyway the best way to learn about a society is to live and understand it first-hand.

"Surprising how can a scholar and a teacher be so greedy?," Dhananjay said to Neel.

"This is Yaduvanshi state. Things are different here. Remember how that guard boasted. This is what's different about this state." They both laughed together. "Let's just find a place to live now and I am also hungry. Aren't you?"

"More than the tiredness of the journey that lecture drained out all my energy," replied Dhananjay.

They were walking into a narrow lane and saw a huge building with a sign that said 'Dharamshala—All visitors are welcome'. It was a guest house.

Looking at the lodge, Neel said, "This could be the right place. It is a 'Dharamshala', maybe they abide by some ethics of *dharma*. So far Shripur has failed to show any glimpse of that."

They both entered the guest-house. At the reception they saw a broad wooden table and a man sitting on a comfortable chair across that. He was an elderly man with normal stature. He wore clean white clothes and satin yellow turban on his head. Small golden earrings dangled from his ear lobes. Neel and Dhananjay greeted him and the man responded back with similar gesture and said, "Welcome to our guest-house. My name is Sampat. How can I help you?"

Sampat's humility impressed the duo and they looked at each other in pleasant surprise. Neel said, "Sir my name is Badrinath and this is my friend Kedarnath. We are from Takshkhand state's capital Takshashila. We are doing research on Aryan Civilization and that's why we have come to your state. We need a place to stay. Can you arrange for our accommodation here?"

"Yes, why not! This guest-house's whole purpose is to accommodate visitors like you. How long do you want to stay?"

"About two to three months."

"Okay, no problem, do you have any identity document?"

"Yes, sure." Neel handed him the papers that the security officer had prepared for them.

Sampat carefully matched the description provided in the papers. He scanned both of them a few times and peered back again into the papers. After a few minutes, he said, "Okay. I can arrange for your stay on the second floor. I am sure it won't be a problem for healthy young men like you. We keep the ground floor for elderly and sick people."

"Second floor is okay. How much do we have to pay sir?"

"You are scholars. You have come to our state for study and research. We can't charge a rent from you."

Neel and Dhananjay were amazed and looked at each other. This was the kind of incident they were not expecting in Shripur. Neel had thought the politeness of Sampat could be cunningness of a shrewd businessman.

Sampat guessed what the duo were thinking. He added, "Don't be surprised. Our Sethji is a very liberal religious man. He built this for people like you. We only take rent from those who can afford it and who have a clear source of income. Seeking money from scholars will be a huge sin for us. Society needs more scholars who can illuminate us with the light of the knowledge. We are simply here to serve you as much as we can." replied Sampat and started to walk. "Please collect your belongings. I will show your room."

They took their leather luggage bags and followed Sampat.

The guest-house was a four-storey building made of bricks. Small stairs at the main gate joined the main entrance that lead to a rectangular open yard. The floor was tiled with stone slabs leaving raw earthen space along the perimeter for flower beds, which were vibrant with fresh colorful flowers of all kinds. There was a paved well on the left with a pulley to draw water. On all four sides of the yard were erected four storeys full of rooms. A set of stairs to get to each floor was on the right. Washrooms were on the lower floor. The dining room was at the front in the yard on the ground floor.

Pointing at the dining room, Sampat said, "This is the dining room where you will be offered twice a day food free of cost. You'll have to come at prescribed times and please make sure not to waste any food. As we believe food is akin to God."

Neel and Dhananjay listened intently to Sampat's words. Now the pain they felt at giving huge bribe to the security officer had subsided. Climbing the stairs onto the second floor, Sampat opened the door of a room and said, "This is your room. Keeping it clean and washing linen and bedding is your responsibility. If you are unwell, just let us know and we will arrange for vaidya and medication for you."

The flurry of charitable services showered upon them made Neel and Dhananjay unable to hide their excitement.

'Atithi Devo Bhava'—Guests akin to God—tradition of the Aryans was still alive. Neel joined hands in polite gratitude and said to Sampat, "We are truly grateful. I am sure your Seth ji is a great soul."

Sampat accepted their gratitude and came back to his office.

The room was a medium-sized hall with two jute-beds, locally known as *khaats*. Each had cotton mattress, white bedsheet and a soft cotton pillow.

Neel sat on one of the *khaats* and said, "Surely, the society, just like the men we encountered seem, is full of contrasts. This has been an amazing experience so far."

"Sure, your Highness, but despite all the contrasts and dichotomies, a society still moves in one direction. That direction always tells the true nature of that society."

"I agree. That's why we are here—to find out the true nature of Yaduvanshis. Which way is this society heading to?"

□

Chapter 10

Shatvari's fluttering fingers on the museless strings of Veena were producing no music that day. She sat lost in her stream of thoughts trying to weave them in a conceivable form. But to no avail. The events that had unfolded on the Pola festival day troubled her mind. Gunjan was still recovering from his wounds and his right arm's muscles were badly torn. That was affecting his livelihood. Damodar emerged in a new light. It was a pleasant surprise. What had gone in Veera's head that he hurt both Gunjan and Damodar so badly? Why did he loathe women so much? Was it because of the treatment he got from his stepmother? But why vent it out on Gunjan and Damodar?

An impatient knock on the door broke her chain of thoughts. It was Damodar.

She opened the door. Even though she was a bit surprised, she tried her best to not look so. She asked, "Damodar, how are you?"

"You haven't been coming for the music lessons, so father sent me to know your well-being. Is everything okay, Shatvari?"

"Oh, yes. It's just that Gunjan is still not well, so we do not have a conveyance to get there."

"That is so. You should have informed me. I could have come to take you. Anyway, now I am here, so please come along."

Shatvari looked at Damodar. He was unusually calm. There was no trace of excitement and excessive eagerness that she observed in all their previous meetings.

"Just wait for a moment, I'll inform my mother," said Shatvari and went in. She needed the break more than Damodar expected.

As soon as both walked out of the house, Shatvari's eyes fell on Damodar's horse carriage. It looked like a small royal chariot. The two giant wooden wheels made of Sal were studded with metal to lend strength. A thick wooden axle yoked the two wheels together. The upper carriage was built of Teak wood and it had fine engraving on each side. The engravings were decked with copper and ivory designs to make it look spectacular. The front seat was a wide red satin-covered padded mattress. Right behind that seat was a passenger's seat that could accommodate up to three people comfortably. The carriage's upper canopy was covered with a silk cloth supported by two metallic poles. A white horse of high pedigree stood at the front with leather reins spread down to its back.

Shatvari was visibly impressed by the carriage. She tried to hide that and realised the reason why Damodar had been so arrogant about his carriage in past.

Damodar rode in the carriage and asked, "Should we also pick your friend Aditi?"

"No she is not in the village. She has gone to her grandmother as we realised we won't be able to go for our classes for some time." Shatvari paused for a moment and asked, "But tell me where did you get such a beautiful carriage? You are only a modest Brahmin's son. This must be really expensive?"

"I was friend with the son of a wealthy merchant in town. He gifted it to me."

"Really! What good friends you have. Normally, even our own relatives don't bestow such costly presents."

"That's the quality of our friendship. We make friends that are dearer than family members and relatives. If you doubt it, you can try for yourself."

"Doubt? Nothing to doubt, I can see the proof with my own eyes right here. But it's better if friendship remains within the limits, otherwise people start to doubt a man's character."

"Me and him? What an incredible joke! I am not that kind of man." Damodar burst into laughter. Shatvari was now clearly enjoying talking to Damodar. She asked, "Now when we are talking about friendship, how come you made a friend like Veera? You don't seem such a man."

"Well, sometimes people do make mistakes in choosing friends. Veera was one such mistake. Actually, his father is a wealthy and influential man of the village. He is also a very intelligent person. I thought maybe his son inherited his qualities."

The mention of Veera changed the mood of the conversation. Shatvari realized that and said, "So are we going straight to your house?"

"That is the intention, so far, yes."

"I remember you once promised to take me around in your carriage."

"Promise, no, but a humble request, yes. Still waiting for your reply".

"Really, then, I give my consent. Where will you take me?"

Damodar's eyes lit up as soon as he heard the permission from Shatvari. He said, "There is a beautiful ancient temple along Mahanadi River. If you don't mind, we can go there, it'll be a great trip." Shatvari noticed the usual excitement in Damodar's voice which he showed for the first time that day.

She said, "Why would I object to a visit to a temple. Just make sure we get back before dusk."

"This is a horse carriage and not a bullockcart. It won't take entire day in just getting there," replied Damodar.

Shatvari smiled and said nothing, even though she knew what he was pointing at.

Damodar pulled in the rein and motioned his steed towards the wide road in the town's direction. The horse snickered back in reply and kicked in all his feet and quickly was running with the wind. Soon the carriage was plying upon a thirty feet wide road made of soil, sand and rocks. Shatvari had never experienced such high speed in her life before. She felt as if her life had again picked up speed, her heartbeats got faster to keep pace with the speed of the carriage. Inhibited at first, she soon let go of her resistance and started to enjoy. Her frail body swayed in tandem with the feet of the galloping white horse. The breeze fondled her hair as if trying to set the lock free.

Shatvari eased her hand behind her neck and pulled the pin that held her hair. The lock of hair erupted as if a river broke a feeble dam. The silken hair touched Damodar's shoulders now and then. Shatvari felt as if her hair were connecting her with Damodar's thoughts in a sensuous way. She withheld her hair back trying to keep still with her head bent backwards to enjoy the thrill of speed and her fast-moving emotions.

Damodar's whole body electrified at the touch of Shatvari's hair. He felt as if she herself touched him to express an emotion they both were incapable to express at that moment. He held the rein of the horse strongly and looked ahead with intent.

They soon reached at the gate of the temple. The young passengers of a speedy carriage didn't realise when the whole distance was covered. The temple was an enormous structure. About five hundred feet wide and four hundred feet high. A peripheral stone wall of fifteen feet high circled the temple complex. The main door opened towards the north direction. A giant pair of Teak wood door of about thirty feet high and twenty feet wide stood with abundant fine engravings depicting the divine gods and goddesses. A towering turret of fifty feet high black stones was erected upon the main door. It had the stone etchings of mythological tales from ancient times. A semi-cylindrical top of the turret had four golden urns.

Damodar stalled the carriage right in front of the gate and moved it along to park it on the right hand side area. He asked, "So, shall we go in?"

"You are asking as if I am an atheist and you'll have to request me to come in."

"One whose beauty can make people believe in heavenly creation of God, can never be an atheist."

Shatvari again wondered why she didn't mind the way Damodar was praising her beauty that day. On previous occasions, it used to make her so uncomfortable. She said, "Seems like you have a long experience in singing songs of a girl's beauty. You must have been doing it for long."

"You can't learn to appreciate beauty. It comes from the heart if it's there."

"Just keep a tight grip on your heart; you are in God's abode."

Shatvari smiled and moved ahead to climb the entrance steps into the temple. Damodar followed her.

Shatvari had already inkling that Damodar liked her. He had been trying to get close to her since the first meeting at Acharya ji's music lesson. It was up to her to take the next step. Damodar was attractive and educated. Their families had good terms. But she knew the difference between love and mere attraction. She was trying to find out if there was any speck of love in her present emotions.

Shatvari was taken aback by temple's splendour. Rising on top of a twenty feet red stone mound, the temple presented a great sight. A wide set of stairs on the eastern side of the temple went up to the top of the mound. At the top four square stone pillars formed a vestibule. The stone pillars had the Ghat-Pallava style etchings on top and bottom and mythological figures of gods in the middle. Next up was a dance hall—Natya Mandir—resting on twelve stone pillars. The pillars had the engravings of Gandharvas and Apsaras in dancing moves. The stone engravings reflected erotic mood of the dancers. In front of the dance hall was the main hall. Right in the center of that hall was the *adytum* that had the four-armed idol of Vishnu made of stone and bricks.

Leaning against one of the pillars, Damodar teased Shatvari, "So you missed your lesson today, if Acharya ji found out that you have come here instead of going for the lesson you could get bit of a stick beat from him."

"The one who is actually responsible for it, should be punished."

"Oh really! So what would be the punishment if you were to decide?"

"Well...you'll have to make up for the loss. You are also a musician, why not teach me something I don't know?"

"I am not an Acharya, but surely I can sing a song if you prefer."

"If your song can teach me something new why not!"

"I have done an experiment with classical and folk music, see what you make of it."

Damodar started an *alaap* in raga Bhairavi. The tune was of a popular folk song from South Kosala. It was about the love affair of Radha and Krishna. The peppy folk rhythm and tempo of the song instantly struck a chord with Shatvari. Despite being amorous in nature, the song spurred emotions of divine love. Damodar was completely lost in the music.

Shatvari had never seen Damodar in that way—lost completely in the devotion to music. That was an indication that maybe he also knew the divinity of love. He surely was capable of understanding the spiritual purity of love. Shatvari felt an innate urge to flow with the music. Her shivering feet now burst into a full-fledged dance. The whole arena came alive with Damodar's mesmerizing voice; Shatvari's oscillating feet; and the spiritually alive Natya Mandir with dancers on the pillars descending down on the earthly plain.

Time flew. By the time they came to their senses, Shatvari found herself leaned against one of the pillars with her hands round it. Damodar was still humming on the other side of the pillar. As soon as Shatvari realised that her fingers were brushing Damodar's back, she quickly pulled them back. She drew back and noticed a Gandharva and an Apsara in each other's arms on the pillar in front of her. She dropped her head down and took a couple of deep breaths. After a few more moments, she said, "I think we should leave now."

"You are very rude. At least some sort of praise of my song is expected. Do I sing that badly?"

"No, not at all. You sing really well. Your music made me dance unintentionally."

"Yes, I noticed. Where did you learn to dance so well?"

"I haven't learnt classical dance formally. As you know our society doesn't allow Brahmin girls to dance. It's not considered to carry traditional decorum."

"I have heard you don't really care too much about the society?"

"Surely, I am not a narrow-minded person but I do like to stay within the periphery of civil society and its traditions."

"You are right. A society will fall apart without the structure of their traditions."

"But when structures become shackles they stop a society from moving further."

"Okay, okay, we'll leave this argument for some other day as we are getting late, it's almost dusk. You should reach home before dark."

Shatvari sat in her room staring blankly at a painting depicting a dance move of an Apasara and a Gandharva. The events of the day kept knocking in her mind. The memories of intermingled poses of Gandharv and Apsara tinkled her sensuality, at the same time the divine hypnotic voice of Damodar echoed in and out.

'How mesmerizing is Damodar's voice? Such an unprecedented unity of grace and devotion! Acharya ji always talked about this. If love can adorn the qualities of faith and surrender, it becomes a surrender to the divine. Will Damodar have faith and surrender towards me in his love? Will his love have the same sanctity as his music? Is he the right man for me?'

While Shatvari was lost in her stream of consciousness, she heard her mother Gautami's voice, "What is the matter Shatvari? You look lost."

Shatvari didn't realize when her mother came into the room and was now looking at her stroking Shatvari's hair softly.

"Nothing, really, Ma"

Gautami was a middle aged woman of shorter than average height. Slightly stocky in appearance. She had a very simple and elegant countenance. Long black hair pleated in a braid that rested on her back. She wore a blue cotton sari. Simple make-up and just the basic jewellery-golden ear-rings, a garland of white pearl round the neck, and glass bangles in her hands.

"What happened? You seemed really happy in the morning when you left with Damodar. Anything Acharya Ji said that dampened your mood?" Gautami sat beside Shatvari still stroking her hair gently.

Suddenly Shatvari realized that she had told her mother that she will be going to Acharya ji. But she actually went with

Damodar. Should she tell her mother the truth about this? Better to tell herself rather she knows from someone else.

"No, Ma, didn't go to Acharya ji's house today. Damodar offered to come along him for his horse-cab's ride so I went to the town with him. We went to a temple together" said Shatvari resting her head on her mother's right shoulder.

Gautami felt better, probably, to know the truth. Maybe she had no problem with Shatvari going out with Damodar.

"So how was your day with Damodar?" asked Gautami smiling at her daughter.

"It was great, Ma. It went like a whiff. Damodar sings so well. Sounds like God himself sings from his throat" said Shatvari turning a little pink while praising Damodar.

"Do you like being with Damodar?"

"I don't mind, really, I don't know Ma." Shatvari blushed slightly and looked down.

"And what about him?" asked Gautami, reading her blushing cheeks.

Shatvari blushed again, deeply. She knew how desperately Damodar wanted to be with her. She got hold of herself and replied, "I hope he does, otherwise why would he take me out"

"If you both like each other, then why not decide to stay together forever? Damodar is well educated, handsome, and from a decent family known to us. This really is a good match" Said Gautami, looking at her pink face.

Shatvari tilted her head down modestly. She didn't know what to say.

'Ma really doesn't know that I have been thinking on the same thing ever since I came back. Or does she know? After all she's my ma' Thought Shatvari. Mother's suggestion eased her heart a bit.

"Your silence says that you agree with this alliance. I will talk to your father. I am so happy for you dear" Gautami's face lit up with excitement.

Shatvari sat in silence with her head down.

"Seems like Shatvari and Damodar like each other", said Gautami to Shastri ji with the a glee on her face.

"Did she say that to you?" asked Shastri ji, pleasantly surprised.

"Not in clear words, but I know my daughter for sure"

"If this is the case then, of course, I am happy with this alliance. I like Damodar-he is a very bright young man"

"So will you talk to Acharya Ji regarding this?"

"Yes, but we should first ask Shatvari and Damodar, what do they think?"

"Don't worry about Shatvari. I am sure she is very happy with this alliance. Acharya ji should ask Damodar about it, you can suggest him that" Gautami looked quite assured.

"Okay, I will discuss this with Acharya Ji. This will be a good relation for both the families", contemplated Shastri ji. Gautami's face lit up with positive expectations.

Shahstri ji felt relieved and happy to hear about Shatvari and Damodar. All his worries regarding Shatvari's relation with Gunjan started to vanish. Ever since he heard about the events of Pola festival from people he had been anxious and worried. He thanked the Almighty that his prayer had been answered.

"How did the sun rise from the West? So, finally Vishwamitra's magic has worked upon Menka", Aditi poked fun at Shatvari.

"Neither am I Menka and nor is Damodar a Vishvamitra. Nothing out of order is happening. You just say whatever makes you happy."

"That's right-you're love is that of Radha-Krishna style. With that sorcerer Krishna. But tell me how did this happen? You never used to bother about that Damodar", teased Aditi further.

"But I never showed any disrespect to Damodar ever. But now I am realising that he has a divine character", replied Shatvari with a glint in her eyes.

"Oh I see, so the black magic is working. Where is the magician these days?", Aditi grinned impishly.

"He has gone to town to invite his friends for the wedding and to make some final preparations"

"So he might be having many girlfriends too in the town, being a spell casting wizard that he is."

"You are simply jealous because you can't find such a handsome man for yourself" Shatvari gave one back to Aditi.

"Don't be so arrogant. I might steal him from you leaving you gasping."

"Always thinking about other people's stuff, huh. Find one for yourself" laughed Shatvari and Aditi joined and they both laughed their hearts out together.

□

Chapter 11

"Why don't we go out and see the town and try to understand the mannerism and thought process of people here? We do not have much time to stay here as you know. So, let's finish our food and set out," said Neel to Dhananjay.

"As you wish your Highness."

Both of them finished their lunch and went out. Strolling through the market they saw a large notice written on a silk cloth hung on a large building. It read: "Everyone is invited to a special dance programme this evening by the enchanting queen of beauty and arts—Nagarvadhu Vaishali. All music lovers are cordially invited."

Neel pointed at the notice and said, "This might be a great occasion to meet a lot of dignitaries and noted citizens of this state. We'll gain good insights."

"But the society is largely comprised of ordinary citizen, what will we gain after meeting the elite class?" asked Dhananjay.

"Yes, but these elite men lead the ordinary citizen. It is true that most of these special citizen do not necessarily respect art, but they still come to pretend their likeness for fine arts. Most leaders of society are these fake pretenders."

"Yes, maybe you are right in a way. Let's go and see for ourselves then."

Inside the huge building and through a wide hallway, there was a five feet high performance stage. Musicians sat on either side of the stage with different instruments, such as, Veena, Mridangam, and Pakhawaj. Rows of chairs occupied the rest of the hall. Special seating with larger and well-cushioned chairs was arranged for the special guests and leaders. Behind these chairs were rows for ordinary chairs for common people. Neel and Dhananjay took their seats in one of the chairs at the back row.

A few moments later the musicians started the program. After carefully tuning their instruments, they all synched into a melodious tune. Vaishali entered the stage from the left. Her feet throbbing effortlessly on the rhythm of the music.

The whole theater erupted in excitement and a wave of thunderclap greeted the dancer. Neel and Dhananjay too joined their hands and clapped. Vaishali was an astonishing beauty. She was dusky in complexion but that duskiness gave her features amazing angular contrasts. She was tall and slender. Her beautiful face had two locks of curly hair dangling on each side. Shining white pearls were threaded in the locks making them look like two vines of Jasmine. She wore red pearl necklace; large golden earrings; and a small nose pin that shone like a pole star. She was appropriately dressed for this occasion. It was hard to decide whether to look at Vaishali or at her dance.

Vaishali's dance matched the rhythmic music played by the musicians. Her dance *mudras* and skilful depiction of various dance postures showed her deep understanding and grasp of the classical music. She perfectly combined her artistry with her divine beauty.

Suddenly, she paused for a tiniest of moment and looked at Neel and Dhananjay in an unusual dilemma. She continued to dance but every once in a while she would find a way to catch a glimpse of the two guests.

Neel noticed this and said to Dhananjay, "Seems like we are looking too attractive to ignore. See how she keeps looking at us."

"Maybe we are looking like two clowns your Highness," replied Dhananjay and both of them laughed.

Neel suddenly realized that people sitting around were gesturing as if they were watching a harlot's dance and not a classical performance. They were keenly watching the shaking of the hips and the movement of Vaishali's curves.

Eventually, Vaishali's performance ended. Amidst the clapping and praises, there were some usual cheesy comments. A lot of people got up and approached Vaishali with various kinds of gifts for her. She accepted the gifts with a pleasant consistent smile on her face. Neel stood up to congratulate Vaishali on how well she performed. Her dance had relaxed him immensely and he was feeling lively again. Both of them walked up to the stage. Neel went near Vaishali and said, "You were really very good. You moved our souls with your dance."

"Who are you, if I may ask? I need to talk to you," said Vaishali looking at Neel with an unusually surprised look.

Neel found it strange that Vaishali didn't respond to the words of praise. Maybe that's not how they praise people here in South Kosala. He smiled at Vaishali and replied, "Sure, tell me what you want to talk about."

"Not here. Meet me at the back garden. It's quiet there."

Dhananjay pinched Neel's elbow and pointed with his head and said, "Go ahead, have a quiet chat."

Neel glanced back at Dhananjay while making his move towards the back garden. Vaishali didn't react in any way to Dhananjay's comment but she just stared at him for a moment and walked out of the hallway. Neel followed her.

As soon as they reached the garden, Vaishali turned around to face Neel. He asked, "So?"

"Please excuse my behaviour but I strongly feel I have seen you somewhere. Your face looks very familiar."

"This is an old trick madam. If you want to be familiar just say so."

"Please try to understand. I am not joking. I feel I know you."

"You are simply mistaken. We are students from Takhskhand. We have never been to this part of the world before." Neel felt the need to tighten his guard and be more careful.

"So why have you come here then?"

"For research and studies."

"Brahmins?"

"Yes."

"Don't look like, though."

"Well, you can't tell looking simply at a man's face whether he is a Brahmin or a Shudra."

"That's right but your whole countenance and personality does not signify you are a Brahmin."

"Actually my grandfather, who was a Brahmin, married a Nishaad woman. As Takhskhand society is very liberal and broad-minded, their alliance was accepted." Neel tried to make up a story to convince Vaishali. He realised how one lie required many more to hide it. Neel saw how the mention of the word 'Nishaad' aroused fresh wave of scepticism on Vaishali's face.

While they were engaged in their conversation a man came running from behind and snatched Neel's leather pouch tucked in his waist. The man grabbed the pouch and went past running. Neel drew a hidden dagger from under his clothing aimed at him and threw it at the man's right leg. The dagger flew and pierced the man's right calf. He struggled to run even a few feet and fell down on the ground. As soon as he fell on the ground, he pulled out the dagger from his calf, got on his feet and ran again. By this time Neel had pounced upon him and held him from his waist. The man tried to attack Neel with the blood-soiled dagger. Neel grabbed his wrist and twisted it. The dagger fell down and the man moaned in pain. Neel snatched his pouch bag and turned towards Vaishali and said, "So your state has thieves too?"

"Mostly thieves, actually."

"Seems like you are not too fond of your state. What do you suggest we do with him? Hand over to the guards?"

"Leave him, let him go. Guards will only thrash him and break his bones for their pleasure."

"But shouldn't a thief be punished?"

"When there are bigger thieves roaming around free, why punish a petty one?"

Neel let the thief go. He apologised with joined hands and limped away.

"So you keep a dagger and your aim is also perfect. I was right in my suspicion. You are not a Brahmin after all. You can't be," said Vaishali.

"You are doubting us for no reason. We are in an unknown country. You just saw what happened. We have to be armed to defend us."

Suddenly, Vaishali almost jumped in the air. Her eyes flashed with a newfound insight.

"Ahhhh yes, I know who you are now...I remember perfectly. You are Neel, the king of Mekal, isn't it?"

□

Chapter 12

"Getting married my friend?", asked Ambrish, the son of town merchant while gently patting Damodar's right shoulder. Ambrish was a stocky young man of average height. Round plump face had an oily skin and wheatish brown complexion. Ambrish wore an elegantly cut hairdo.

"Yes, that's why I am here to invite you my dear friend of friends!", replied Damodar with excitement and happiness. Ambrish was his dearest friend. How could he hide his excitement from him?

"I am happy for you mate. But do you know what happens after marriage? Any idea of the things you must know beforehand?" Ambrish had a twinkle in his eyes.

"I know that marriage brings forth a lot of responsibilities. One has to share all his happiness, sorrows, and everything with a life-partner."

"Oh my innocent fool, that's not what I am asking dear. I meant what happens soon after the wedding? Do you have any experience to tackle that?" Ambrish raised his eyebrows and winked at Damodar that he understood instantly.

"I am not that much of a simpleton, Ambrish. But having such experiences before wedding? Is that appropriate?"

"So you are telling me that you'll meet your wife on the first night with no experience or know-how of what to do? You don't know that this is the time to win over the bride once and for all. Those who get the first night right rule the entire life."

"But before marriage? How that is possibly appropriate? Is this not against the traditions?"

"Everything is possible, my dear friend. In towns, we have courtesans to give such experiences. They are beautiful conjurers adept in the erotic art of love. Young boys and girls from royal and rich families visit these courtesans to know more of such experiences to be better prepared for love life after marriage. This is a tradition in itself my friend."

"I don't feel this is a right tradition. Let me remain a simpleton with no experience." *"I am better off as an innocent fool."* Thought Damodar.

"Don't talk like an ignorant village boy. If you disapprove of the traditions followed in towns then why did you come and study here? What did you come here to learn? See, every girl has countless dreams about her marriage. We men can't come close to grasping their imaginations when it comes to love and marriage. These courtesans can make you aware of those feminine secrets. In order to lead a happy married life you have to understand such desires and dreams of your wife"

"I know what you say, but is this appropriate? What if something goes wrong...?" Damodar still didn't look convinced.

"What can go wrong? You are not going there to fall in love, just spend some time, and get on your merry way. A new courtesan has arrived in town. Her name is Amodini—incredible beauty! I have heard stories of how mighty kings and princes line up to be with her. If you are ready, I can arrange a visit for you."

Damodar thought for a moment, initially hesitated, but eventually nodded in affirmative.

Amodini was a stunning beauty. Tall, slender, and fair-complexion as if white milk and rose nectar combined to create an aura of majesty. Long neck and face decked with a pair of intoxicating large eyes—Damodar had never seen such an exotic beauty.

'Wow! Truly incredible. Who wouldn't fall for such a luscious beauty!' Damodar was awestruck.

Ambrish went ahead and greeted Amodini and introduced Damodar as his friend who studied together with him in town but now lives in his village.

No sooner than Ambrish had expressed his greetings, Amodini cast a sensual look at Damodar, "Damodar! Hmm...Looks like a very decent man, your friend." She then came face-to-face with Damodar. "You have something that I haven't seen anywhere else. You do not look like from a royal or a merchant family."

"That's right, I am from a simple Brahmin family. My father is an Acharya of classical music."

"We too have an intricate relation with music. I hope you too might know some music being Acharya ji's son", asked Amodini widening her amber lit eyes.

"Yeah, I can do my bit, not much."

"This modesty is what makes you different. I am sure you breathe music every moment."

"So you think you can gauge people that well?"

"This is what I have been doing all my life—trying to gauge people. Seen more than my fair share of life", Amodini again cast a sensuous look and took his hand in her hand.

The mere touch of Amodini's hand sent tidal waves across Damodar's body, as if many strings were plucked at the same time. He had never been touched by such a lusciously beautiful woman in his life. Before he could get a hold of himself he heard Ambrish jumping in the conversation, "You are right Amodini, Damodar is a master musician just like his respected father".

"Let's see how much music runs in your veins my dear. Can you match the rhythm of my feet with your beats?"

"You are trying to challenge me?" Laughed Damodar.

"All those who come here, go back after losing everything. Don't harness hopes of winning", said Amodini, still holding the same bewitching look in her eyes.

"If you dare to bet, let's try our fortunes!"

"As you wish—if you win I will always ever dance only for you."

"And if I lose?"

"Then you will play Pakhawaj here for me all your life." Said Amodini with an impish smile, and both Ambrish and Damodar erupted in a playful laughter.

Amodini's place was no less than a grand theatre. White marble floor was covered with soft velvet carpet with very fine embroidery. Large cushions wrapped in silk covers lay on either side of the velvet carpet. Each cushion had a couple of round pillows. Some musical instruments sat in one corner of the grand room. On all four corners of the carpet, four pillars stood as if holding the floor and the roof together. The red pillars had beautifully etched poses of celestial Gandharvas and Apsaras. The walls were also made up of red stone and depicted engraved poses of erotic dancers.

Damodar sat on one of the large cushioned mattresses, took a deep breath and let out a long sequence of notes forming a melodic tune. He started in a fast tempo and picked a melodious composition in Teental. Amodini's feet picked up the rhythm and started to move in incredible dance poses. Melody and rhythm started to play with each other in a fascinating duel. Soon both started to grow in confidence and stature as if to dare each other. The contest thus seemed entrapping not only both the artists, accompanying musicians but also all the engraved celestial dancers on the red walls.

As the music and dance rose to a shared, thrumming crescendo, Amodini abruptly drew back towards Damodar and put her right foot on his left thigh "I am impressed! I have to confess whole heartedly that I have not seen such a master musician as you are. Bet or no bet, I so willingly would serve you dancing all my life".

"So you accept a graceful defeat?" said Damodar while looking at the silver anklet in her curvy leg.

"Sometimes the game takes you at a point where a win and a defeat looks just the same. Where a defeat feels just as sweet", Amodini shook her anklet.

"Seems like you two have found a perfect tuning and I am not required anymore", said Ambrish and he rose to leave.

Amodini didn't seem to care what Ambrish said. Damodar leaned forward and politely bade Ambrish good-bye.

"How come you chose to come to me while there are a few others in town?" Amodini asked Damodar, as soon as Ambrish left.

"I wasn't aware of all this, to be honest. Ambrish brought me here, if truth be told."

"Ohh, so the credit should go to your friend, you didn't want to come, mister", said Amodini stroking Damodar's left palm with her right.

"I didn't say that, exactly."

"Didn't I tell you, all my life I have learnt to understand how men think? Trust me, it's an art in itself. I can tell looking at your face that it's your first time ever."

"Alright, alright…I agree you are great at this 'art'", confessed Damodar while raising his head down.

"Then tell me what is it that brought a man like you here?"

"What is it that brings people to you?"

"People come to us for a lot of reasons. Those in love, come to learn the art of loving; those hurt in love, come for comfort; happy people come to celebrate; sad souls come to mourn. What brings you here?"

"You said you are a master in reading people, try again?"

"Well…you have a beloved?"

"Are you asking or telling me?"

"I am telling you", laughed Amodini, "You have a new found love. You need to learn the ropes quick and you have been told that this is the best way to do that."

Damodar didn't say anything. He kept looking back with a gentle nod and a sideways smile.

"Do you take liquor?"

"Is that a question, or an offer?"

"It's a very old joke." Amodini sneered, "I didn't get a reply, yet".

"Sorry, I don't drink."

"A very strange man! The harlot houses of Shripur run on liquor. It flows faster than the breath of people who come here."

"You are more than enough to intoxicate me, who needs liquor!"

"Didn't I tell you—you have something that others don't. I hope you are ready for the real game now", said Amodini in a sensual and saucy tone.

"If you are the host of the game, why not you prepare me yourself."

"You sure are a naïve player in this", Amodini pulled his collar and gave him a sideways mischievous glance.

Cuddling Amodini in his arms, Damodar pulled the silken duvet from his shoulders. Her soft embrace was smoother anyway: reveling in her arms felt like basking in the winter sun. Her breath smelled like a moist sandal stick, her silken hair flowing like a gentle breeze of spring. He pulled her sweet face close to his. Her lips pulled his in to dance, holding them in and sucking slowly. Damodar had never imagined that the first experience of life would be so intoxicating. The idea of getting up and having another look at her luscious beauty crossed his mind, but he brushed it aside, preferring to clutch her in his arms sturdily.

'Why would I need liquor when Amodini is here? She herself is so intoxicating, she has taken hold of me like a wine. Do all harlots shower so much love on their clients? Or has she just found attunement with me? How did she find the perfect rhythm to lead me in so many melodies? Amodini is not teaching me the art of love making. She is playing this game so intensely that she has forgotten who is teaching whom. Will the game end today? Or is the board just set for a new round?'

Damodar pondered this for a while, clad in the warm embrace of Amodini, and then pulled the duvet over his shoulders.

"How did the first experience go, my friend?" asked Ambrish tapping Damodar's shoulder who was sitting there lost in some distant thoughts.

Damodar kept looking in a far distance. Ambrish pressed his shoulder and asked again, "What's the matter, are you tired?"

"No, I think I should now get back to my home."

"As you wish. But keep in mind this is also your home, you can stay as long as you want."

"I know, but I think it's time to get back", replied Damodar, and, then paused to think and added, "I am thinking I should go and thank Amodini one last time before I leave."

"Courtesans are thanked using the currency of coins, not with words and warmth. We have paid for her services. What else left?"

"Nothing, just...", whispered Damodar.

"Oh my country fool! Don't tell me you've fallen for a courtesan? Don't you understand that this is their profession—To entice every person, they meet and make them feel as if he's the most important person for her. Forget her, go back home and step in new phase of your life."

"Perhaps Ambrish is right. Maybe I am reading the events of last night in my own personal manner. Maybe I am just that—yet another customer for her. Ambrish had rightly said—just spend some time, and get on your merry way. I think I should do the same."

Damodar bade goodbye to Ambrish and started on his journey back to his village.

Two days had gone by since Gunjan's bandages were removed. He felt completely recovered now. He wondered that he didn't meet Shatvari during all this while. She also didn't pay a visit to him. That surprised him. How come she didn't bother to even ask about his health? Shatvari's warm embrace still flashed in his memory. It was a never felt before emotion. Shastri ji was right in telling him that life can't be fully understood in books only. Some things must be experienced. Shastri ji's thought reminded him about Shatvari and how inappropriate it would be to think about her with such feelings. Shatvari is also his guru. A pang of remorse struck him. Were there any unfounded rumours in the village regarding this? Did she go through the taunts of the villagers because of him? Maybe that's why she didn't come to meet him. His heart felt heavier. He would go to Aditi. She was the only one who could tell him what happened.

Gunjan stalled his cart in front of Aditi's house. Aditi's father Vishwamohan was also a Brahmin, but neither was he a scholar of the status of Shastri ji, nor did he garner such respect from the villagers. Although Shatvari and Aditi were fast friends, Shastri ji never really considered Pandit Vishwamohan of his stature. Not that he disregarded him as a person, but he didn't agree with Pt. Vishwamohan's understanding of the holy texts and his interpretations of the scriptures. Pt. Vishwamohan was one of those clerics who defined religion in a very conservative manner. Shastri ji strongly defied this conservatism. Pt. Vishwamohan's financial position was poor. Society hadn't gone down to the level where it could lend ears to a narrow-minded cleric. He barely had any clients. His small two-room house was a simple and modest affair with bare walls and fading paint work.

Gunjan knocked on the door and waited. Aditi opened the door and seemed delighted to find a healthy Gunjan standing in front of her.

"Gunjan, you look very fine now, I hope you have recovered fully?" asked Aditi looking surprisingly happy.

"Just a result of all the blessings of you people."

"Is Gunjan being sarcastic? I too didn't go to see him while he was recovering" wondered Aditi.

"I went to visit my grandmother in the adjoining village that's why couldn't come to see you."

"It's okay, I am sure you would have prayed for my wellness", replied Gunjan and asked, "Do you know how is Shatvari?"

Aditi's face lit up with a mischief and her black eyes shone teasingly.

"Shatvari! She's dying!"

"What are you saying?" asked Gunjan unable to hide his shock, "I am sure you are again having fun with me, please tell me honestly".

"You are a simple fool, Gunjan. Did you not die on anyone, ever?"

Gunjan somehow got Aditi's prank.

"We unfortunate poor Shudras are killed by poverty, we barely have time to die on anybody?" replied Gunjan with a much sombre face, "But what are you hiding? Why don't you tell me what has happened?"

"Shatvari has fallen in love with Damodar. She is going to marry him soon."

Gunjan felt uncomfortable upon hearing those words. He felt disappointed. But soon regained his senses to ask why he should feel this way. Shatvari was not his love interest. He had decided never to be amorous with her. There was no possible relation between them apart from that of a guru and a disciple. She was an educated beautiful Brahmin girl and he was a mere Shudra cart man. Damodar was the right match for her. The news should have delighted him.

"This is good news; very good news in fact", said Gunjan trying hard to look happy.

"Rubbish. You have lost one passenger now. The princess now has her own horse cab to go around in."

Aditi's mischievousness couldn't deter Gunjan from thinking about Shatvari and Damodar. He was trying hard to feel happy about the news but failed.

"Okay then, I should take my leave, if you meet Shatvari, please tell her to invite me in the wedding", said Gunjan with a heavy heart.

"Don't worry, she is your guru, won't go anywhere without taking her fees."

Gunjan didn't reply. He walked back slowly to his cart and moved away. On the way, he kept thinking about what he could actually give to Shatvari in return.

"Shatvari...how come are you here?" asked Gunjan bemused on finding Shatvari standing at his doorstep.

"I think you misunderstood me, Gunjan. I wanted to come to see you. But what happened that day bothered me. I do care about the society and what people might say. They don't care. I worry about you. I will go away from this village once married but you have to stay here and earn your living."

"You are getting married?"

"Yes, with Damodar. Who told you?"

"You didn't, but, yes, congratulations!"

"That's why I came. Are you not happy with the news?"

"If you are happy, then I am happy too."

"Gunjan, I won't be able to teach you music after the marriage. You understand I will have new responsibilities."

"So with you, I will also lose my music."

"Why do you think so? You have learnt much, you have enough skills even to teach others now"

Gunjan replied nothing and kept looking down. A wave of disappointment was clearly evident on his face.

"Gunjan, have you heard of *guru dakshina* that I can ask from you? It's a time-honoured tradition of disciples repaying their gurus. What will you give?" Shatvari tried to lighten the air with this question.

"Ask whatever you want. I have nothing much to offer anyway, as you know."

"You have so much to offer Gunjan. Promise me this that you will never break-away from music. You will revere it as a divine gift and become an accomplished singer and musician. You will not confine your talent to yourself but also share it with others."

"You are asking for too much all at once. What if I fail to keep the promise?" Gunjan looked down again. His voice sunk to a whisper.

"You'll have to bear your guru's curse, then", joked Shatvari.

"One whose existence itself is his nemesis can't be cursed further."

Shatvari was perplexed to find such a change in Gunjan's behaviour. His newfound pessimism baffled her. She didn't realise why the news of her going away saddened him so much. He was the kind of person who lived happily within his means regardless of circumstances. He had no ambitions that kept him awake. Did she arouse any feelings in him that would remain unfulfilled if she left? Did he start to love her and the news of her wedding made him sad? Shatvari glanced upon Gunjan's disappointed face and said, "Don't lose heart. You have no idea what you are capable of. You can give so much back to the world."

Shatvari for the first time felt an unknown uneasiness on parting ways with Gunjan. She left quickly.

Gunjan kept looking at Shatvari's enticing gate. But this time it didn't arouse any amorous feelings in him. All he had was these words of Shatvari ringing in his ears.

"You have no idea what you are capable of. You can give so much back to the world."

"Can giving to the world make you happy? Can you find happiness in other people's happiness? Shastri ji says that we are all part of the Brahma—the Supreme Self. If we are all part of one then surely we all are no different. Where does the difference between myself and others come from? All these differences and disparities are manmade. God made us all equal."

The moment of epiphany literally changed Gunjan's life. He decided to dedicate his life for others. One God and equality of all human beings will be the backbone of his philosophy. He will take his music to the world. He will confront the traditions of inequality on the basis of caste, colour, and creed. Whatever he endured in his life so far, he will not let others go through this. □

Chapter 13

Neel was taken aback to hear his name from Vaishali. How could she recognise him when they had never visited South Kosala before? Maybe there were Kosala's spies in Mekal.

He came face-to-face with Vaishali and asked a bit more sternly, "Who are you exactly? How do you know the Mekal king Neel?"

"First, please tell me honestly. You are the Mekal king, your Highness?" Vaishali's eyes got wet and tears of happiness rolled down her cheeks.

Neel noticed the tears and wet eyes of Vaishali. He was not sure what to make of that but he realized that Vaishali had a deep bond with Mekal.

"Why don't you tell me what's your relation with Mekal? Who are you?"

"Your Highness, I belong to a lowland village of Mekal. They captured our village, made us prisoners and brought us here. They abused my body and soul and forced me to become a *Nagarvadhu*." Tears continued to roll down from Vaishali's eyes. She was looking down and gently sobbing.

Neel's face tensed after listening to Vaishali's plight. His arms flexed and fists clenched. He took a moment to reply to her. He said, "Vaishali you should not suffer any longer. I feel I am a culprit. As your king, it was my responsibility to protect you in the first place. I now promise you that I will not return from here without liberating you."

"Don't take all the blame, your Highness. I always believed that you will definitely come here some day to rescue us. Seeing you here has made me so happy, you can't believe." Vaishali wiped her tears with the back of her hand. Her eyes reflected the joy of finding Neel and starting telling him the agonising tale of the past days.

Neel changed the subject and asked Vaishali, "You have been here for some time now. Maybe you can help us now."

"What kind of help, your Highness? It's not only my pleasure but my responsibility to help you in any way I can."

"Vaishali in order to defeat these Yaduvanshis we must find a smart plan. We can't defeat them in a face-off battle as they are a very strong army. So if we understand them and find their weakness, we can chalk out a strategy to beat them."

"Sure I can be of some help to you. I know some things, but am not sure how much they can help you."

"The fact is that we have been telling people that we have come here to take up a research upon Aryan Civilization. This also serves our purpose of finding more about this society and its values. We can understand their inner contradictions and conflicts to make our plans."

"I understand now. I think I can introduce you to a person who might be of great help. His name is Krishnamurti. He is my guru here who taught me music, dance, culture and everything I know."

"Great! So do we have to tell him our real identity?"

"No. Just tell him what you have been telling others."

"Good, so when can you arrange the meeting?"

"Tomorrow morning."

Neel agreed to meet Krishnamurti the next morning. He thanked Vaishali and walked out of the building with Dhananjay. They both slept that night in keen anticipation of the next morning.

"Guru ji, meet my friends Badrinath and Kedarnath," said Vaishali to Guru Krishnamurti while greeting him respectfully. Turning around she added, "And he is my revered Guru ji Krishnamurti."

Both Neel and Dhananjay joined their hands to greet Krishnamurti.

Vaishali added further, "Guru ji, Badrinath and Kedarnath have come from Takshashila to understand the Aryan culture and its historical development. If you can spare some time to discuss the topic with them, it'll be of a great help."

Krishnamurti was a tall man of fragile frame. He had fair complexion and long face with a wide forehead smeared with red tilak. His long curly hair were neatly tied in a ponytail.

"What kind of information can help your research? Please feel free to ask", Krishnamurti told Neel and Dhananjay.

"We are looking forward to understand the present state of the Aryan society. Its social, political, economical, cultural, and historical background also. We are young students with limited knowledge and experience. Your insights will be hugely beneficial to us," said Neel.

"Okay. Let's go inside in the study room and discuss there."

Leaving the duo with Guru ji, Vaishali took her leave and left. Krishnamurti initiated the discussion.

"Development of any civilization happens in random ways and not in a linear straight line as most people tend to believe. There are peaks and troughs in its journey. There are periods of rapid growth followed by cessation. There are upheavals and turmoils. Sometimes ethics rise and dominate and at other times values are completely depleted. Aryan Civilization has gone through all these phases of development to get here."

"We've heard that at one time Aryan society genuinely stood for morals and ethics?" asked Neel.

"The definition of values and morality can be very subjective and it changes with time and place. What is morally right and justified in one society can be unacceptable in another. No society can be perfectly moral. Just like basic human nature, which has both the positive and the negative aspects at the same time. The delicate balance between the two defines the success or failure of a society. To strike this balance, Aryan society strived to create a social system of idealized human callings, the Varna system. Every person was given a role based on character and qualities. To expand values, principles were put in place. To curb wrongful things, certain boundations and rules were evolved."

"The Varna system in principle is a model approach, but how has it worked practically?"

"As you can imagine, it hasn't been as successful as was expected. It's impossible to keep human beings within predefined limits of any kind. That's why it was made flexible enough to adapt to changing times. For example, if someone is not satisfied or happy with the work or profession he has been assigned, he can choose to change it. There have been many Kshatriya scholars of ancient holy texts—a job originally and socially assigned to Brahmins. Similarly, many Brahmins and Shudras waged wars and triumphed in warfare. But that also gave rise to many issues. The changing roles also affected the overall social ethos. Ambitions arose and collided. Each strata of the society wanted to rise and become the ruler. There have been battles for supremacy, but eventually the basic structure prevailed."

"That's interesting. Would you please tell more about the kind of battles and clashes within what groups?"

"Collisions have happened since the formation of the Aryan society. The oldest in the series of such collisions has been clashes between the Aryans and the Panis. The Pani population was a leading trading community based in the West of India. They were prosperous and affluent. They traded with foreign countries and used the sea-route to make their business prosper. The collision between these two communities continued for several hundred years but as the Panis were not originally warriors, they withdrew and migrated out of India. They continued to do trade with Greece, Arab and Egyptian people. Those who stayed back mingled with the Aryans over a period of time. The present Vaishya community was born out of these Panis."

"There must have been an influence of Pani community over the Aryan culture and Vedic religion. How progressed the process of blending of two cultures?

"Panis were a really smart community of businessmen. They were hard toilers as well. With their hard work and tact, they made amends with the Aryans despite the original differences. They quickly grew to become one of the most respected communities in the Aryan society. They again networked with their foreign partners and started to trade overseas. They have played a vital role in the prosperity of the whole Aryavart. They merged well with the Aryan culture but also kept their own basic tradition and cultural legacy intact. Their philosophical viewpoints were different than the Aryan philosophy. They deeply influenced the Aryan philosophy. In the beginning, Arya Brahmins only believed in Vedic philosophy and considered everyone else that included the Shraman Panis, to be non-conformists. Gradually, the Shraman philosophy influenced the Vedic philosophy enough to become an integral part of the Vedic texts, such as, Vedas and Upanishads."

"But Shraman philosophy is about self-mortification and austerity and Panis are business people with financial ambitions. They worship the deities of prosperity, Lakshmi and Kuber. So, how can Shraman be their guiding way of life?"

"In actuality, Panis are a hard working and toiling class as I just told you. Shraman philosophy is also a way of life based on *Shram*, which means hard work. They do have financial ambitions but they are not luxury-seeking indulgent people. Rather they believe in a life of abstinence and restraint, which is exactly what the Shraman philosophy suggests. Money is just a means to get social respect. Their life is based on the pillars of hard work, discipline, and austerity. In contrast, the Vedic philosophy propagated joy and happiness. It believes the universe as a manifestation of Brahma. They are one and the same. Hence, the universe is as joyful and ecstatic as the Brahma. Life is like an eternal festival. Vedic sages worship nature. The archetypal Aryan incarnations personify these aspects of Vedic philosophy. Krishna's whole persona is joy and ecstasy. He dances, plays his flute, engages in love affairs which are eternally playful. On the other hand, the Pani sages have gained enlightenment as a result of serious devotion and austere practices. There is a stark difference between the two philosophies as you can see. One is a way of joyful and easy going life, while the other signifies diligence and discipline."

"So do you consider Shramanic lifestyle better than the Vedic way in some ways?" Dhananjay asked.

"No, I didn't mean to say that, nor do I believe in that. No philosophy can present an ideal way of life. It cannot be the absolute truth. It can point you in the direction of truth, but itself it's not an absolute. It's a perceptive reality at best. It changes meaning depending on who looks at it. The universe has importance for the joy as well as a need for discipline. Life is both a festival and a diligent devotion. It's a matter of perception. To each his own. Those who find themselves aligned with joyful and festive ways of life choose Vedic way of life and those who'd rather like to live a disciplined and simple life look at Shraman philosophy."

"So is there an emergence of Shraman philosophy again? Are the Panis going back to their original ideas?" asked Neel.

"Yes, you can say that. There is a newfound sympathy with the Shraman philosophy and a lot of Vaishyas are drifting gradually towards their original philosophy."

"And how will this affect the Vedic Aryans? Will it not result in new forms of tension grounds between the two communities?"

"Yes, it could give rise to collision as well as some co-operation. It's kind of an interesting paradox. A lot of Khstariyas have followed the Shraman way. They fulfilled their social hierarchy duties despite that. A lot of Brahmins believed that Shraman is in fact complementary to Vedic philosophical way. Upanishads and Vedanta are born out of such line of thought."

"How and when this Varn-vyvastha transformed into a caste-based system? The discrimination based on caste and all such debased traditions spurted out of the original system. How do you think that deformity took place?"

"It's a long story. At one time Aryan society was very broad minded and devoid of conservatism. There were less limitations in marriage and sexual matters as well. People from one community could easily marry or have conjugal relations with others. It was not a matter of exception but a widely used free practice. The religious values and traditions had space for broad-minded thoughts. They believed that religion is universal and eternal and their social system can apply to the whole human race. For that it had to be flexible and adaptable. That was a huge factor in the expansion and development of Aryan culture beyond Aryavart. Lot of minor cultures blended into Aryan society. The religion, philosophy, spirituality, science, and trading took Aryan civilization above most of the contemporary civilizations in the world. As it grew and many different cultures and civilizations merged, the social hierarchy got diluted. The original principles on which it was based lost along the way somehow. That resulted in discrimination based on caste and creed. The social division based on caste and race started to take shape.

The Aryan society grew faster in the Southern areas. Hot and humid climate, fertile soil, coastal territory aided the development of Aryan population there. The Southern society was amongst the most developed in the world at one time. It was a sea-trading route connecting many traders around the world. But the proximity to sea also affected it adversely. Sea cyclones and storms over time destroyed large parts of the territory. Gradually, they eroded liberal traditions and turned Aryan culture into a narrow-minded discriminating society over time."

"I can understand social division, but how untouchability crept into the great Aryan Civilisation?

"That is a long sordid tale. The biggest victim of this kind of discrimination is the Dalit or Chandaal community. They are forced to live in cremation grounds. Some believe that they do black magic and understand the mysteries of ghouls and ghosts that roam the crematoriums. That led to more and more discrimination against them. They are considered so lowly and ghastly that people even avoid going anywhere near lest their shadow should cast an evil effect."

"I agree. The conditions of Chandaals are really pitiful. I wonder if they have learnt to live with this pathetic state. Do they not burn with revolting pangs of agony?" asked Neel.

"I have come to know that they have begun to organise. There is a growing anguish in Chandaals. They hate the upper caste, especially, the priests. This hatred and anguish is taking them to the path of *Tantra*. They see *Tantra* as the saviour as it could bless them with extraordinary powers and attainments to change their state of being. Maybe they consider that they can use these spiritual attainments to reclaim their place in the society and avenge the misdeeds done against them. Being a patriarchal society, the condition of women is even more ghastly in the Chandaal community. That has resulted in more anger in the women there. A lot of South Kosala Chandaal women have formed a group that aims to help each other to spiritual Tantric attainments and take revenge from the upper caste."

Suddenly, it occurred to Neel that it was Monday and they had to go to the security office for attendance. He joined hands in appreciation and asking for the leave, "Guru ji, sorry to interrupt you, I think we must leave now we have to go to the security office."

"For registering your attendance?" I know that's mandatory for all foreigners. When will we see a day when men will learn to completely trust other men! Perhaps, man is the only creature that creates its own cage."

They took leave from Krishnamurti and walked out. Krishnamurti bade goodbye cordially and did not ask for any fee or gift of any kind.

Dhananjay and Neel looked at each other in a feeling of respect and newfound vision. Maybe Yaduvanshi society is still alive simply because of people like Krishnamurti and the rich altruistic owner of the guest-house they were lodging in.

□

Chapter 14

Breeze swayed around intoxicated. A haunting tune rose from the bosom of Mahanadi's waves. Shatvari's breath ran amok and longed to meet Damodar's warm breath. Damodar's arms were wrapped around her slender waist. His lips were caressing her navel. Slowly, his lips felt their way round her waist like a serpent slithering up a sandal tree. Shatvari's breath effused a sweet incense. For a while she got lost in this incense not knowing when Damodar's lips moved up from her waist and reached her lips. Her tender lips started to melt in his lips. Shatvari felt as if Damodar's breath had struck up the same melody that had made her burst into a dance. She felt the same urge again, but of a different kind this time. Her silky hair desired to spread on his shoulders. Her slender waist wished to sway in his arms.

Damodar's fingers slid up and found the knot of Shatvari's blouse. A quick flick of the fingers and the blouse slipped down to her waist and then to satin sheet. Her delicate bosom melted in Damodar's wide chest. Her body throbbed and heaved in his strong arms. Damodar caressed hair off her shoulders and face. Her embalming fragrance and the warmth of her body sent a tidal wave through Damodar and a sudden memory encroached his sensibilities. A memory of Amodini hovered over the presence of Shatvari in his arms, memory of Amodini's fragrance, her warmth, and her hair. Damodar tried to brush her memory aside but it stormed back, more vividly. Gradually, Shatvari disappeared and Amodini took shape as he closed his eyes. Coming down from his eyes, Amodini started to pervade his entire being. His hands, his breath, his lips, and the entire body felt only Amodini.

Oblivious of Damodar's internal conflict, Shatvari kept swaying and spreading her fragrance in his arms. With interlocked lips and the play of hands dancing on an unknown tune of love, they were lost in their own ideas of love. Damodar's hands slipped down to the roundness of Shatvari's hips. As he started to caress and feel her even more with his hands, lips, and all his senses, everything stopped for a moment. Amidst the fast beating of two hearts, everything stood still. A whisper of sweet sound took shape from Shatvari's lips and with an 'Aah' the magic was broken. Damodar's hands grasped her hips even tighter.

Damodar and Shatvari settled in Shripur after their wedding. Damodar took a music teacher's position in a respected school. Realizing Damodar's caliber, he was soon awarded with the title of Acharya followed by Chief Acharya at the school. His fame spread beyond the premises of the school and soon he became a respected personality in the music circles of Shripur. He put in a lot of hard work to compliment his natural talent. He would practice for hours every day and Shatvari supported him in every step.

Ambrish was still a friend of the household but they would not meet as frequently as before. Damodar's heart occasionally found itself wondering about Amodini but those moments would fade away just like due drops with the sunrise.

After some time, a grand musical festival was organised in Shripur. Many renowned musicians were invited to perform. Damodar was also invited. He accepted the invitation gladly knowing that this was not only a great opportunity to showcase his talent but also to learn the nuances of various musical styles from the other performing musicians.

The festival was organized in Rangmandir a huge theater. Vocalists, musicians, dancers, and other artists used to come here to perform from all over South Kosala and adjoining states. For them it was a temple of sorts. At the day of the festival, Damodar wanted to peruse the venue just like a devotee would want to go round his place of worship before a grand ritual. The main hall was circular and had the performance stage right in the center and seating facility around it. The front row was meant for special guests and was visibly large and well decorated. The rest of the chairs were normal. Outside the hall, there was a hallway that connected with other smaller performance theaters. They were meant for rehearsal performances.

While roaming through the hallway, Damodar heard the dancing steps emanating from one of the theaters. He tried to recognize the ghunghroo rhythm. It was familiar. He went towards the door of the theater and leaned forward to peep in.

It was Amodini. She was rehearsing and was totally lost in the dance. Damodar felt a pleasant surprise. Amodini's beauty was still hypnotic. A slender waist as delicate and fragile as a Jasmine vine; a heaving bosom throbbing through a thin purple blouse; a short royal blue saree draped only up above the knees flaunting pearl white silken legs of the dancer. Damodar felt her beauty as if a divine light was flickering through immense and impenetrable darkness. He stood there watching her moves. He wondered whether to focus upon her or her dance moves. Her dance complemented her physical form in its divinity and grandness. It imbibed aesthetics and creative skillful agility of a master who knew what she was doing. She was unaware of his presence. But soon she noticed Damodar standing at the door and looking in through a gap.

The sudden union of gaze caught her off balance and she fumbled and fell on the ground. As she fell, one of her silver anklets tied to her ghungroos broke free and slipped away. Damodar rushed to the spot in a flash. He tried to help her stand but she herself got up and adjusted her dress.

"Are you hurt Amodini?" asked Damodar.

Amodini was still looking down mending her clothes. "Yes, seems like some strain in my waist but nothing that won't heal with time," replied Amodini rubbing her waist.

"Thank God, it's nothing serious. Yes, time heals everything. Here, get up and tie your anklet."

"Why not you do it yourself? I might feel better." Amodini moved her leg towards Damodar and for the first time looked straight into his eyes with a gentle smile.

Damodar sat down bending one knee and held her ankle on his thigh.

Amodini put her leg on Damodar's thigh and moved it further elegantly. Her saree slipped further up her knee making her thigh in open sight. Emerging out of the royal blue saree, her naked skin gleamed like a full moon coming from beyond a veil of dark clouds. Amodini slightly rubbed the back of her foot onto Damodar's thigh. It sent a flutter of waves down his spine. His heartbeats raced and he could feel the hair at the back of his neck.

She kept looking at him and smiled. "So how have you been Acharya ji?"

"Who told you that I am now an Acharya?"

"Your fame moves faster than you Acharya ji. What if you won't remember your old friend, even though you have been in our town for some time now."

"Nothing like that dear. Just been busy, you know."

"Never missed me? Never felt like meeting again?"

"You know that I would have. But then thought how proper that would be."

"Got married?"

"Asking me, or telling me that you know?"

"Good, so you remember our old ways of communication. I know you got married to your beloved. Are you happy with her?"

"Well, you are the master. Tell me what do you think?"

"I can tell that you still have the memories of the night we spent together. If we hadn't met today you would have certainly come to meet someday soon, I am sure."

Amodini looked at Damodar's face. She knew she had fired the erotic arrow at the right moment. But she needed to see the signs of affirmation.

"Won't you tell something about yourself? How have you been?" asked Damodar.

"So finally you want to know how I have been. Seems like you forgot your bet. You won the bet and walked away from the reward."

"Oh, that was just a joke, nothing serious."

"Maybe for you, but I took it most sincerely."

"Well, so you can fulfill that promise now. Dance here in this festival as if you are doing that just for me."

"Will you be able to match the rhythm of my feet with your heartbeats?"

Damodar felt the same flurry of emotion as he did feel when he met her for the first time. The entire experience came down thunderously upon him.

"The promise from your side was to dance for me. I don't need to sing any more."

"That entirely depends upon you. If your heart can stop its breaths from throbbing with the rhythm of my feet, you can stay away. Else I will wait for you there." Amodini raised her eyebrow as if throwing a challenge to Damodar. She then gently walked out of the room.

Damodar sat there motionless. Amodini was adept at reading the minds of men. He was more than eager to get on the stage with her and create the same magic of music synchronisation that they had created when they first met. But he was a married man with a stable household. His respect and fame in the society also put him ethically beyond such adventures of engaging with a courtesan. On the other hand, that was the inherent role of a courtesan—to please the respected men of the society. They were not merely treated as an object of lust. They were highly trained artists with skills in classical dance and music aimed at the finer sensibilities of the elite men. Still, he knew whatever he felt for Amodini was not simply a emotionless attraction for a random courtesan. The thought troubled him. Heart and mind moved in contrasting directions.

The festival opened with Amodini's performance. Many renowned musicians accompanied her on the stage. They were playing and enjoying the rhythm of her feet. But Amodini's eyes were searching for Damodar in the crowd. For a while the hope remained alive in her eyes and she kept up the routine but when she realized that it was in vain her whole body almost gave up. She was dancing just for the sake of it. The aura and hypnotism of her usual performance was lacking. The dance lost its soul. People in the crowd noticed it and were visibly bored.

Sitting in the last row of the auditorium, Damodar, too felt that Amodini was not dancing as she usually did. He also knew its reason.

"I met Amodini?" said Damodar.

"Who? That courtesan Amodini? After all you couldn't keep control on your silly self my friend," replied Ambrish.

"Yes, I met her at the recent festival. I controlled my heart but her feet were dying to harp on my command."

"I see. Now even they fall in love. What special quality have you got that she is dying to come to you? They make the royal princes and kings die for them and you are saying she is mad for you. Are you sure, that you are not being befooled?"

"I think I have learnt enough from life to know the difference between confusion and genuine feelings. I have seen a sincere desperation in her eyes."

"And what about you?"

Damodar didn't reply. He kept looking ahead in the vacuum.

"Seems like the matter is more serious than I thought. What do you want to do now?" asked Ambrish.

"I am going to see her once."

"I hope you know the consequences. Keep a tab on your heart my friend. It's a no-return journey."

"You may be right. But I think I have stepped on that journey already. So why not go and see it through. Maybe I'll find a way back."

Amodini looked up to find Damodar in her dance theater. An expression of surprise mixed with joy appeared on her face.

"See, your helpless poor feet dragged you here to me finally. I told you, you won't be able to stop yourself for long," said Amodini.

The expression on her face changed to one of arrogance and

pride. She felt as if Damodar came on his knees asking for her there.

"Well, not that helpless but it was important for me to come. Something needs to be done."

"At least some truth even if not the whole. What was so important that you felt like coming here?"

"Wanted to talk a few things with you."

"All that you want to say can't be said with your words. Leave it. I understand."

"So let this be our last meeting, I can't betray my wife."

"You sound like you have rehearsed that a few times. But you are failing. Are you not betraying your own self?"

Damodar didn't reply. He looked away from Amodini and looked at a window that brought in some fresh air into the hall.

Amodini held his hand and pulled him down. "Sit here please."

The touch of Amodini's hand raised his sensation that he had determined to suppress. He moved slightly away from her. She moved even closer and asked, "Have you started drinking yet?"

"No not yet." Damodar kept looking away.

Amodini moved her face closer to Damodar's face and rubbed her cheek ever so slightly. Damodar felt he would melt away any moment.

"You will have to start soon then. Who would intoxicate you in my absence?" Amodini put her arms around the neck of Damodar and pulled him towards her. "Let your heart open up to its core and come to me. You can then decide for yourself what is right or wrong."

Amodini pulled him closer and put her lips on Damodar's lips. Luscious lips kissed away Damodar's doubts and hesitation. He sprawled over her body in the emotions of the moment like molten candle wax.

Damodar sat in his house with his Veena.

"You look lost in distant thoughts. Is anything wrong?" asked Shatvari.

"I have to prepare for an important program. Can't think of anything."

"Important program...you are quite busy in these programs these days. You don't seem to bother about the household or even me."

"So my wife has a concern about her husband?"

"Really. I didn't say anything to mean that. Should I be concerned?"

"Well, you meant that, didn't you?"

"If you felt that, I was just joking. But you do look lost in thoughts beyond my knowledge these days."

"There are a lot of things in life. Not sure you should know each."

"I am your wife. I have full right to know each and everything happening in your life."

Shatvari sat down beside him and said, "Okay give me the Veena, I'll help you with your practice. What's the subject of your program?"

"Lost in her thoughts" whined Damodar, "Can you not leave me alone for a few moments?"

Shatvari thought it was right to go away from there. But she kept thinking about this. What could be the reason of Damodar's frustration? Nothing had changed in their personal life that could disturb him. There were no apparent issues. But he was definitely disturbed. She wanted to know its reason. Suddenly, she thought of Ambrish. He was the closest friend Damodar had in Shripur. He would know for sure.

Damodar was lying on the carpet beside Amodini's feet. He slowly rubbed his cheeks onto her silver anklet. He was looking up at her face while Amodini's thighs were clearly visible from within her saree.

"Ambrish says royal kings and princes fall down to their knees for you."

"If that were the case, there would be golden crowns instead of silver anklets here," laughed Amodini.

"And here you have a poor Brahmin. Tell me honestly, what did you find in me that you preferred me over all those rich kings and merchants?"

"They don't love women like us. For them we are just an object of pleasure—a harlot. Moreover, they don't breathe music as you do. As I do. I can kick away any number of soulless crowns but a heart fluttering with the divine notes of music is life for me."

Amodini caressed Damodar's cheek with the sole of her foot. Damodar's shivering lips were desperate to get a feel of her silky thighs. "Well, I tried my best to hold tight to my heart...." Damodar continued to move up from her ankles, calves, and up to her warm thighs.

"But it slipped out anyway..." thought Amodini and pulled her leg back and Damodar slipped back to her calves. Amodini laughed and added further, "I spotted you right in the first meeting that each cell in your body was dying to throb at the rhythm of my feet."

Damodar softly planted a kiss on Amodini's ankle and said, "When the breeze that touches you becomes musical how can one not be mesmerised with your magic. People often die to grab the beauty of body but fail to see the music that emanates from it."

"Music would come from each part and you are stuck only at my feet." Amodini pulled Damodar towards her and her ample bosom took him in.

Ambrish's four-storeyed house was a grand building. It was encircled by ten feet high redstone wall. Once inside the house, Amodini couldn't help but see the abundance and grandness of the place. She wondered how rich Ambrish might be and whether that was the reason why Damodar became his friend in the first place. But that wasn't a good thought as Damodar was a simple Brahmin scholar interested only in music. She wasn't sure what was true in a way. If he was actually a simple Brahmin how come he had friends like Ambrish? Maybe Ambrish was the reason of Damodar's disturbance in some way. Was Damodar harbouring any ambitions? Was there an unknown facet of Damodar that she was unaware of? Such flurry of thoughts troubled her mind as she walked further into the house.

Suddenly, Shatvari's eyes caught a glimpse of a large room on the left hand side of the yard. The scene took her breath away. She felt the ground beneath her feet slipping like sand. It was Damodar. He was lying in a woman's arms as if a lousy snake was entwined around a Sandal tree. She was resting on Damodar's chest with her breasts pressed between them while they locked their lips in a timeless passage of play. Damodar's eager hands were fumbling to pull down her wet saree down from her busty hips. The pair was so engrossed in the amorous act that they didn't realize that Shatvari was standing right on the doorstep.

□

Chapter 15

"What are you thinking?" asked Dhananjay while walking out of Krishnamurti's house. Neel looked puzzled. He put a counter question, "What is your opinion?"

"I think Yaduvanshis have their enemies within them."

"Maybe, but who are they?"

"Can't you figure out?"

"Maybe I do, but I want to know who do you think are their enemies?"

"You know it very well that the Chandaals and Dalits are their most potential enemies lurking within their own backyard. They have been exploited for generations. They are girding up to organise themselves. At the first opportunity, they will go all out on the Yaduvanshi higher castes and would do everything to destroy them."

"That's exactly what I am concerned about. Chandaals' fury is not simply confined to Yaduvanshis. They are angry with the degeneration of the whole Aryan Civilization. They are gradually opting for a path of aggression and violence. They are learning black magic. Today they are fighting the rule of the debased Aryans and tomorrow they might just turn their swords against us too. They will fight and oppose any form of state rule and entire system. We should be very wary of them."

"So you take them as our enemy as well?"

"Not necessarily as enemy, but certainly not as friends. You have to understand that an enemy of Aryans would not always be our friend. Moreover, we are not against the Aryan culture and its great civilization. We have to learn and imbibe a lot from that culture. Their science is highly developed. Their philosophy is of the highest order. We are against their insensitive ideology of imperialism and their caste-based inhuman discrimination."

"And how do we fight them then? Who will help us?"

"I pin my hopes on the Vaniks, the enterprising business people."

"But why will they stand by us? They are peace-loving merchants why will they fight their masters?"

"Dhananjay, their philosophy is based on diligence and labour. They believe in hard work to earn their living and status. Any sort of theft and manipulation is against their ideology. They are against any form of exploitation to grab assets of others. They are firmly against any form of violence. All we have to do is to explain to them the policies of expansion of the Aryan kings. They must be made to understand that the present Aryan culture will ruin the Vanik way of thinking eventually."

"But Vaniks have already moved on leaving their original philosophy behind."

"No that's not the case. You didn't pay proper attention to Krishnamurti's talk. Shraman philosophy is on the rise again. This is the best opportunity to get them against the Aryans. As you know that the main strength of the Aryans is their economic prosperity. Most of the trade and business is directly influenced by the Vanik community. If they go against the Aryans, the whole empire will come tumbling down."

"What's your plan then?" Dhananjay's eyes lit up with excitement.

"First let's finish our conversation with Krishnamurti. We'll plan once we know enough."

Neel patted Dhananjay's shoulder and they both moved towards Krishnamurti's house.

"Do the Chandaals and Dalits feel this anger against only the South Kosala upper castes or, do they feel betrayed by the whole Aryan community?" Neel asked the question to carry on the discussion with Krishnamurti.

"Most of them are in it together. The Chandaals and Dalits from other states are in secret pact with each other," replied Krishnamurti.

"This must be a cause of concern to the Aryan kings. This can result in a mutiny and a revolution any time. Are they prepared to combat this internal threat?" Asked Dhananjay.

"Not sure if they are," replied Krishnamurti adding further that, "Aryan rulers have their own problems and internal conflicts. The biggest rift is between Raghuvanshis and Yaduvanshis. Both believe in physical expansion of their state boundaries. Yaduvanshis employ force and raw aggression while Raghuvanshis use tact and shrewdness. Yaduvanshis are losing their fundamental values in the tryst with the army power. The focus has been merely on destroying and capturing other states. Raghuvanshis are exploiting the overtly ambitiousness of Yaduvanshis. They are making it worse by supporting the downward spiral by sprouting corruption in the society to drive it on a path of self-destruction. They pay handsome bribes to senior administrators of South Kosala to promote corruption in the overall system. They are driving our youth get used to prostitution, drugs and gambling."

Neel and Dhananjay looked at each other and passed a confirmatory smile as they had already seen the signs of widespread corruption in South Kosala.

"Many thanks for your valuable time, Krishnamurti ji. You literally helped us scan through all the pages of Aryan Civilization's history. Right now we have enough to ponder upon and write our thesis. Now we'll roam about in the state and assess the political, economical, and social circumstances here ourselves. If we have any doubt, we'll find our way here again." Neel got up with folded hands in a gesture of thanks.

"As you wish. I am happy that both of you are so serious about your research. You are most welcome anytime."

Both gratefully walked out.

"We will have to meet the Vaniks", said Neel to Dhananjay and Vaishali.

"Why?" asked Vaishali.

"We will have to show them the face of reality which they have been ignoring."

"Which reality?"

"The reality of oppression and exploitation. Oppression can't be tolerated for long. Oppressed class often seeks solution in violence and revenge. Their first target is often the rich and affluent class. The indulgences of the affluent class of South Kosala must be arousing envy in them and will surely become the first target of their vengeance. We have to make the Vanik's realise this", Neel explained.

"But how will we meet Vaniks? And why would they listen to us? For them we are merely some students living on beneficences from them", asked Dhananjay.

"Leave that to me. All rich men and their debauchee sons line up before my house", said Vaishali with a smile of arrogance.

However, Neel didn't like the way she mentioned her profession but he knew he had no other option.

□

Chapter 16

Watching Damodar and Amodini in that state sent a bolt of lightning on Shatvari. The whole universe came tumbling down at her head. She was shocked. A stream of tears rolled down from her eyes spontaneously. The love for Damodar was melting down as saline water down her anguished cheeks.

Shatvari's moans caught Damodar's attention. He was awestruck and didn't know what to do. He wanted to rush and go towards her but he stayed as he was—entwined in the arms of his beloved.

Shatvari needed nobody to console or explain anything. She started to run. She just ran aimlessly outside the house towards her home. She was cursing the whole universe, all the ideals, all the talk of love and sacrifice. Religion and spirituality existed only in the books. In reality, men lived only to fulfill their beastly sensuousness and carnal desires. She loved Damodar like a god. She trusted him at the core of her heart. He not only betrayed her but also the very idea of a sacred bond that ties two souls together. Where was that bond of Shiva and Shakti? Where was that surrender to Brahma! Everything was a big lie.

Shatvari decided to leave Shripur and return back to her village. She took her essential luggage and left on her journey back home the same day.

Gunjan dedicated his life to music. He imbibed the insights of philosophy and spirituality into his music and recited the songs of love and social unity to people in simple language. Gradually, people started to follow him. The section of the society that was kept away from the nuances of spirituality and deeper cultural understanding found great insights in his songs. People at the lowest rung of the society found solace in his music and devotional songs. He was looked upon as a social saint. Renowned intellectuals, such as, Shastri ji respected his ideology. On the other hand, fundamentalists, like Pandit Vishvamohan looked at him as an opponent. They took him as a challenge to their orthodox social system.

Shatvari noticed a vast mass of people gathered around a Banyan tree as she entered the village. They were all swaying to the tunes of a devotional song. She had never seen anything like this in the village. Religious ceremonies did happen time-to-time. But she had never seen the common folks gathered like this. Shatvari was curious to know the face behind such a godly voice. As she walked up to the Banyan tree, she was surprised to find Gunjan singing devotedly with his eyes closed. Shatvari felt very happy to see Gunjan engrossed in devotional music. Still, she wasn't able to overcome the pangs of sadness that were there when she entered the village. Gunjan's melodic voice couldn't quite get to her grief. Her eyes were moist with tears waiting at the periphery. As soon as the song was over, Gunjan scanned through the audience with gratitude and he saw Shatvari. He was surprised to see her standing there with wet eyes. He rushed forward through the crowd and asked her, "Shatvari...how come you are here? And how come your eyes are wet with tears?"

"Nothing...just overwhelmed by your music, Gunjan", Shatvari replied while wiping her eyes with the back of her hand.

"How are you and how is Damodar ji?"

The mention of Damodar's name brought back all the sadness rushing back to her face. She tried to look calm and replied, "All is okay. How are you?"

"I am fine as you can see. Paying back my debt owed to you as my guru." Gunjan looked straight into Shatvari's eyes and asked, "I realise you are trying to hide something from me. I don't think you are happy."

"Nothing much, just ordinary things. You tell me how come you have started with your group of followers. Are you preparing to be a leader?"

"No...," Gunjan smiled and said, "Whatever I have learned from you and Shastri ji, all that you taught me about religion and spirituality, I try to weave that in simple songs so that people can relate to that. I tell them that the universe came into existence out of love and for love itself. With these thoughts in mind, everything will look divine and holy."

Hearing such philosophical thoughts made Shatvari even more restless. Her recent life experience was contrary to all such thoughts. Her divine love turned out to be a fake entity. The person she treated as a god turned out to be a beast. She wanted to unfold her heart to him. But she kept quiet with a great effort. She simply said goodbye to Gunjan and went to her parents' house.

"Maybe love is blind to worldly logic. Maybe this blindness made me worship Damodar", spoke Shatvari while leaning against Aditi's shoulder. Shatvari's eyes were still wet.

"I think humans do not have a constant form. We have many guises inside of us. Circumstances make us gods at one time and devils at another time", replied Aditi.

"But are we simply driven by circumstances? Is there no room for introspection and patience?" asked Shatvari.

"Sometimes some emotions ride over all the intellect and patience. People make mistakes under the influence of such emotions. Maybe something similar happened with Damodar."

"A mistake can be realized and corrected. When one repeats the same mistake without even an attempt to stop it, you can't call it a mistake anymore. It becomes a sin."

"How do you know Damodar doesn't realize his mistake? Or for that matter, whether he is trying to make amends?"

"If that were the case, he would not have repeated it again and again. I am sure he has been neck deep in this for some time now. It was not the first time." Tears rolled down Shatvari's eyes and she made no attempt to wipe them off.

"So what do you want to do now? Even the gravest mistake can be rectified. You have to give him a chance to realise and amend himself."

"But will we have the same love and respect for each other? Once a thread is torn, it can't be joined without a visible knot."

"That depends upon the fact whether Damodar ever had love for you in his heart. If he repents and comes back to you that will prove his love for you. Just like a holy river cleanses all the impurities of its path, love can wipe all the sins and follies from a relationship."

"What if his coming back is simply a social arrangement?"

"Arrangements are done out of compulsion. What will force him, except love, to come back to you?"

Shatvari had no answer to that question. Aditi was right. Damodar had no such compulsion. There was only one possible bond between the two, that of love. Only if it's still there.

"Do you think love is always divine?" Shatvari asked Gunjan.

"Yes. Love is God's gift to us and that's why it must be divine."

"If that is so then why one can't faithfully love only one person. Why do people go from one to another and another seeking love? Why do people forget love for lust?"

"Lust is also a part of love. Fulfilling lust is also a way of love."

"But can lust become love without faith and surrender?

"Yes, why not. Only if there is no ego and selfishness."

"What do you mean? How can love be divine without faith and surrender?"

"Why do you seek surrender to only one person? God can't be tied to one person. So is the thing with love."

"What does that mean? Is there no place for faith in love? Does marriage mean nothing?"

"It's not like that..." Gunjan paused a little while gazing straight into an exasperated Shatvari.

"Then?"

"Actually, the whole cosmos is just a reflection of Brahma. One Brahma, one Universal Consciousness. Everything is Brahma. Nothing is separate. The individual soul and the universal are not separate. People don't realize this but they do feel it in their inner being. The individual soul is always longing for the Brahma. It's always searching, seeking and restlessly looking for it. That's why we have so many desires. All are born out of that original desire to merge in the Brahma. What you call love is also one such desire. Out of the *Maya's* illusion, we seek love in different people, one after another. We are constantly attracted to newer people. The search is always on. As the search doesn't realize what the real search is, the circle goes on. If one realizes that all are same and one the search will end."

"So you mean to say that until one realizes the Brahma, he or she can't be fully faithful in love? Then what is the need of marriage when one can't be faithful?"

"There must always be a vow for faithfulness. That's what marriage propagates. The attempt to faithfully seek your love in one person is actually a path to knowing Brahma."

Shatvari felt that their opinion was coming to a point where they could agree to some extent. It was strange that once she was Gunjan's guru and now he enlightened her on the topic of love and philosophy. She felt slightly relieved. She started to think that Damodar's fault has been his ignorance. He couldn't find our love sufficient and that's why he had to seek it elsewhere. That simply meant that he was just a simple man with worldly flaws. Not a God that she took him for.

Shatvari's parents found out about all the events. Damodar's father Acharya ji wasn't aloof to it either. They all tried to talk Shatvari into going back to Damodar and restore her household but she wouldn't listen to anyone. She believed that if her love had any strength, it would pull Damodar back to her. Whether he came with repent or begging on his knees is another matter. She wouldn't initiate the matter at all.

In the meantime, Shatvari started to meet Gunjan frequently. His talks were soothing to her estranged heart. She started to get engrossed in devotion to God. She started to believe in the thought that what we call love was actually a yearning for the Almighty. It's just a matter of expression.

A lot of people from the village started to talk about Shatvari. Not only was she living with her parents leaving her husband in town, she was associating with another man, that too a Shudra. Tongues wagged. Aditi's father Pandit Vishvamohan also felt it going beyond the social rules. He was already not happy with the growing fame of Gunjan, now his frequent meetings with a Brahman girl made the matters worse.

"Why is Shatvari living with her parents? Why not go back to her husband?" Pandit ji asked Aditi.

"How would I know? It's their internal matter."

"These things are not simply internal matters of a family. These are social matters. We all live in a social order. It's not right for a married girl to come live with her parents for so long."

"She is living with her parents, why do you care?"

"If every girl started to do that, our whole social system will collapse. What about her frequent meetings with that Shudra cart man!"

"What about it? He is no more simply a cart man. He is a saintly figure now."

"How can a Shudra take up the job of a Brahmin?"

"Maharishi Valmiki was also a Shudra."

"Right, so now you will also teach me philosophy. I am telling you in clear words Aditi, I do not want you to meet that girl anymore."

Aditi didn't reply. She bowed her head and went out of the room.

Soon Shatvari found out that she was pregnant with Damodar's child. The feeling of motherhood made her even more anguished as the father of the unborn child was not with them. That erupted into thoughts of doubt and nervousness. She felt the urge to go back to him. But she had decided not to do that until he came with apologies. Even if he did come back, maybe that would be for the sake of the child and not for her.

Soon the whole village found out about the news of her pregnancy. People started to link the child with Gunjan. Pandit Vishvamohan grabbed this opportunity with both hands. He had obvious issues with Gunjan and he was jealous of Shastri ji's social reputation as well. He felt he could kill two birds with a single stone.

Village chief Jugalkishore and head of Panchayat, Sarpanch Ramprasad were present in the meeting called by Pandit Vishvamohan.

Jugalkishore was a short and stocky man of dark complexion. Protruding belly and round face gave an impression of a man enslaved by luxuries. On the other hand, Ramprasad was a tall and lanky man of dark complexion and sharp features. He had an aura of alertness on his face.

"This cart man Gunjan is hell bent on destroying all our social traditions. He goes around his Shudra community reciting the Vedic knowledge as if it's a child's play." Pandit Vishvamohan was loud and clear in his tone.

"Yes, we have also heard him saying that a lot of rituals, were irrelevant and useless. He stresses for devotion and meditation instead," Jugalkishore said.

"That is all because of Pandit Aditya Shastri ji. He gave the lessons in holy texts to this Shudra. On top of that his own daughter has left her husband and is now staying with them. If that wasn't enough, she is very cosy and a frequent visitor to this cart man, Gunjan." Pandit Vishvamohan wanted to come right to the point.

"There is no doubt that Shastri ji is a very learned man. He would have pondered long and hard before imparting Gunjan with the Vedic knowledge. He would have tested his abilities before making him his student," stated Sarpanch Ramprasad.

"Can Shastri ji decide who can or cannot study the Vedas? Our eternal tradition and culture does not allow this at all," replied Pandit Vishvamohan.

"Traditions are created and modified by learned intellectuals of the society. I believe that someone like Shastri ji has the deserving right to guide us in the right direction even if that meant changing the traditions," insisted Ramprasad.

Jugalkishore felt that the discussions was getting hot. He suggested, "Why should we argue about this here? Why not call the Panchayat and let it be argued in front of the whole village?"

Panchayat was called and the whole village gathered around the five members of the Panchayat. Gunjan and Shatvari were summoned as the accused. Shastri ji and Acharya ji served the dual role of the relatives of the accused as well as the religious social experts. Pandit Vishvamohan was also invited to give his expert opinion.

Village chief Jugalkishore started the proceedings by addressing the whole gathering. "Today's Panchayat has been called to assess the accusations labeled against Gunjan and Shatvari. Gunjan has been accused of imparting the Vedic knowledge to Shudras. He, himself being a Shudra, has no right to interpret and spread his Vedic knowledge to people. Shatvari has been accused of leaving her husband and living with her parents. On top of that she maintains friendship with another man despite being pregnant. Now I hand over the matter to the five members of this Panchayat and the invited experts to discuss and come to a mutually agreed solution."

As soon as Jugalkishore finished, Sarpanch Ramprasad addressed Shastri ji, Acharya ji, and Pandit Vishvamohan, "First of all I would like to hear the opinion of our experts here. Shastri ji what do you have to say about the accusations?"

Shastri ji thought serenely for few moments and then said, "According to the Vedic Shastras, a person can't be truly labeled Brahmin by birth. A person's aptitude, intellectual level, and abilities should decide the social hierarchy for him. There are many examples in the history of Aryan culture where people born into non-Brahmin families went on to become great Rishis and Maharishis. Maharishi Valmiki, Maharishi Vishvamitra, Rishi Jabaal and many more...."

Even before Shastri ji could finish, Pandit Vishvamohan interrupted by saying, "That was a different era...at that time Aryan society was not so vast. It was easier to manage the small population. That's why it was allowed to change from one social community to another. Now our society is an ever-expanding population. We must have a definite system in place to keep the society in discipline. If everyone did as they please, we'll have no system left and a chaos will set in."

"But life's ultimate goal is to follow your path as per your inherent abilities and aptitude. If we forcefully kept people in social systems irrespective of their abilities, how will the society move forward? If we do not allow people to realize their true potential, they will be dejected resulting in frustration in the society. That kind of all-pervasive frustration and anguish will culminate into some sort of revolt. You might know of numerous such examples from history", said Shastri ji.

"Abilities and basic aptitude come from parents and ancestors. And every soul takes birth based on its *karma* in previous births. A person born in a Shudra family will have the aptitude and hereditary instincts of a Shudra," stressed Pandit Vishvamohan.

That made Gunjan stand up and speak directly to Pandit Vishvamohan. He said, "If you are challenging my abilities, why not test it by doing a Vedic Shastrarth with me. We'll all find out who stands where."

"Shastrarth with a Shudra! You want to spoil my *dharma,* you fool!" shouted Pandit ji.

"Pandit ji don't refer to Vedas when you talk about upper and lower classes. Vedas and Upanishads never teach discrimination," Shastri ji spoke in favor of his student.

"Shastri ji you might not remember that Vedas clearly say that Brahmins were created out of God's mouth, Kshatriyas from the arms, Vaishyas from his thighs, and Shudras from the feet. Hence, Shudras must stay at the bottom of the social system," explained Pandit ji.

"You are talking strange Pandit ji. We all know that the holiest place in the entire universe is at the feet of the Almighty God. Then how come someone arising out of God's feet is the lowest? He could be right up there at the top," Shastri ji replied back.

Pandit ji kept quiet. Sarpanch Ramprasad asked everyone, "So what should we do with this cart man Gunjan?"

Shastri ji said, "I have complete faith in Gunjan's spiritual abilities. If you have any doubt, you can invite Pandit ji to have a Shastrarth with Gunjan. Otherwise, considering his intellectual and spiritual insights, he should be declared a Brahmin in front of everyone here."

"And what about your daughter Shatvari?"

"I suggest Shatvari to allow Damodar one more chance. She should forgive him this one time and restart her domestic life again."

Shatvari was never in agreement with that suggestion. By now she had completely distanced Damodar from her heart. She was always thinking and waiting for her only child. She was upset to hear her father's words. She said, "Is this not a very male-dominated society? A woman who is holier than the Ganges is asked to pass through the fire to prove her sanctity, while a man who has been proven guilty of acute adultery is offered forgiveness and another chance!"

"Everything is contextual. What happened in past had its own relevant and appropriate context. Religion teaches, forgiveness and patience. It's my humble request that you give Damodar another chance, especially when he is fully regretful of his mistakes."

"Simply being regretful and repent for your sin is not sufficient," replied Shatvari.

My dear, I suggest you listen to your father's advice and respect the decorum in this Panchayat," spoke Sarpanch Ramprasad to Shatvari. He addressed the villagers and said, "I now request everyone to stay put as we will now discuss this matter with all the present members. We will reach a decision in a few minutes."

After discussing all the aspects with present members, Sarpanch Ramprasad stood up and stated, "After hearing all the opinions on the matter concerning Gunjan and Shatvari, we have come to this conclusion that Gunjan should be declared a

Brahmin based on his knowledge and abilities. Shatvari is also ordered keeping in mind the culture and traditions of our society to allow Damodar the chance to remorse and amend his mistake. Panchayat also requests Shastri ji and Acharya ji to help Shatvari and Damodar to reunite in their domestic life. With this decision, the Panchayat is dissolved for today."

□

Chapter 17

Shatvari was pleased with the decision to declare Gunjan a Brahmin. She felt after all there is justice in this world. But she wasn't happy with the decision made for her. She wasn't in anyway willing to go back to Damodar on her own. She was willing to fight with the whole world and even the God himself.

Gunjan's popularity increased manifold. The Shudra community got inspired by this decision. His fame traveled as far as the state capital itself in a matter of days. The Shudra in the capital also accepted him as their hero. But the priestly and higher caste community also got the news and they got alert.

Shatvari declined the Panchayat's decision to go back to her husband. Shastri ji sent her to her in-laws' house in order to save some prestige in the society.

Damodar was burning in the fire of regret. How could he loose his childhood love for a lusty temporary affair with a courtesan! Even though he had stopped meeting Amodini, he knew the damage had been done. His social prestige took a clear hit and people started avoiding him. Even his friend Ambrish stopped meeting him. He felt lonely and stressed. He took refuge in alcohol.

One day when he found out about Shatvari's pregnancy, his anguish reached its peak. He couldn't stay away anymore. He wanted to get to his child by any means. Whatever it takes he would get over to Shatvari and ask for forgiveness on his knees.

"I am ashamed of everything I did to betray you Shatvari. Please, if possible, forgive me just once," said Damodar with his head bent down.

"It took you such a long time to realize this." Shatvari spoke without any display of emotion.

"I did realize it a few months back, but could not muster courage to face you."

"How many different faces you have to show me?"

"Shatvari, I am not what I made you think about me."

"Wasn't my love genuine that you had to go to a prostitute to satisfy your lust? In fact, you never loved me from the core of your heart.

"Don't say that please. I realise that I have made a big mistake."

"It wasn't simply a mistake. You committed a sin. You insulted the vows we took in front of the holy fire. You made it unholy with your deeds."

"For quite some time I am burning in the fire of remorse."

"You are a Brahmin. You must know that remorse is not enough to wash away the sin. You have to pay penance."

"What would that be?"

"Stay away from me and our child."

"For how long?"

"Until your child decides to meet you."

"Will you be able to raise the child alone?"

"I have been living with the unbearable burden of your sin alone for so long. It has made me stronger. Raising my child will be much easier."

Damodar didn't reply. He left with a heavy heart.

Shatvari gave birth to a beautiful baby boy after some time. She gradually forgot her miseries and spent most of her time in raising the child.

Everything was still not okay. Some conservative minds of the society were not happy with the soft decision of the Panchayat. Pandit Vishvamohan was one of them and he was determined to do something about the matter. One day he went to meet the village chief Jugalkishore and said, "Mukhiya ji, the popularity of Gunjan has been on the rise ever since the Panchayat declared him at par with Brahmins. He has been spreading the religious knowledge to his fellow Shudras. If something is not done soon, there will be many more Gunjans out there. What should we do then? How will you manage the society? Also, Shatvari has openly rejected the Panchayat's decree."

"You are right Pandit ji, but what can we do anyway? Panchayat stated out its decision and if Shatvari has rejected it, we can't force a woman. After all she is living with her in-laws now", replied Jugalkishore.

"We can file a complaint in the state court. I have inside news that the state priests and other Brahmin chiefs are also not happy with Gunjan's fame spreading so fast."

"If that is the case, I will go to Shripur tomorrow itself and lodge our complaint before the state court."

Jugalkishore went to Shripur the very next day and placed his application in front of the King Rudrasen. Rudrasen was a young king of about thirty. Young kings are either philosophical thinkers or rowdy strongmen. Rudrasen belonged to the latter category. After hearing Jugalkishore's plea, he summoned the royal priest and senior ministers for a consultation.

"What do you all have to say about the Panchayat's decision?" asked the king.

"I believe that the decision to declare Gunjan at par with Brahmins is very unfortunate. He is now openly provoking Shudras against priests and Brahmins", replied the royal priest.

"I also agree with the royal priest in toto. On one hand, he is encouraging Shudras to do the work of Brahmins and on the other hand, he is associating with a Brahmin woman. People believe that they have illicit relations and her child is also his progeny", said the chief minister.

"Hmmm" Rudrasen pondered over the matter, took a deep breath and said, "I also think so. Then what should be done now?"

The royal priest took the initiative to speak first and opined.

"The wrong should be amended. It's not fair to declare a Shudra a Brahmin. On top of that he has relations with a Brahmin girl, which are unforgivable. If this is allowed to go unpunished, we'll have anarchy and our social hierarchy will simply collapse."

"You are right. I have decided what should be done", the king sounded resolute. The faces of the royal priest and the chief minister lit up with the anticipation of a desired verdict.

Veera found out about the news of Gunjan and Shatvari's complaint in the state court. He was delighted and deep down desperate to see them suffer.

The court was convened the very next day. All the accused and their relatives were asked to come. Pandit Vishvamohan and Jugalkishore were also invited.

King Rudrasen stated the accusations out loud—"This court has come together to hear the arguments drawn against the cart man Gunjan and Brahmin girl Shatvari. Gunjan has been accused of studying the holy texts despite being a Shudra and interpreting the texts in his own way. He is spreading his interpretations amongst the Shudra community who are not supposed to seek any scriptural knowledge. Apart from that he has also been accused of maintaining illicit relations with Shatvari who is a married Brahmin girl."

Shatvari was shocked to hear this. "What sort of baseless accusation is this? Me and Gunjan?" She got up and wanted to defend the accusations right away but the king asked her to settle down. "Devi, you please sit down. You too are accused of the same sin. Your son still doesn't have the father's name."

Acharya ji interrupted the accusation. "This is not right, your Highness. I am the father of this child's father and I have no doubt that he is my Damodar's child. I would give this child my family's name."

"If that is the case then why don't you call your son and ask him to publicly accept the baby. Where is he?" asked the king.

Nobody knew where Damodar was. He had left Shatvari and gone away.

"If your son was this child's father, he would have come rushing to him. The fact that he doesn't live with the child and is not even present in this court to accept him proves that the child's father is someone else. Such a child with no legitimate father has no right to live in a civil society, as per the holy Shastras," said the king to Acharya ji.

"I beg your pardon your Highness, but this is not true. I have complete knowledge of the holy Shastras and nowhere has such a thing been mentioned," Shastri ji added.

"I have consulted state priests and my ministers and they all agree that such a child cannot live in our society. Lawmakers and royal priests have all the rights to amend the Shastras. This has been happening since centuries." The king took his stand.

"I have heard everyone and all the relevant arguments in support and against the accusations. I am firm with my decision." The king asked the royal priest to write the decision down. They discussed one final time and finally wrote the verdict on a copper leaf.

The royal priest stood up and asked the court to read out the verdict.

"The court finds Gunjan guilty for studying and wrongfully interpreting the holy texts despite being a Shudra. He is also guilty of having illicit relations with a Brahmin married girl. He is ordered to be expelled from the society. Pandit Aditya Shastri helped Gunjan study the holy texts and so he will be stripped off his Shastri status. Shatvari's child is also expelled from the society and Gunjan will accept the responsibility of the child and will live in the Chandaal community with him. Shatvari is accused of leaving her husband and making relations with another man, that too, a Shudra. She is hereby ordered to become a *Nagarvadhu*."

Everyone looked surprised at this verdict. Nobody expected such a cruel decision. Some faces drooped down in acute disappointment while some others lit up with joy. A few eyes were moist. The king's decision was the final word. Pandit Vishvamohan and Veera were visibly delighted.

Shastri ji could not bear the embarrassment and he walked himself in the river Mahanadi and drowned himself. His wife also followed him.

Aditi found out about her father Pandit Vishvamohan's conspiracy and she fought with him. But she couldn't do anything else.

Gunjan was worried about the child and Shatvari. He cared nothing about himself. But how will Shatvari live a life of humiliation. He tried to console Shatvari, "Don't worry. We will leave the state tonight after dark. We will go to the adjoining state Kalinga and start a new life."

"How will we live there? What will we do?" asked Shatvari.

"We'll do anything. I will drive a cart, do farming, and teach music, whatever we can. I will not let you live a life of a *Nagarvadhu*. Trust me I have always took you as my guru and I will protect your honour."

Gunjan's words made Shatvari even more emotional. She took his hand and said, "I could never understand you truly Gunjan. You are such a great human soul."

"Don't say that. You always gave me respect. We should now have some rest and we will leave as soon as it's dark. We will move towards the east to Kalinga." Gunjan wiped Shatvari's tears with his hand.

Their secret plan somehow found its way down to Veera. He assembled his men and waited for the opportune moment.

As the night dawned upon the village, Gunjan took Shatvari and her child towards the east direction. It was pitch black. Gunjan had deliberately planned to move without any light. Their steps were falling on uneven farm land. They kept moving while Shatvari tightly clutched her child in her arms. They felt hopeful of getting away from the village. But fate had something else in store for them. Soon they noticed some fire torches at some distance moving towards them. Next, they could hear a cacophony of a crowd. Gunjan wasted no time in deciphering that the crowd was coming to stop them. He quickly jumped behind a tree and motioned to Shatvari, "you walk fast towards the east. I will hide here and keep an eye on them."

"But Gunjan how can I leave you alone?"

"Don't worry about me. You can't do anything anyway. I will hide here and make sure they can't see me."

Shatvari left Gunjan there and moved on with her child in her arms. She was ambling in total darkness across strange farmland.

The crowd came nearer and Gunjan saw that Veera was with his accomplices with torches. Veera ordered the men to search for Gunjan and Shatvari. They all had thick wooden batons and fire torches.

"They must be somewhere here. We heard them running from here." Veera shouted to his men and motioned to look around.

"Yes, but all we can see here is bushes and trees," said one of the men.

"They must be hiding somewhere behind the trees or bushes. Just look carefully," replied Veera.

Shatvari somehow kept on running and crossed that field and reached a bit further away. She tried to look back for Gunjan but with her child in her arms all she could do was to keep moving forward.

Gunjan was still hiding behind the tree and waiting for Veera and his men to disperse away. He was a bit relieved that Shatvari had gone far away by then. He didn't care about his life anymore.

When Veera's men couldn't find Shatvari and Gunjan in the fields, Veera shouted, "Torch the crop and the trees. They must be hiding here somewhere. Let the bastards burn to death and go to hell."

Gunjan heard this and got worried that if Veera burnt the field, it would be a disaster for the field owner farmer and his family. His whole year's hard work would turn to ashes because of Veera's anger. He decided to come out of his hiding and face Veera.

"Veera have some mercy on the farmer whose crop you are thinking of burning. You are a farmer yourself, have some empathy," shouted Gunjan while coming out from behind the tree.

"Huh. How can a man who maintains illicit relation with another man's wife talk about empathy!" Veera replied.

"Veera think before you speak."

"Yeah you want to teach me how to act. You are running away in the dark with your beloved and you tell me how to behave. Where is she? She must be here somewhere as well, we'll find her out."

Veera pointed to his men to spread around Gunjan.

"You'll have to pass over my dead body to reach Shatvari." Gunjan moved forward and stood in front of the men. One of the men jumped forward and tried to hit Gunjan with his fire torch but Gunjan swayed back in time and bent down to get between his legs and toppled him over. Gunjan snatched the fire torch from the fallen man and waved in front of the others to shoo them back. He madly started to try and hit anyone who came closer. But how long could a lone man survive attacks by an armed mob. A wooden baton hit his head from behind and Gunjan slumped to the ground. Shatvari heard the agonizing shriek from across the silent fields. She trembled for a moment and her feet stopped moving.

All the armed men pounced upon fallen Gunjan. They started to unleash their fury with their sticks on Gunjan's helpless body. His shrieks became calmer and calmer. The men went on as if under a fit of demonic rage. The rage settled only when they realized there was left nothing more to beat. Gunjan was lying dead on the ground laced with blood.

Shatvari withstood all this while hiding with her child. She knew there was nothing she could do. She couldn't even let her moans escape her throat for the sake of her child.

After some time when Veera's men wiped sweat from their foreheads and dusted their hands of Gunjan's murder, they walked off. They didn't care for searching on for Shatvari.

Shatvari walked towards the lifeless body of Gunjan. The blood was still oozing out from his body. Shatvari's eyes flooded with tears and she burst into a thunderous fit of scream. She somehow got hold of herself. She couldn't let Gunjan lie there. She summoned all her strength and started to pull Gunjan's body towards the crematorium on a solitary bank of Mahanadi.

As she reached the cemetery, the ritual keeper of the Dom caste came forward running and asked, "Who is it that you are dragging here in the middle of the night sister? Is it your husband?"

Shatvari couldn't reply for a while. She kept looking at Gunjan's bloodied corpse and finally said, "Last rites for him."

"Last rites can only be done in the morning now", said the Dom and added, "Your child is shivering with cold, sister, give him to me."

Shatvari hesitatingly gave her child to him. A Brahmin woman's son in an untouchable Dom's lap.

Gunjan's last rites were completed in the morning. Shatvari sat by the burning pyre. Her eyes were staring into the fire that was taking Gunjan away from the physical world. Her eyes were devoid of any tears and face without a fleck of any emotion. She sat there until the whole body turned to ash. She got up, took a handful of hot ash from the burnt pyre and rubbed on her body and took a vow. "Gunjan, today I am taking a vow and I promise you that I will avenge the injustice done upon you by this cruel society. Until then this *shamshan* ash will not be removed from my body. I will keep the fire of your pyre burning in my heart. My every breath will remind me of the atrocities. From now on this *shamshan* is my home and the Chandaals will be my only family. I swear to bring justice to this community of Dalits and Chandaals. This is my penance and my worship."

While listening to the pathetic narration tears were held up in Shatvari's son's eyes. Two streams of tears started rolling down at his cheeks. His voice was choked by the sobbing. However, with immense effort, he composed himself and asked his mother, "Why didn't you tell all this to me much earlier?"

"With the fear that you could go for the search of your father. I didn't like to see the person, who had betrayed me." Asserted Shatvari.

"But why didn't you forgive him when driven by deep repentance, he rushed to you and asked for your forgiveness?"

"Betrayal is a sin. That sin could only be forgiven after a sincere penance." She replied.

"Have you any inkling of my father's whereabouts?"

"I don't know. How come I know?"

"I have to meet him. I will find him out." The young man resolved.

"You will not go anywhere. I am still burning with a sense of revenge from all these lords of society and the religion. That's why I named you Shatrughan, the destroyer of the enemy. You have to be with me in taking this revenge. We'll have to destroy them."

"You will fight with the whole society, the whole system, the entire civilization? There are people like my father and your father too in this society."

"They are exceptions, made irrelevant. This whole society is sick. The disease of discrimination based on caste and creed. The disease of social rift. We will have to set it right. You will have to stand with me in fulfilling this vow."

"But why should it be violent? You used to sing the songs of love, affection and devotion."

"When people stop respecting all the gestures of love, affection and devotion, then the only recourse left is to march on the path of armed struggle."

"What do I have to do?

"To find out that Yantra (Magic wand) gifted with supreme Power."

Shatvari closed her eyes, took a deep breath and proceeded with her *sadhana* (spiritual practice).

□

Chapter 18

"Shripur's rice can certainly make one salivate just from the fragrance", said Neel to Dhananjay while raising his nose to enjoy the aroma of the food being cooked in the kitchen.

"Free meal can make anyone drool, we are just unemployed students", replied Dhananjay with a smile, "But seriously I am fed up of eating the same vegetables every day. I long for roasted gazelle meat."

"Not in this modest inn of Vaniks, my friend! This all is what you'll get here."

"Let's go out somewhere, then. Even if it means spending a bit of money. Don't be such a miser."

No sooner than Dhananjay had finished his sentence, they heard somebody banging on their door. Both looked at each other fearing somebody might have overheard them. Neel rose slowly and opened the door.

Two armed soldiers stood at the entrance of the room.

"Yes, what do you want?" asked Neel probing their expressions.

"Are you two staying here posing as students from Takshashila?" asked one of the soldiers looking straight into Neel's eyes.

"What do you mean—'posing'—we are students from Takshashila", said Neel faking confidence. *'How come these bastards came to know our reality.'* He looked a little puzzled and worried.

"Both of you have been summoned by our state's minister of defence. We have reasons to believe that you are living in disguise".

"On what basis? Your minister's office gave us the identification papers in the first place. You can see for yourself, if you want."

"We don't need to see anything. The minister wants to see you and he will decide afterwards," replied the soldier motioning Neel and Dhananjay to come along with them.

"Listen, you are mistaken for sure..." Dhananjay tried to explain but was interrupted by the soldier, "We are never mistaken. Maybe you are mistaken in believing that you could mislead Yaduvanshis so easily. You better come along peacefully, or...."

Dhananjay glanced at Neel. They knew the best course of action for the moment was to do as the soldiers commanded. They moved along in front of the soldiers. Neel elbowed Dhananjay softly and whispered, "See, you set your eyes on my pocket and it's going to cost us a lot now."

"And what about my roasted gazelle meat. It's going to be prison food now," replied Dhananjay in Neel's ear.

"What are you two whispering? Don't try to make any plans to run away, you will be immediately killed, make no mistake," ordered the soldier.

"Let's see who gets killed', thought Neel and smiled back at Dhananjay. His sharp mind started sorting out a strategy for escape.

Soldiers pushed Neel and Dhananjay towards a horse carriage. The carriage-driver sat at the front with the reins of two horses held tight in his right hand. Two soldiers were already seated at the seat behind the driver. Neel and Dhananjay were asked to sit backwards on the middle seat so that they were facing two soldiers in front of them who can keep watch on them. The carriage moved towards the royal palace.

"What do you feed your horses, compared to our Takshashila horses they look like donkeys?" Neel asked one of the soldiers, sucking his cheeks inward to make a funny gesture.

"Speak less, otherwise you two will be yoked instead of the horses," said the soldier giving him a daunting look.

"What do you feed them, anyway?," asked Dhananjay making the same funny face as Neel did.

"Shut up, don't you hear" frowned the other soldier.

"I was simply asking in case we have to get down and do the job of your horses. At least we should know what to expect in our diets." Dhananjay still had a mischievous smile on his face.

"Whips and lashes," his frown deepened into a glare, "Just shut up and stay quiet. Don't try to divert our attention."

"I feel like itching my right thigh. Can I?" asked Neel putting his right thigh over his left.

"Are you stupid to ask such a question? Don't be smart, or, we'll sort out all your itching," replied the soldier.

"So is that a yes? I can scratch my thigh to ease the itch. I didn't want you to think I am reaching out to a hidden dagger in my *dhoti*," replied Neel while inserting his hand in his loincloth.

He winked at Dhananjay, and almost like clockwork they both reached for their hidden daggers tucked in the belt of their loincloths. Before anybody could react they stabbed both the soldiers sitting in front of them with their sharp stiletto daggers. Both soldiers, taken by surprise, could do nothing else but to fall away screaming on either side of the moving cart. The two soldiers got alert and unsheathed their swords out. Neel and Dhananjay had already snatched swords from the two fallen soldiers. They both now wielded their swords with royal elegance and pounced upon the soldiers.

Neel struck the soldier in front of him but he stopped the blow with his sword raised up in the air above his head. Neel quickly struck another blow, this time kicking with his right leg onto the soldiers left thigh. This put the soldier off-balance and allowed Neel to deal another heavy blow with his sword. The soldier stopped the blow but his resistance gave way to Neel's power and the soldier's sword flew away from his hand. Other soldier saw his unarmed mate standing hapless in front of Neel, and so, he tried to have a go at Neel but was stopped by Dhananjay's sword. Neel sensed the opportunity and stabbed the soldier standing in front of him, killing him instantly. The last remaining soldier was now surrounded by Neel and

Dhananjay. Realising there was no way out, he begged for mercy, "Please don't kill me, I will do whatever you say."

"Get us out of Shripur, can you?" asked Neel.

"It'll be nearly impossible because of the current tight security arrangements," replied the soldier kneeling in front of them.

"Then we don't need you," said Neel and pierced the soldier's heart with his blade.

Neel quickly checked for the pulse of the rest of the three soldiers lying on the ground. They were already dead. The cart man had already fled the scene. Leaving the dead soldiers there, Neel and Dhananjay disappeared behind a large building to hide.

"We can't stay here for too long, your majesty! We have to find a way out," Dhananjay looked worried and anxious.

"Yes, but how? Every exit has high security. By now every soldier in town would have been intimated about us," said Neel looking distressed.

"What I am really wondering about is how they found out about us? Nobody, except Vaishali knows about us being here," Dhananjay was still puzzled at the soldiers finding out their reality.

"We will have to meet Vaishali right away," Neel clenched his fists with anger looking extremely worried.

"Commander, there is a messenger from North Kosala requesting to meet you," informed a soldier to Ranveer—the commander-in-chief of Mekal army. He was responsible for the well-being of the state of Mekal in absence of Neel and Dhananjay.

"North Kosala? We don't particularly have a good relation with them. What could it be?" asked Ranveer a bit puzzled.

"No idea commander, you can ask the messenger yourself. I will send him in if you permit," replied the soldier.

"Yes, send him in," ordered Ranveer.

Ranveer was around thirty years, average height and stocky build, and dark sun-tanned complexion. His sharp sparkling eyes could pierce a man's heart. His whole countenance reeked of abounding energy and freshness.

The soldier brought the messenger from North Kosala and left him inside Ranveer's tent. The messenger bowed and greeted the commander. Ranveer accepted his greetings and bowed back to greet him.

"Tell me, what's the message from North Kosala?" asked Ranveer staring the messenger in his eyes.

"A news, commander, not simply a message," replied the messenger.

"What's the news, let me hear it?"

"Pardon me commander, but the news is not good. Your ruler his Highness Neel and his friend Dhananjay have been captured by the South Kosala army in Shripur," said the messenger with bowed head.

"What are you saying? How is that possible? I can't believe it, his majesty and Dhananjay can easily tackle a group of 10-20 armed soldiers." Ranveer gave him an incredulous look.

"But yes commander, you are underestimating the strength of South Kosala's infantry. Their number runs in thousands."

"How do you know of this? Who told you that his majesty and Dhananjay have been captured?" asked Ranveer. His gaze was intense.

"Our spies are spread all over South Kosala state. They informed us about the event," replied the messenger.

"Why just convey it to us? What are you planning for their safety?"

"We are Raghuvanshis. Old friends of you Nishaads. We sincerely want to help you." The messenger tried to convince Ranveer.

"Help? How can you help us in this situation? How can we trust you? Too many doubts" again Ranveer gave him the same sceptic look.

"You have to trust us commander. We gain nothing from lying to you. We want to help you to rekindle old friendship of Nishaads and Raghuvanshis," said the messenger giving him a firm look.

"So...what is your plan of helping us?"

"You'll have to meet our commander. Only he can share details of the whole plan. I can arrange a meeting soon if you want."

"Where does he want to meet?"

"If you want, he can come right here in your camp. He can come to meet tonight itself," replied the messenger.

"Okay then, I am ready to receive your commander. You can bring him in tonight," said Ranveer in a positive tone.

"With pleasure, commander," replied the messenger and back stepped out of the tent with his head bowed down.

Ranveer drifted into a wave of worry and discomfort.

This is a worrisome news. I wonder what they must be going through. How will we free them from the clutches of Yaduvanshis? North Kosala's messenger has assured to extend every possible assistance. But how will they help? Will we have to step into a war with South Kosala? We are hardly prepared for it. Will it be right to get into a battle simply on the basis of a news from North Kosala? Should I send a spy to South Kosala to verify the messenger's information? But that might result in further delays. It's a matter of life and death of his Highness and his friend Dhananjay. It's a question of the very existence and integrity of Mekal. We have to do something fast. We'll have to plan something concrete with the commander of North Kosala army. This must be kept a secret until we have a well-thought out plan. Especially, the citizens of Mekal should not find out about this. It is, indeed, a disappointing news that can create statewide panic.

"Greetings commander! We welcome you in the kingdom of Nishaadraj Neel," said Ranveer joining his palms together to greet the commander in his tent.

The commander of North Kosala army was a tall and well-built man of around forty years. His name was Indrajit. He was of fair complexion. A delicately shaved beard, wide forehead, and long hair tied together neatly made him look like a man of prominence. He was accompanied by about fifty armed soldiers who stayed outside the tent.

"Greetings commander! How are you?" replied Indrajit with palms joined together.

"What do you think I am feeling after listening to the news you sent?" replied Ranveer looking worried and anxious.

"That's why I am here. We are here to help you in this moment of distress"

"So what is your plan commander? How can you help us in this situation?"

"We have a plan to free his Highness Neel and his friend Dhananjay from the clutches of Shripur's army. There is a huge festival at Mahanadi's bank outside the fort of Shripur, day after tomorrow. Princess of South Kosala Pallavi will be coming to that festival. We plan to kidnap the princess. We will negotiate the release of his Highness and his friend in return of the princess. This will result in meeting our goal without a battle or bloodbath," explained Indrajit.

"Kidnap the princess! But don't you think there will be heavy security for her there?" asked the sceptic Ranveer.

"Don't worry about security. Our battalion will be ready there as and when needed," assured Indrajit.

"I am short of words to thank you my friend. How many soldiers should I take along?" asked Ranveer holding both hands of Indrajit in his hands.

"You can send about fifty. We will brief them. Maybe we won't need that many but we should be prepared for any eventuality." Replied Indrajit with a smile.

"Your Highness!" asked Vaishali looking shocked at finding Neel and Dhananjay at her doorstep.

"How are you Vaishali? We were concerned about you?" asked Neel still looking worried.

"I am okay, your Highness, what about you?"

"Yaduvanshis have found out about us, Vaishali," replied Neel looking anxious.

"How did that happen? Nobody knows about you here except me. Are you...?" asked Vaishali looking puzzled and confused.

"No, Vaishali. We can't doubt you. Rather we were worried about you. If they have found about us they'd soon find out that you are helping us. That will bring trouble to you," said Neel showing concern towards her.

"Don't worry too much about me your Highness! I have learnt over the years how to tackle these Yaduvanshis. But what about you, what will you do?" asked Vaishali.

"We will have to get out of here as soon as we can. The security is too tight and it'll get harder as the time progresses," replied Neel.

"You can stay at my house for at least a couple of days. In two days, there is a cultural festival in Shripur, outside the fort in a Vishnu temple on the bank of Mahanadi. There will be a lot of cultural programs. Artists, musicians, dancers will come from all over the country. They will all congregate here in the town and leave together towards the temple tomorrow. I can mix you two in disguise with them and you can leave the town easily," suggested Vaishali.

"Two days here? But I think they are already looking for you. They will come here for sure," added Dhananjay.

"Nobody will know. I am going to serve the guests. I have a basement in my house where you can hide. I will lock the door from outside. Nobody will know," assured Vaishali.

Vaishali's confident assurance relieved the duo. Neel looked at Vaishali with tenderness and asked, "What do you mean by 'you are going to serve the guests'?"

"You know what I mean, your Highness! Let it go," whispered Vaishali tenderly while looking down.

"Vaishali I promise with all my heart that I will avenge Yaduvanshis for all the humiliation you have to go through here," replied Neel while clinching his fists and a tear drop rolled down his royal cheek.

"This is the last thing you should worry about now your Highness! You must think about escaping out of here," replied Vaishali gently looking up at Neel's face.

A conglomeration of artists from all over the country was gathered in Shripur's guest-house. The festival was an ancient tradition of Shripur. Some people believed it to go as far back as the time when Shripur used to be a great center of cultural activities in the Aryavart. Artists trained in almost all forms of art and magic were there. Best of singers, musicians, poets, writers, actors, magicians, impressionists, illusionists and comedians.

All the guests were accommodated in the best comfortable royal arrangement. Vaishali and other courtesans were asked to look after and entertain the guests. They were to do their best to please them. No complaints expected.

As the dusk fell on the town of Shripur, the gathering of myriad art forms came alive. Vaishali and other damsels started serving wine to the guests. As the wine made its way in, interesting expressions of art started to spurt out.

A poet from Maithil recited a poem on women touching upon the aspects of love and beauty. Round of praises flew in the air. Somebody put up a request to compose the poem into music. A musician from Vidarbha created a quick melody for the poem and a vocalist from Avanti prepared himself to sing it. Amidst all this an artist from North Kosala rose with a suggestion to arrange for a dance to reflect upon the beauty of women form. They wanted a lady to dance to the newly composed tune.

"What is your name beautiful lady?" asked the poet from Maithil addressing Vaishali.

"It's Vaishali," she replied.

"Would you give us the pleasure of your dance on my verses?" requested the poet.

"Yes, but..." Vaishali hesitated.

"Leave your if and but. If an angelic beauty like you would dance on my poem the words will come alive," said the poet.

Vaishali thought for a while about the instructions to please the guests in whatever way they wanted. So she affirmed to dance for the assembled artists.

The singer from Avanti hit melodious notes of a *raga* and Vaishali's feet fluttered on the floor matching the rhythm of the music. The poet's verses were coming to life as hoped by him. He knew no limits to his excitement. Wine, music, and the courtesan's spell-binding dance aroused him to the extent that he rose and started to sway with Vaishali. For a moment his dance amused a few but soon it turned into indecency. Vaishali felt uncomfortable and tried to move away from the poet but he kept following her. He started to pull her with her arms and wrap his arms round her waist.

"With all due respect, you are crossing the limits of decency now!" shouted Vaishali out of sheer desperation.

"Aah, so the limits of decency are set by dancing courtesans in South Kosala now?" blurted out the poet sneering at Vaishali.

Some people didn't like all this. One of the artists who requested Vaishali in the first place to dance, got up and addressed the poet, "My dear respected poet, you are speaking under the effect of alcohol. It would be better if you sat down and not impair any longer the decorum of this house."

"How can one not be, when such an intoxicating grape vine is swaying around!" said the poet grabbing the left wrist of Vaishali.

Vaishali twisted her wrist to get away from the poet's hold but harder she tried, stronger he clutched her. Eventually, when she couldn't try any more to free herself, she turned towards the poet and lent a thunderous slap on his left cheek. The hall went as quiet as a dead man's heart.

Vaishali was a Nishaad woman of pride and integrity.

The poet felt extremely insulted but being slapped by a woman in a full view of the house was too embarrassing too. He let go of her hand nervously.

Vaishali knew she might be in trouble for offending a state guest publically. She huddled in a corner still breathing heavily.

The artist who stood up for Vaishali came forward and said, "I think you should go out from here to have a breath of fresh air. I will accompany you, if you don't mind."

Vaishali herself wanted to get out of there. She accepted the artist's offer. They walked off to a garden behind the guest-house.

"You did absolutely right. Such profanity deserves this," said the artist.

"But he is our state guest. I am not feeling good after insulting a guest like this," Vaishali said in a soft voice.

"Being a guest gives no right to insult a woman. By the way who are you, if I may ask?" asked the artist.

"I am Vaishali. I am the courtesan of Shripur. As you know a *Nagarvadhu* is a state entity. Available to anybody and everybody. So how can one be insulted, I guess," said Vaishali.

"Every civil society allows its citizens to live respectfully irrespective of their profession," said the artist.

"Well, leave all these talks. Tell me about yourself. What do you do?" asked Vaishali.

"Oh, I am just a simple artist. I perform magic and hypnotism shows to entertain people," replied the artist.

"So you are a magician! You know how to hypnotize people and you call yourself a simple artist!" said Vaishali with a surprise.

"No, you are a real artist. I saw how your dance hypnotized one and all there," replied the artist.

"Don't sing my praises, tell me about yourself. What kind of magic you do?" asked Vaishali.

"I am a different kind of magician. It is not as intoxicating but surely marvellous, I would say," said the artist.

"Tell me more. What exactly can you do?" asked Vaishali.

"I can make you forget your name and address. Do you want to see?" asked the artist.

"That's not possible, is it? No, I don't believe," said Vaishali.

"I am here to prove, if you want to see the proof," offered the artist.

"Why not! I am ready too," replied Vaishali.

The artist asked Vaishali to sit on a stone platform and then moving closer to her asked her to look into his eyes intently.

Vaishali did as he asked her to do. She felt a strange attraction. Soon after he touched her forehead softly and Vaishali drifted into deep sleep and knew nothing of what happened thereafter. When she woke up she found herself lying on the stone platform in the garden.

There was an attractive young man standing in front of her. The artist was nowhere in sight.

Vaishali got a bit nervous. She stood up hurriedly. Was this all a ploy to hypnotize her? Has the artist found out things she would have never said in the state of consciousness? Suddenly, the thought of Neel and Dhananjay dawned upon her. She felt the ground beneath sinking underneath her feet.

"Who are you lady and how come you are lying here in this state?" asked the young man with utmost politeness. His voice brought her back from the stream of her own thoughts. She scanned the young man's face. It pulled her into another wave of hypnotism but she managed to control her senses and said, "All that doesn't matter, can you please take me to my house as soon as you can?"

"Yes, why not, but what is it that's troubling you so much?" asked the young man.

"As I said, I need to get home as soon as possible please," reiterated Vaishali.

"Where do you live?" asked the young man.

"Please arrange for a carriage, I will give you the directions," replied Vaishali.

The young man brought Vaishali outside the guest-house. There was a flamboyant horse carriage with four horses parked outside. He asked her to get on board the wide rear seat of the carriage and said, "Please relax, we'll take you home quickly now."

Vaishali leapt quickly into the horse carriage. The young man took his seat on the left of Vaishali and waived the coachman to move on. He then turned towards Vaishali and asked, "So tell me what it is that has made you so worried?"

"Actually, I was with that artist from North Kosala in the garden. I don't know what he did but he hypnotised me in some way and I don't remember anything. I feel nervous and very strange," replied Vaishali.

"North Kosala? We don't particularly have good relations with them. We have to be formally friends to keep old traditions in mind. But these people are the ones we must beware of", said the young man.

"I am feeling so nervous. In my house..." and Vaishali suddenly realised that she was talking to a stranger again. She had already tasted betrayal after trusting the artist from North Kosala.

"What were you saying regarding your house? What is it in there?" asked the young man.

"See…..in my house...I have all my belongings and jewellery and all that I have. I fear that he might have got the information out of me. I am now worried about my house and belongings," replied Vaishali looking visibly perplexed.

"Oh! Don't worry about that. Even if he manages to break into your house and steal anything, he can't get away. Shripur's guards can't be fooled by a mere thief," the young man explained trying to console Vaishali.

The very fact bothered her—how to fool the guards and help Neel and Dhananjay escape from Shripur. She kept quiet to what the young man said. She kept asking the coachman to drive faster.

She kept telling the directions to her house. Soon they arrived at her house and the carriage pulled by. Vaishali jumped off and rushed to the locked front door of the house. She checked the door and the lock and took a deep sigh of relief. She turned back and said, "Thank you very much indeed for your help. I don't know what I would have done without you."

She realized that it's a matter of etiquette to invite the young man in her house, even though that would not be an appropriate thing to do at that moment. She still asked him, "Please come inside" and she motioned towards her house.

"No, thank you. Not today. Maybe next time," replied the young man.

"But how? You didn't introduce yourself?" asked Vaishali.

"My name is Udayan. My father is the king of South Kosala," replied the young man and motioned the coachman to move.

Vaishali was awe-struck at this disclosure from Udayan. Realising that she had just shared a ride with the prince of the state, made her thrilled. She had heard about him. About his handsomeness and abilities in all areas. Such an attractive young man, she felt being hypnotised once again. She felt like meeting him again for sure. A soft smile passed her lips.

Walking inside the house, she quickly scanned for any signs of intrusion. Everything seemed okay. That meant Neel and

Dhananjay were fine. She walked down the stairs into the basement room where they were hidden. They were sitting comfortably and talking. The sight finally soothed her tense nerves. No sooner than she could utter a word, she heard the sound of footsteps above her. Somebody was entering the house. She had left the front door open. Or was she still under the spell of Udayan's aura? She needed to check. She waived at Neel and Dhananjay to stay put. She ran upstairs to find six armed soldiers looking around for something in the house. As soon she appeared one of the soldiers asker her, "We have information that there are some enemies of the state hiding in this house?"

"Enemies!" exclaimed Vaishali and thought whether South Kosala had any friends at all. She tried to look surprised and added, "I think you have been misled, there is nobody hiding here."

"We'll find that out soon once we have searched the house thoroughly," said the soldier.

"Do as you wish," said Vaishali trying to look at ease and not perturbed at all. But she was scared. If their search led to the basement then it'll be all over. They searched the entire upper area and found nothing. They had seen her coming upstairs from the basement so they knew about the basement. She had to do something to distract them somehow.

"They must be down in the basement area, let's go to search there," said one of the soldiers and they proceeded towards the stairs. Vaishali ran after them. She stumbled and fell just before the stairs and cried in agony, "My foot…aah..I think it's broken."

"Hey you, are you playing any tricks on us," asked one of the soldiers.

"Can't you see I fell in front of you? I am sure my bone is fractured. I can't even move it. It's hurting so much. Aaah!" Then she looked seriously at the soldier and added, "Are you going to stand there now or arrange for a *vaidya* to treat me?"

One of the soldiers, who seemed like the leader of the pack, asked another soldier to go to fetch a *Vaidya* quickly.

Vaishali felt a slight sense of relief but she knew how to conceal it. She knew at least one soldier is gone. Now only five to deal with.

The leading soldier asked another soldier to stay there and keep an eye on Vaishali while the rest went down to search the basement.

"What is your name soldier?" asked Vaishali looking up at the soldier assigned to keep an eye on her.

"Gajraj," replied the soldier.

"And the name is very appropriate I must say," replied Vaishali looking at his round abdomen.

"What do you mean?" asked the soldier tucking his belly in and widening his chest.

"Oho, you took it the wrong way Gajraj. I meant you adorn the divinity of Lord Ganesha."

Gajraj felt happy at this. His chest widened.

"Ganapati is the God of art and culture. Do you have any inclination towards any art form? Or you only know how to swordfight?" asked Vaishali examining his sword with her piercing eyes.

"Why? You think fencing is not an art form in itself?" Gajraj asked angrily.

"You get annoyed too quickly. I only meant if you have any interest in dance, music, or poetry?"

"I don't mind watching dance."

"You might now know I am a state courtesan. If you like to watch dance, you are welcome to come to my dance theatre. You'll enjoy very much."

"So you dance?" asked Gajraj.

"Told you I am a *Nagarvadhu*. That's what I do—dance to please my guests. What else do you expect me to do—fistfights!" replied Vaishali and this brought an easy laughter on Gajraj's face.

"Is that sword sheath made of ivory?" asked Vaishali looking at his sword dangling from his waist belt.

"Yes," replied Gajraj.

"Very beautiful. Such fine artistry on it! Would you mind showing it to me for a moment? I love ivory engravings," requested Vaishali.

"I am not such a fool lady to hand over my sword to you!" Gajraj got angry again.

"I am not asking for your sword, I simply want to see the ivory sheath. You can keep the sword if you want," replied Vaishali in a stern voice.

Gajraj thought what the harm in handing over the sheath. It helps to have good relations with a *Nagarvadhu*. Some cheerful evenings can be had. He took the sword out of the sheath and held it in his right hand and handed over the sheath with his left hand and said, "Here you go, enjoy it as much as you want."

"Will you please bend down and hand it over, I can't get up as you can see," requested Vaishali.

As he bent down to hand over the sheath, she held his dress and pulled him further down towards her and started shouting at the top of her voice, " Help, help!"

She started to get louder and this scared Gajraj. He didn't know what to do. Out of utter confusion, he fell down upon her. In the meantime the soldiers came back to check out what was happening. They saw Gajraj lying over Vaishali with his sword in his right hand.

"Save me from this beast! He was trying to molest me and threatened me with his naked dagger," Vaishali screamed at the soldiers.

"What are you saying? Why are you accusing me of this?" Gajraj got up and tried to explain.

"What do you think, we are blinds. Can't we see you were lying on her wielding your sword...this disgusts me to no limits soldier," shouted the leader of the pack.

"You don't believe your own soldier while you are trusting this loose courtesan?" Gajraj said while getting up on his feet.

"Gajraj, learn to respect women. Is this what you are taught in the army?" the chief replied angrily.

"The army teaches us to defend our own respect at all costs. This woman here is wrongly accusing me of something I didn't do."

"If you cared so much about your self-esteem, you would not have done this devilish act."

"You are doing a devilish act by trusting this lewd woman over me," shouted Gajraj puffing with anger.

"How dare you speak to me like that?" yelled the chief and took his sword out and pointed at Gajraj's chest.

Gajraj wasted no time in stepping back and swung his sword and struck his chief's shining blade with all his might.

As the swords clattered in the upper area of the house, Neel and Dhananjay, who had been listening to the events thus far, ascended up the stairs. They pounced upon the two fighting soldiers and before anybody could react, stabbed the soldiers with their own daggers. Both the soldiers collapsed on the ground moaning in acute anguish.

Vaishali lost no time in sensing the opportunity and kicked one of the nearby soldiers in his right knee. He fumbled down and as soon as he got down aching in pain, she picked up a sword and pierced his bosom. Expecting the other two soldiers to get into action, she pushed the two idle swords on the ground towards Neel and Dhananjay.

The two soldiers jumped over Neel and Dhananjay, but they changed their stance like trained dancers, bowed their heads down, swung around, and with a silken swing of their blood thirsty swords slashed the throats of the two soldiers. Blood gushed out and both of them collapsed on the floor.

"We can't stay here any longer now, your Highness, we have to get out as soon as we can. I will do your make-up and arrange for you two to depart with the artists in disguise," said Vaishali while getting up.

"And what about you? Where will you go? Now they would know for sure you are involved," asked Neel.

"Don't worry about me, your Highness."

"No we can't leave you here to be slaughtered, Vaishali."

"Don't be so stubborn your Highness."

"It's my order, Vaishali. You are coming with us."

"If that's the case your Highness...your wish is my command," replied Vaishali.

□

Chapter 19

Vaishali helped Neel and Dhananjay to get into a disguise. Silk clothes replaced their white cotton ones, yellow cotton turbans for the headgear. She trimmed some of her own hair to make fake mustache for the two. She put kohl in their eyes as per the prevalent fashion in South Kosala. Overall, she made them look a lot older.

Neel scanned his new look in a mirror and said, "You have been of great help so far and I am sure you are going to be our great accomplice in the escape. Never know how many more guises we'll have to change to befool these Yaduvanshis. Tell me what are you going to dress like?"

"It'll be nearly impossible for me to change my looks. I'll be getting out in the darkness of the night," replied Vaishali.

"How will you do that alone?"

"Chandaals come here every night for cleaning. I will change my appearance to mix with them and reach their shanty."

"How will you get in touch with us?"

"You will have to contact me there."

"Okay, so this is the final plan. All agreed."

A boat arrived at the shore of river Mahanadi. The boatman quickly jumped off and tied the boat to a wooden pillar. Both ends of the boat had a wooden design like a crane's neck raised up previewing the waters. At the front end was an image of a lion engraved in wood. A small wooden room was in the middle. The door of the room was covered with royal blue satin curtains. A flag was on full mast on top of this wooden room. The flag had a crescent moon in yellow in the middle, a royal signature of some sort. Two bodyguards of robust build also descended from the boat. They were lightly armed with a sword tucked in the waist and bow and arrows at the back. Another adjoining boat that stalled alongside had more armed soldiers on it. As soon as the boats were at the shore, one of the guards said with bowed head "We have arrived princess, you can come out now."

An exotic beauty emerged from behind the royal blue satin curtain. There was something benign in her personality that made her seem like a timeless deity. It was a confluence of the majestic and the erotic. She seemed to walk straight out of the pages of *Kamasutra* (an ancient classic on the art of love-making). Her infinite presence was carefully entwined within the decorum of royal culture. Her magical beauty required no extra make-up but she was very artistically adorned. A sky blue scarf embraced her bosom and her slender waist that had the most artistic curves on both sides as if carefully sculpted by the skilled hands of a master sculptor. A satin yellow *Choli* (blouse) and a dark purple saree held her sacred form within wraps. As soon as she descended upon the shore, an unusual melodic *raga* mixed in the air as if the Samaveda's verses were being played on Veena and Mridangam by the celestial musicians to welcome her. The sand beneath her every step seemed to rise up to feel her feet clad in soft deerskin sandals. Her anklets throbbed on her ivory calves every time she raised her feet. Diamonds studded in her golden bangles; necklace with royal blue pearls, and dangling golden earrings all synced in harmony to the music of her majestic form. The breeze that came from the Mahanadi behind her caressed her dark silken hair into the spontaneous dance moves of Odissi dance. She moved on and glanced at her bodyguards who felt too awed to hold their stare for more than a moment.

Three more beautiful young girls followed the princess. The princess looked back at the guards and instructed, "Wait here, until we get back from the festival."

The guards looked disappointed as they heard this. One of them replied, "But princess we have been strictly ordered to be with you at all times."

"I understand your responsibility and I appreciate your sincerity. But please respect our freedom as well. We will call you if we need anything, be assured."

The princess moved forward. The three other ladies followed her.

Once they were at quite a distance from the guards, one of the princess' friends said, "You broke their poor heart. Even Gandharvas can leave their Apsaras behind to be with you, they were ordinary guards."

The princess looked delighted and blushed. She smiled and said, "Since when have you started to sympathize with young boys! I know how many of them you might have wounded with your killer beauty."

All the ladies joined in the melodious laughter and walked on towards the festival venue.

A large ground near a temple courtyard was made into the festival venue. It looked like there existed a large pond that had dried up. The ground was sandy and hollow from the middle and raised up banks marked the perimeter. A stone and brick wall of about fifteen feet high and five feet wide encircled the whole area. Just like an open amphitheater the wall had stairs from inside all around so that people could sit on them. Some of the stairs had soft rugs and carpets for special guests. On one of such special seating was seated King Rudrasen and his royal family. Rudrasen was now a middle-aged man with distinct features and strong disposition. On his right was his son prince Udayan with some of his friends. On the left of the king was the princess Pallavi with her mates. Some other royal guests were also sitting around them. The rest of the theater was jam packed with eager crowd. Most of the men and young lads had especially come to get a glimpse of the beauty of the princess. They were literally jumping over each other to have a glimpse of her, even if just for a moment.

Soon the proceedings started with an announcement made from a stone podium.

"All the ladies and gentlemen, we thank you and cordially welcome you to South Kosal's yearly festival. Our respected His

Excellency King Rudrasen welcomes you all to this great event and we hope you all will enjoy it well."

The thunder of claps echoed in the festival ground. The announcer continued, "Another speciality about today's event is the fact that princess Pallavi will be watching over the participants keenly in order to pick up a suitable groom for herself. It's a *Swayamvara* for her."

Just the mention of the word *Swayamvara* lit up the eyes of the congregation in general and the young men in particular. Everyone felt lucky to be present there as a possible aspirant. Suddenly, they all became self-conscious.

"We have the best warriors present here to participate from all over the country. Princess Pallavi has put a certain task to judge the spirit of the warriors. Any warrior who can control the intoxicated elephant without any weapons will be the winner of the princess' hand. Those who are willing to take up this challenge please come forward."

This announcement sent a wave of nervous silence around the venue. Facing an inebriated elephant was no child's play. It meant almost certain death.

"What a vanity fair! Is she so proud of her beauty that she can make young men put their lives in danger to get her?" asked Dhananjay.

Neel and Dhananjay were participating in the disguise of artists from a distant state of Kamboj. It was adjoining Persia and people of South Kosala had limited knowledge about the state or its people. The duo had introduced themselves as Shreedutt and Gurudatt.

"There is no dearth of crazy people in this world. People are willing to lay their life for no cause, this is an illustrious cause—a beautiful one. The princess is one of the most sought after diva all over the nation," said Neel.

Soon a young man rose from his seat, came forward and said, "I am Vishvajit the Prince of Vidarbha. I accept this challenge."

He was a tall and strongly built young man. Pallavi looked at him and appeared impressed by the prince's demeanor and good looks. Not to mention his courage.

"You have put up a very stiff and risky challenge princess," said one of her friends.

"Yes, it's not easy. It's meant to test not only the physical courage but also the mental smartness. I know what I want," replied the princess with visible streaks of pride on her face.

Vishvajit entered the arena. A young elephant of shiny gray coat was brought in. The elephant weighing at least three tonnes stood in chains held by a bunch of soldiers. Just to imagine a huge elephant drunk with country liquor running around crazily was enough to shake a lot of young men with fear. The elephant was offered liquor in an earthen vessel. While it greedily gulped down alcohol, all the attendants rushed out of the arena as fast as they could. Vishvajit found himself standing alone in front of an almost mad elephant. As soon as the elephant saw him, it charged with full fury to trample him down under his big feet. The prince just jumped on his left in time to save himself. He knew he had to find a way to get on the back of the elephant. As soon as the elephant turned back, Vishvajit lunged forward and tried to jump as high as he could to reach the animal's back. But he fell short and shuddered on the ground. The elephant saw this and quickly turned and started to run him down. The prince again jumped away to his right and saved himself. But the elephant now understood his game and without wasting much effort swiftly turned around where he stood to grab the prince with his trunk. The prince grabbed the trunk with all the might he had and was left hanging on it while the elephant tried to jerk him down on the ground and crush the prince with his feet. While the prince tried in vain to climb up the trunk to reach the elephant's back, the elephant was vigorously shaking his big head and swaying his trunk to send the prince down on the ground. Eventually, the elephant succeeded in his plan and the prince fell on the ground with one mighty sway of the trunk. Luckily, for the prince, he fell a few feet away from the animal and while the elephant realized where his victim was, the prince got up despite an acute sharp-rising pain in his lower back, and galloped to get as far away as he could. The elephant saw him running away and set to chase him. Vishvajit had given up the challenge and now was running for his life. He quickly jumped over the wall of the arena and lunged out and limped away.

Watching the prince run for his life in such a pitiable manner amused princess Pallavi and it was evident she enjoyed the game.

Dhananjay was visibly upset by this sadist behavior of the princess. He said, "This is the height of insensitivity. She should show some sympathy towards the poor soul who nearly gave up his life for her hand.

The announcement was made, "Prince Vishvajit could not tame the elephant and has now bowed out of the challenge. Is there any other brave man out here who would like to take up this mighty challenge?"

The whole arena was silent.

The announcer continued again in a louder voice, "Is there nobody in the whole of Bharatvarsha who can meet the princess' call to win her heart?"

"Now it's simply not a matter of this princess' pride, it's a matter of saving the pride of our nation," said Neel while getting up from his seat.

"What do you mean, rajan?" asked Dhananjay.

"I am going to tackle this tipsy elephant and this princess' high pride."

"You think you can control this almost mad beast? I don't think we both can do that together with our combined might."

"Might is not in the biceps my friend, it's here at the top. Don't worry about me."

"Your Highness, think it over again. This is not simply courage, this is arrogance too. You are going to bet your life for the sake of a silly princess."

"When it's a matter of pride, who cares about life." Neel stood up, raised his right hand and announced, "I am Shreedutt, a resident of Kamboj. I will take up the challenge."

"Very well young man, but are you aware of the great challenges and the danger. Mind it that you cannot carry any weapon of any kind," asked the announcer.

"Yes, sure, I am aware of the rules and I promise I am not carrying any weapon with me."

The princess eyed him up with a cursory glance. He was a tall, strong, wide and dusky young man with sharp features. She wondered whether this young man was simply a brave warrior or another love-smitten madman crazy for her. Especially, after watching the state of Vishvajit it would need some guts to get in front of the elephant. While she was looking intently at him, Neel stared back and for a matter of moments they looked at each other. She quickly looked away.

Neel kept on looking at her. He was truly astounded by her beauty. Maybe she had the right to be proud and arrogant. But true beauty must imbibe modesty. He became even more adamant in his resolve to shatter her pride.

Neel quickly descended into the arena to face the drunken elephant. He felt resolved and confident. Not a trace of fear touched his psyche. A wild shriek of the elephant brought him closer to the imminent danger rushing with full fury towards him. As soon the elephant came close enough to strike him down, Neel jumped to his right and ran towards the backside of the elephant. He tried to hide in the elephant's blind spot where he couldn't see without turning around very quickly. The elephant turned around but Neel immediately jumped around again to get by his tail. Neel kept doing this for a while to tire the elephant and bring him back to his senses. Gradually, it was evident that the elephant was becoming sober and started behaving in more predictable manner. He went after Neel but wouldn't really try to thrash him down. Neel realised this and started to stroke the trunk and head of the elephant. In a moment of calmness when the elephant stood motionless enjoying the caressing of Neel's hands, Neel swiftly jumped up and sat on his back and vigorously patted his head. The elephant shook his head in affirmation, raised its trunk and let go a loud cry of joy and submission. The arena burst into a wave of thunderous claps. The face of Princess Pallavi glowed with the light of a thousand suns.

King Rudrasen looked towards the princess and she nodded back in approval. In a matter of moment, the announcer came rushing to the arena where Neel sat atop the subdued elephant.

"Congratulations young man! You have proven your cleverness and courage in a great manner. You have won the challenge and the princess has given her approval to choose you as her groom."

"Thanks for your nice words. I actually have no interest in marrying your princess. If she wants, she can marry this tamed elephant," replied Neel while patting the elephant's trunk.

Soft murmurs and sounds of mute laughter passed around the ground. The news reached the princess and her pink face turned amber red. She got up stamping her feet down and thought aloud, "Who does he think he is? I will crush his arrogance and make him a tamed beast like that elephant."

She got up and went to sit alone. Neel, too, joined Dhananjay in the audience.

"Your Highness, why did you reject the offer to marry the princess? This was a great opportunity to amend relations between our two states. Moreover, you won't get any girl as beautiful as the princess in Mekal," asked Dhananjay.

"See, firstly we are living here in disguise. If they find this out, we'll be crushed under this very elephant's feet. Secondly, by making marital relations I don't want to be the part of their sins. We want to teach them a lesson and stop them in their policy of exploiting other people's lives and their lust to expand their boundaries," replied Neel.

"Oh...I didn't think about that, really."

"Now just wait and watch what happens."

Both enjoyed the last words uttered by Neel and kept sitting in their seats.

Rudrasen was visibly angry because of the incident. If he was not bound by the ethics of respecting a guest's honour, he would have got the young man cut into pieces. He felt for his daughter Pallavi. She must be furious and embarrassed beyond limits. He wanted to talk to her but couldn't publicly go and console her.

Pallavi sat alone thinking of how to make Neel come begging for her and apologize for his arrogance. While she was lost in these thoughts, a dusky tall young man approached her.

"I beg your pardon princess for directly coming to talk to you, but I was upset by the arrogance of the young man," the young man said.

Pallavi looked up while still sitting. She wasn't offended in any way. She felt maybe this was the right opportunity to make Neel jealous. She smiled and showed eagerness to talk to the young man. She asked, "What is your name?"

"Prahlaad."

"Then you must be a devotee of Lord Vishnu, are you not?"

"Is there anybody who doesn't worship the Lord Vishnu in some way? Whatever our religion or culture, we all do pray to the same God."

"Really! It reflects your broad mindedness. Where did you pick up such great thoughts?" Pallavi seemed more interested in showing off her pleasure to Neel.

"Thoughts originate in mind and soul, one doesn't need to learn them from anywhere. Thanks for the compliment."

"You are one very interesting young man. While we are talking about Lord Vishnu why not go and visit his nearby temple. I can't sit here any longer anyway."

Pallavi got up holding his hand and Prahlaad followed her in haste. She glanced back at Neel who was looking in her direction but with a total indifference.

Prahlaad was glad and satisfied at his conquest. He knew that the princess had no clue that she was holding the hands of a Chandaal who was not supposed to even cast his shadow on the royal princess.

One of the princess' friends who looked for her everywhere suddenly raised her voice and shouted in despair, "Has anyone seen the princess? I can't find her anywhere."

All eyes turned to her and the king yelled from his seat, "Where is my dear daughter? She was here a few moments ago?"

Neel and Dhananjay also looked around and were confused. Neel had seen the princess talking to that young man just a while ago. They went out together somewhere. Could he be behind the princess' disappearance?

"All the soldiers fan out and search each house if you have to," ordered the king to his soldiers and to Udayan, the prince. He also rushed into action at the unpredicted event.

"I think we should also try and look around for her," said Neel to Dhananjay.

"But how do you suggest we do that. We don't know where she might have gone?" asked Dhananjay.

"I have seen her departing with that tall and dusky young man. I distinctly remember his face. Maybe somebody can help us recognize him. We need help."

"Who can help us? Our best ally here is Vaishali."

"Yes, that's good idea. We are going to meet her tonight anyway."

"Is the Mekal's battalion ready to go for the princess' abduction?" Indrajit asked one of his soldiers.

"Yes commander, they are all set. They are hiding not far from the festival venue, waiting for our signal," replied the soldier.

"Then what are we waiting for! Pass on the signal to start the guerrilla attack and kidnap the princess."

While they were still discussing, a spy soldier came running in towards the commander and said, "There is some bad news, commander. The princess has already been kidnapped."

"What? By whom? How did that happen?" thundered Indrajit.

"We don't know for sure but she was last seen with a Chandaal from a ghetto near Shripur," replied the spy.

"Oh, so the Chandaals are also in the game. They would have taken her to the shanty I guess. How are the Yaduvanshis searching for her? Do they have an inkling that this is the handiwork of Chandaals?"

"They are looking around for her vigorously. They are searching each house. They will surely get to the Chandaal ghetto too."

"Then we'll have to get to the Chandaals before they do. We'll have to divert the attention of Yaduvanshis."

Indrajit looked back at the soldier he was talking to earlier and instructed, "Order the Mekal soldiers to start guerrilla attacks on the South Kosala soldiers."

Then he ordered the spy to start looking for the princess and make it quick so that they get to her before her people.

□

Chapter 20

As soon as Neel and Dhananjay reached Chandaal slum, they started their lookout for Vaishali as planned. The Chandaal community lived by the river Mahanadi. It was congregated around a *Shamashan*, which was the primary cemetery of the area and where many Chandaals worked. The houses were dilapidated huts made of twigs and mud. Narrow lanes with open sewer lanes separated rows of houses from each other. Dogs and rodents roamed freely. Neel's heart shuddered at the sight. He wondered at the state of people who lived their whole lives there.

"Where could she be, Dhananjay? How should we search for her here?" asked Neel.

"I am not sure. We cannot ask anyone or even shout out for her," replied Dhananjay.

While the two were discussing the matter, they found some people looking at them trying to work out what the duo were up to.

"If we walked around like this, they will surely doubt us. But how can we find her this way?" Neel was visibly worried.

Suddenly, they heard a female voice calling out Neel's name. It was coming from behind a hut.

They both looked at each other and jumped to proceed towards the hut.

"Vaishali! I can hardly recognize you in this attire. You are surely a master of disguises," said Neel. Vaishali was dressed as a Chandaal woman.

"Rajan, I have been waiting for a while here. I was getting worried," replied Vaishali.

"Everything fine Vaishali? Why do you look worried?"

"Rajan, these Chandaals have kidnapped the Princess Pallavi."

"Aahh, so that young man was from here. He was a Chandaal youth?"

"Who are you talking about Rajan?"

"I saw him there at the festival talking to the princess. He was tall and dark with strong muscular body. Very bright eyes."

"His name is Prahlaad."

"Do you have any idea where they could have taken the princess? Somewhere around here?"

"No, your Highness! They have taken her to Kaal Bhairav pier, which is far away from here in the north-west direction. It's a spiritual center of Kapalikas. Ordinary people are too scared to venture out there even during the daytime. Chandaal chief Shatvari's guru Kapali Gorakhnath stays there."

"We will have to get there anyhow."

"You want to rescue the princess?"

Neel nodded in affirmation.

"But why?"

Neel kept quiet but Dhananjay looked at Neel and said in cheeky tone, "Your Highness has fallen in love."

They all kept quiet for a moment then Neel spoke, "We'll have to arrange for some horses to get there."

"We will have to go to the capital to get horses. Going there in these circumstances is full of danger. We will have to arrange for a bullock cart from here only I suggest," said Vaishali.

"Bullock cart? That will take a long time to get to the pier," said Dhananjay.

"We do not have an option I am afraid. Vaishali is right, we must not waste time looking for horses. Let's find a bullock cart and start on our way as soon as we can," said Neel.

Mekal's soldiers, who had been waiting to attack, rushed into action as soon as they received the orders. They pounced upon the security guards and soldiers at the festival venue. As they were dressed in ordinary clothes and mixed with the crowd, the attack came as a shock to the South Kosala soldiers. People ran around and panic set in everywhere. It was impossible to figure out who was attacking and why. The royal guards were in a big fix as they had to guard the royal guests while at the same time the common public was being butchered by the unknown assailants. Somehow the royal guests and family members were quickly ushered out of there and brought safely to the nearby temple. Some guards stood by to protect them while the rest carried on to fight the Mekal soldiers.

Udayan was on his way to find the princess when he was informed about the attack. A dilemma struck him—whether he should carry on and go to find his sister, or, use the soldiers to protect the royal guests and family members from the unknown enemy. It was a matter of hundreds of lives as well as the prestige of South Kosala to protect the visiting guests.

He turned around and addressed his soldiers, "We have just been informed that unknown enemy soldiers have attacked the festival venue. It's a matter of our state's prestige and honour to save the innocent lives of our citizens and also to protect our guests. I order that half of you must proceed as we plan to search for the princess and the rest come with me to the festival venue."

About fifty soldiers went on to look for the princess, the rest followed the prince back to the venue. As soon as they reached there, they saw people running around to save their lives. Udayan saw a person with a shining sword pursuing a South Kosala soldier from behind. The person with the sword was about to jab the soldier when Udayan leaped at him and kicked with full force. The sword fell away and Udayan held the attacker from his waist trying to wrestle him down on the ground. While the two were in a tussle, Udayan noticed another attacker running towards him with a sword pointing at his back. Udayan lifted the attacker in his arms and turned him around to face his accomplice's sword that pierced his chest. A loud moan and he died in his arms. Udayan quickly jumped to grab the other attacker who suddenly turned around and kicked Udayan on his thigh. Udayan fell away on his stomach and the attacker pounced over him and sat on his back holding Udayan's neck. Being an expert wrestler, Udayan swiftly turned around beneath the attacker and pushed him hard with both his hands.

The attacker bounced away. As soon as the attacker fell to ground holding his back, Udayan grabbed him and asked, "Tell me who you people are? Why are you attacking us?"

The attacker didn't answer. Udayan twisted his neck a bit and asked even more sternly, "So you won't answer like this. Just a few lashes on your naked back and you will speak out."

The attacker looked at Udayan with utter contempt and puked with full force on Udayan's face and said, "Use all your lashes and swords, but you can't break our vows."

Udayan was taken aback by this reaction. The captured assailant was so full of hatred that he didn't care for his life to protect his vow. While Udayan pondered over this, he suddenly realized that he must go and checkout on the royal guests and his family. He decided to deal with the captured attacker later.

As Udayan walked into the temple premises, King Rudrasen walked towards him and asked, "How come you're still here prince? Are you not worried about the safety and whereabouts of your sister?"

"I beg your pardon your Highness, but as a defence minister my first priority was to ensure the safety of our people and our guests," replied Udayan.

"What about your responsibilities as a brother of a sister kidnapped by our unknown enemies?"

"Your Highness, being a Kshatriya warrior my first duty is towards the citizens of my state. Family comes second. This is also the *Rajdharma*. I have, however, sent an armed unit in search of the princess."

Rudrasen took a deep breath and calmed down a bit and added, "Okay, now you too can proceed towards finding out the princess. We are all safe here."

"As you command, your Highness," Udayan bowed and left.

Pallavi gradually opened her eyes and looked around. It was an old temple. It was evident that only few people ever came there. Her hands and feet were tied to a wooden pole. The rope was so tight that it turned her wrists and ankles blue with clotted blood. She noticed a dilapidated idol of Kaal Bhairav seated on a dog. It was an aggressive face. Black serpents were coiled around Bhairav's arms, ankles, and neck. A garland of human skulls around his neck and another on his chest. In his right hand, it held a blood-soiled dagger and in the left an amputated human head. Pallavi also observed some snakes and scorpions lying lazily in the dark corners of the temple. Some bats were hanging upside down from the roof which was covered with cobwebs. The sight ran a shiver through Pallavi's spine.

A Kapalika sat with a circle of human bones in front of the Bhairav idol. His eyes were closed and he was lost in deep trance. He wore a black headgear and his entire body was covered in black clothes. A garland of human bones was dangling around his neck. A talisman threaded in a black thread was also hanging from his neck. A large stick with crooked head wrapped in red cloth was placed on his right. It was decorated with red flowers and small sandal pieces. A middle-aged woman and two young men were also sitting in front of the Kapalika.

Pallavi was shocked to see one of the young men. It was the same youth who talked her into walking out of the festival venue. She realized that it was all a conspiracy to kidnap her. She wondered if that young man who tamed the elephant was also a member of the sinister plan.

The other young man sitting there was Shatrughan, and the middle-aged woman was Shatvari.

Suddenly, the Kapalika opened his eyes and said loudly, "Kaal Bhairav is asking for a human sacrifice at his altar. Arrange for a human sacrifice."

"Human sacrifice at the altar? But why?" asked Shatrughan.

"Because Kaal Bhairav is asking for it, you fool!" thundered Kapalika staring at Shatrughan with his bloodshot eyes. He then added with a slightly softer tone, "You have a soft heart, because you are the son of a Brahmin. You will have to toughen up to attain *siddhis* that I am going to teach you."

Kapalika now addressed Prahlaad and said, "You take Shatrughan with you and arrange for a human sacrifice. Take my disciples waiting outside. They are expert swordsmen and will come handy if needed. Make sure the person you bring for the sacrifice is not harmed in anyway."

Prahlaad and Shatrughan stood up, bowed and walked out of the temple.

Pallavi's face twitched out of stress at the mention of human sacrificial ritual.

Shatvari noticed that Pallavi was now wide awake and taking account of her surroundings. She walked up to her and asked in a stern voice, "Tell us what all you know about the Yantra of Maharshi Vasudev."

"Which Maharshi? What yantra? I know nothing about all that," replied Pallavi.

"Don't try to befool me young princess! Don't you know who Maharshi Vasudev is?"

"No, I do not."

Shatvari stepped back and thought maybe the princess really knew nothing about the yantra and Maharshi Vasudev. King Rudrasen might not have told her anything about this for some reason. Shatvari thought about relaying all that to the princess but was apprehensive if the princess would trust her words at this point.

Pallavi kept looking at Shatvari with scorn, "Why have you brought me here? Why are you treating me like this?" Pallavi raised her shackled hands to ask Shatvari.

"You will find out with time."

"With time, what does that mean? How can you keep me tied like this here? Who are you—humans or beasts?"

"Beasts!" Shatvari screamed at the top of her voice." We are even below animals. You keep swans and deers in your mansions and treat them with love. We are Chandaals and you want to avoid even our shadow. You would cuddle pillows made of animal skin, but you abhor us so much that you won't even wear shoes made out of our skin."

Shatvari's eyes shone like embers. Pallavi watched her burn with fury. She kept quiet.

"Sit here with your mouth shut dear princess. Sure let me know if you need to eat or drink," Shatvari controlled her emotions. She went back to sit in meditation alongside the Kapalika.

Udayan divided his battalion in four units and sent them in all four directions. He instructed them all to lookout for the previous search units and coordinate efforts with them. Heading one of the units, he moved towards the north-east. He was pondering over the events of the day. He raced his mind around but couldn't think of an enemy who would kidnap the princess. Why would somebody kidnap her anyway was beyond his comprehension. That soldier also reminded him of a section of people who hate them so much. He was wondering if they had only external enemies, such as, Raghuvanshis of North Kosala who are known to create instability in their state. Mekal was also an enemy state. But Vidarbha and Utkal were friendly neighbours.

While the prince explored all possibilities in his mind, a horseman wearing black clothes galloped past him. The horseman dropped a shiny gold-like object towards Udayan. Before any of the soldiers could react, the horseman had vanished in the jungle.

It was a golden bangle. It was wrapped in a piece of a purple cloth. Udayan unwrapped the bangle and saw some writing on the cloth. "Old Mahadev Temple". Udayan looked up thinking that Pallavi also wore a purple colored attire. Could it be her attempt to send a message. But then why the messenger just disappeared so quickly. Old Mahadev temple was straight ahead in the direction they were moving. He decided to go up there and find out what was going on.

Udayan asked his soldiers to proceed towards the temple.

The old Mahadev temple was a small premise made of black stones. It was a beautiful ancient design built on the shore of river Mahanadi. A huge jungle spawned from right in front of the temple and spread all the way up the mountains in north-east. When they reached there it was evident the temple hadn't been visited by anyone for years. He asked the soldiers to search the area thoroughly.

While they were busy looking for any signs of the princess, the same horseman emerged from behind the bushes and again ran past Udayan. He shot towards the dense jungle like an arrow. This time Udayan wasted no time and kicked his horse to chase the horseman down. He tightened the rein of his horse, leaned forward and was flying through the jungle behind the galloping horseman. The black attired youth knew that the prince was following him with full speed. They would go left, right, up the mountains, then down in the valleys but Udayan couldn't get near the horseman and he had ventured miles away from his unit. Udayan suddenly realised that he'd soon be crossing the boundaries of his state and enter an unfriendly territory. He slowed down thinking of turning around.

Before he could motion his horse to take a turn, a net of ropes descended upon him from the trees above. A group of armed men jumped from the trees around him and grabbed him. He knew instantly that it was too late now. That was all a ploy to trick him down here and capture him.

He tried to fight his way out but soon they tied his hands and put a mask on his face. Two strong set of arms held him from either side. On the left was Prahlaad and on the right it was Shatrughan.

"South Kosala's prince Udayan has been captured by the Kapalikas. They were searching for someone for the human sacrificial rite. Now, both the prince and princess are in their captivity," informed a bubbling spy soldier entering Indrajit's tent.

"Bravo! On one hand, Udayan is their defence minister and on the other he is the dear son of King Rudrasen. The princess is the apple of the king's eyes. If both the prince and the princess are removed, it will wreak havoc on the king and his state for sure. We will have an easy victory over them." Indrajit's eyes lit up and he looked determined to get it done.

"What about the king of Mekal—Neel?" asked the soldier.

"Keep an eye on him. He is still important for us until we have South Kosala in our hands completely."

"As you wish, commander."

Udayan was ushered in by Prahlaad and Shatrughan. Pallavi was shocked to see the face of his brother as they removed the black mask.

She had heard all the conversation for the human sacrificial rite. It didn't take her long to realise that they had captured Udayan for exactly that same ritual. She screamed out the name of her brother.

As soon as Udayan saw her sister tied to a wooden pole, he was surprisingly shocked. He quickly glanced at her clothes and jewellery. Everything was intact. He realised it was all a ploy to capture him.

Udayan glanced at her sister and tried to smile helplessly. He tried to convey a message of strength and confidence.

The Kapalika was ecstatic seeing Udayan. He instructed Prahlaad to tie him in front of the Kaal Bhairav idol. "We will commence the sacrifice after midnight."

The mention of human sacrifice perturbed Udayan. He was never aware that there were people in his state who engaged in such brutal rituals. Who were these people? What for have they captured Pallavi? He had to find some way to get out from there before midnight.

It was almost dusk. Sky was a sombre grey and with orange streaks at the horizon. Neel, Vaishali and Dhananjay sat in a simple wooden bullock cart pulled by two white oxen. They were right by the Kaal Bhairav pier. As they approached, Vaishali said to Neel, "We have to be cautious here, as these Kapalikas have supernatural powers of all kind."

"Keep your heart and mind focussed on the mission Vaishali. Nothing is mightier than a stable mind," replied Neel.

They tied the bullock cart some distance away from the temple and quietly walked towards the temple. As they approached, Neel could see that Pallavi was tied to a pole. Right in front of the Kaal Bhairav idol was tied another young person. He walked closer to the temple and saw it was a young man in royal attire.

"Who is that young man Vaishali?" Neel asked pointing towards the temple.

Vaishali looked closely and almost shrieked in shock. "This is the Prince Udayan."

Neel put his hand on Vaishali's mouth and asked her to calm down.

"So both the very important royal members are here in captivity. We will have to rescue them both somehow. Let's wait and chalk out a flawless plan."

They hid there just by the door in the bushes and tried to figure out what was going on inside.

"Be warned! There is someone around us," said the Kapalika still with his eyes closed.

"Who is it, guruji?" Asked Shatvari.

"Someone is here. Be warned, I say!"

"But who? Humans, ghouls, or demons," asked Shatvari looking around.

"Humans are more dangerous than all the ghouls. We have to keep these two safe until the ritual is done. Go outside the temple and guard the place. Nobody should come near before midnight," ordered the Kapalika to his disciples.

No less than fifteen men with swords walked outside the temple and spread around to keep vigil.

"Now what will we have to do, your Highness?" asked Dhananjay.

"Nothing we can do, as they are five times our number," replied Neel.

"Then, should we just sit and watch them murder the prince?" asked Vaishali.

"Better to let one person die as opposed to all of us getting killed."

"Since when have you become so selfish your Highness?" Vaishali was visibly upset and raring to go.

"Keep calm. Let me think for a minute. Dhananjay, how many swords and daggers do we have?" Asked Neel.

"Six."

"That won't be enough. We will need more weapons."

"What are you thinking rajan? What's the plan?"

"As they are far more in numbers we cannot win in an in-person combat. We will have to fight from a distance."

"But we do not have the weapons, like bows and arrows, to attack them from a distance."

"That's what I said, we need more weapons. We will make bows and arrows. Vaishali, you go and find sturdy sticks from the nearby bushes. Dhananjay you go and fetch the ropes from the cart."

As they gathered the material, they quickly made a bunch of arrows using their sharp daggers to chisel top of sticks into sharp-pointed weapons. They made three strong bows as well.

"When are we going to attack, your Highness?"

"Right now. It's almost dark and these guards are drowsy and visibly tired. This is the opportune moment to strike."

As the night moved towards midnight hour, a blanket of darkness engulfed the whole area. Some flickering earthen lamps lit the temple inside but outside only the moonlight spread over the area. Shatvari, Shatrughan, and Prahlaad were preparing for the ritual. Pallavi and Udayan were wide awake and silently praying for some miracle or divine assistance to save their lives.

Suddenly, a torrent of arrows from somewhere in the bushes flew through the air and hit the guards. They were taken by surprise and the sturdy-pointed arrows pierced their bodies. Some ran to hide themselves in order to save their lives; some were too shocked to do anything and stood baffled.

Pallavi and Udayan's eyes lit up. The divine help they had been praying for had arrived.

Soon the shell-shocked guards were attacked by Neel, Dhananjay and Vaishali. They found an already dwindling unit running around to save their lives. They took them by surprise. Neel slashed a few throats in a matter of moments and pierced no less than two guards' chest with single jabs. Dhananjay was no less a swordsman. He was moving around like an expert warrior with a shining long sword in hand. It was an easy job for the two brave young men trained in warfare.

While Neel and Dhananjay destroyed the guards outside, Vaishali quickly sneaked in and cut the ropes of Udayan's and

Pallavi's bondage. Kapalika and Prahlaad saw Vaishali freeing Udayan. Kapalika shouted aloud and Prahlaad rushed to attack Udayan. It so happened that Udayan picked a nearby sword to save the first blow by Prahlaad. In the meantime, the Kapalika also joined in and Udayan found himself swordfighting with both the Kapalika and Prahlaad at the same time. It was evident that he was well trained and his agile body with sword fighting skills matched the two fighters. Out of nowhere somebody hit Udayan's left shoulder from behind. His sword fell away and he himself rolled down the ground moaning in acute pain. Sensing the opportunity, Prahlaad changed the grip of his sword to hold it like a dagger and ran towards Udayan to pierce his heart. As he back lifted his sword to jab it down on Udayan, someone sliced his sword from behind into Prahlaad's body. The Kapalika saw Shatrughan standing behind Prahlaad holding the sword with expressions of loathing and fury.

Shatrughan's attack on Prahlaad shocked everyone present there. Shatvari's face was flushed with surprise. The Kapalika's face was burning with anger. He shouted, "You fool!" and ran towards Shatrughan with his sword. Before he could kill Shatrughan, a sword pierced his body from behind. It was Shatvari. She murdered her guru to save her son. But she instantly realized what she had done. She knew there was no point regretting now.

Shatvari managed to shout out to Shatrughan, "Run now, run for life, why are you still standing here."

Shatrughan dropped his sword and ran out of the temple, in the jungle. Shatvari ran after him. Soon they both disappeared in the dark dense forests.

Neel and Dhananjay killed most of the guards and the rest fled to save their life. As they both walked inside the temple, Neel's eyes found Pallavi. He kept looking at her while she could hardly look back and kept her head down with shame and embarrassment as if atoning for her arrogance at the festival.

She somehow managed to speak. "We thank you from the bottom of our heart for saving us. Still, don't think I have forgiven you for hurting my ego."

"You think only the rich and the royal class has the privilege to have a self-esteem?" asked Neel.

Pallavi looked up amazed at what Neel had asked, "What do you mean?"

"Maybe my words can't make you understand. Let the time explain it."

"So you are Shripur's *Nagarvadhu* Vaishali?" Asked Udayan smiling at Vaishali.

"You figured it out, right."

"Yes, and also the fact that you have sheltered the enemies of South Kosala to live in your house."

"Yes, the same set of enemies saved your life today. If they were truly enemies, they would not have risked their life to save you and your sister, I am sure you can figure that out as well."

"But they were spying in our state, isn't that true?"

"Where is it said that spying is done only for the purpose of enmity?"

"I am still not sure they were doing it to make friends with us. If they did, they could have just come and met us right away."

"You think you are friendly and your state encourages friendliness?"

"Of course, there are political rivalry between states but we do not believe in bloodbath for the sake of it."

"Political rivalry for political reasons, is that why you capture weaker citizens from other states to enslave them? Is that why you play with their self-esteem and make harlots of their wives, sisters and daughters?"

"Slavery? Harlots? What are you talking about?"

"Don't be so naive, prince. If you have no idea what I am talking about then you have been living in a delusion."

"I know what you are talking about. Trust me I discussed this with his Highness and he had promised me to abolish all such practices."

"Yes, he promised you and then went on to capture eight Mekal villages and enslaved thousands of people. Children were snatched from their mothers and made to work in farms; young girls were auctioned in open bazaars in front of their shackled fathers; young brides were spoiled even before their henna could dry. Your brothels are populated by the women captured from our villages. This *Nagarvadhu* you are talking to is one shining example of how such an atrocity forces a simple girl to become a crowd pleasing harlot."

Udayan looked at Vaishali with a palpitating heart. He never knew such a rage and fury was boiling within her. He said, "You don't know all this has shocked me. I will talk to my father about it for sure."

"I hope so, prince. Now please allow me to leave as I have to go with our king Neel back to Mekal."

"No, Vaishali, I cannot allow you to go like this."

"Are you arresting me for treason?" Vaishali smiled.

"Can I do that to you? I want you to stay and help me achieve a lot of work for our society's upliftment. I need your help and direction."

"So you have it all planned up." Vaishali looked at him while moving on.

"You spoiled the whole plan, you fool, you know that." said Shatvari to Shatrughan.

"Did you want me to let an innocent person be killed for no reason?"

"Reason! Do you have any idea what his father has been doing to us? This Prince Udayan's sin is that he was born in that family of grave sinners."

"But why punish a son for his father's sins and what about his sister?"

"Are you not suffering for the sins of your father?"

"That still doesn't make it proper to believe that every son or daughter must pay for the sins of their father. If this is carried on the world will never be rid of hatred and revenge."

"But someone must be punished for the sins. Sins can not go unpunished."

"Even then I don't think sins will disappear if you go on punishing. The remedy for sins is not punishment but an atmosphere of reforms and rectifications. We need to create a positive environment. We must forgive and let the next generations have some time and space to move forward in the right direction. If you keep taking the path of revenge and every next generation would have to respond to it, what will be the future? I firmly believe that the civil society should be devoid of fear, rage, and hatred."

"I see, my son that you have learnt the language of high ideals. Don't fall in this trap. It serves no one. All these ideals are created by the high class people, who rule over us. They create these rules and change them as it befits them in order to exploit and enslave us to the condemned life of dalits and Chandaals."

"I am not talking about ideals and high values; I am talking about listening to your conscience. The fire of revenge burns down the conscience. People you supported to take revenge were going to also kill your own son. Didn't you see that? Why did you kill your guru to save the life of your son? If revenge was supreme for you, then why did you kill him to save your son and put all your plans in jeopardy? Because I am your son? Your mothering affection made you pick up the weapon to save your dear son. If you pick up weapons with the same feeling of love and compassion for the entire generation of your son, it will bring peace in the world. However, if you pick up weapons with a feeling of hatred and revenge, it will bring only destruction. I urge you to restrain all the emotions of revenge and hatred. Then I will be with you in any fight or mission you want me to execute."

Shatrughan took a deep breath and started to walk away.

"Where are you going now?" Asked Shatvari.

"Away from the air polluted by hatred and fury."

□

Chapter 21

Vaishali returned to Shripur with Udayan. Now she was not a courtesan or merely a *Nagarvadhu* but also a social worker. She was not just an object of men's lust anymore. She found herself helping men overcome their emotional conflict. While till now she was only accessible to the rich and the powerful people of Shripur, now her doors were open for everyone.

Udayan got busy in reorganising the security and safety of Shripur. He also took upon himself the responsibility to awaken the youth of his state and enthuse them with vital energy and nationalistic ideals.

Neel and Dhananjay had returned to Mekal after assigning Vaishali the task to carry on the unfinished job.

King Rudrasen kept on pursuing his expansive ambitions.

It was the first quarter of the night. Vaishali was sitting in her theater alone lost in her own thoughts. She was wondering about the changes she could bring in her life and consequently the visibly positive change in the lives of the people coming to her. Apart from money, she was now amassing deep respect from the society. People no longer looked at her with only lusty passions.

While she was busy pondering over her streams of thoughts, a lad of about seventeen years stepped in.

"What is the matter Aniruddha? You are back again? I hope everything is fine at your home," asked Vaishali.

"I don't feel like staying at home. My heart is restless wherever I go there," said Aniruddha.

Aniruddha was of medium height and a delicate build. His attractive face had just started to show traces of facial hair. Curly dark hair dangled back on his shoulders. He wore golden sturdy earrings in his ears; pearl-studded golden garland around his neck; gemstone ring in each of his fingers. Overall his appearance indicated that he belonged to a wealthy family.

"It's nothing new for a boy of your age. You must be in love with someone," said Vaishali.

Aniruddha stood silently for a moment and then said, "Can you get me a cup of wine?"

"You are already drunk."

"Not much. Nothing from your hands."

"What's so charismatic in my hands?"

"Something is special for sure that drives me here again and again. A cup of wine is useless until your hands touch it." Aniruddha grabbed Vaishali's hand.

"Leave my hand Aniruddha."

"Why, today I can't even hold your hand!"

"If you don't leave my hand, how can I go and get you a cup of wine?" She went towards the bar and filled a cup for him. "You have taken to wine too much lately. You should try to focus on something positive."

"That's why I have come here."

"So there is nobody else left in the whole town to entertain you?"

"I swear, apart from you I never have even thought about going elsewhere. I don't know what pulls me here everyday. My days go restless and nights sleepless without meeting you." He held her hand again and started to stroke it gently.

"Do you know what you are saying?"

"Yes, I know. If this is love then yes I am in love with you."

"Don't be so naive. You know I am a *Nagarvadhu* and much older than you in age."

"Love can't see all these things. It's driven only by heart."

"You are simply not driven by heart. You love me charmed by my body. I have sympathy for you. I don't want you to misunderstand this sympathy for love."

"There are many harlots in the city to offer their body to me. I promise I never even thought about them. If you become mine Vaishali, I can lay down all my wealth on your feet."

"That is not your wealth, but is inherited from your father. Don't squander it because of your ignorance."

Vaishali's talks fell on Aniruddha's deaf ears. He slumped down on the floor and wrapped his arms around Vaishali's legs and said, "I don't know anything. All I know is that I can't live without you."

"Get up Aniruddha. One of the town's most respected merchants, Seth Ambarish's son shouldn't stoop so low. Don't tarnish his respect by bowing down to the feet of a courtesan. It doesn't suit you."

"And does it suit you to break someone's heart like this." Aniruddha's eyes were moist with tears.

"Wait...for a while, let me at least have some time to think over it."

"Please do. You have all the time. I am waiting here."

They both sat silently for a few moments.

Vaishali thought hard and then broke the silence and said, "What will your father think of our relationship?"

"He has no time to care about such things. He is so much engrossed in making money that he has forgotten all relations already."

"Hmmm...still...he is a respected man and your father nonetheless. Alright...let's go."

"Where?"

"Here neither your father nor the king will let us live together. We will have to escape from here."

"Yes, but where?"

"Trust me, can you? Just do as I say".

They left with the first rays of the dawn. Vaishali packed her bare essentials in a leather bag. Some food for the journey and some weapons for self-defence just in case something happens. Everything was loaded on a horse cart. Aniruddha sat closely beside Vaishali on her left. He was feeling ecstatic in the company of Vaishali.

"What's the impatience for? Sit properly. You will get many opportunities to get closer," said Vaishali giving a playful smile to Aniruddha. Vaishali let loose the reins and whipped the horses. The cart was on the way.

"It's a difficult terrain my dear boy. There are man-eaters in these forests. Are you afraid?" asked Vaishali.

"I'll happily die alongside you if needed."

"What about when you are not with me?"

"I keep thinking about you."

"What about the time you had not come to know me?"

"Used to wonder if I can meet somebody like you."

"Who else is there in your family apart from your father?"

"Nobody."

"Mother?

"Left us while I was a child."

"To where?"

"God's abode."

"Aaaah...how old were you then?"

"Four."

"Really! only four. Any brothers or sisters?"

"None."

Vaishali couldn't think of what else to talk about on the matter. She wondered how lonely he would have been all these years.

The morning turned to noon. The sky was covered with clouds. Sun was only a distant haze. A cool breeze through the forest trees caressed their faces. Vaishali stopped the cart by a freshwater lake. She said, "Let's stop here and take some rest. Horse must be hungry by now. We should also eat something."

"Are you going to ask me to hunt an animal now?" asked Aniruddha.

"No, but are you scared?"

"Not scared, I just can't imagine killing an animal to eat."

"We have to kill to feed ourselves."

"Yes, but I can't see the sufferings or pain of any animal."

"So you won't hunt even if you have nothing to eat?"

"I don't know. So far such a situation hasn't come."

"Don't worry, even today you won't have to hunt. We have enough food."

"Do you hunt?"

"Yes, I am a Nishaad woman. Hunting is our favourite past time."

"That's how you hunted me down so easily," an impish smile emerged on Aniruddha's blushing cheeks.

"Yes, but we don't believe in hunting tame animals", Vaishali glanced at him with a similar playful smile. Aniruddha looked away blushing even more.

Vaishali let loose the horse. He went on to graze.

"Don't just stand there. Go and get the food and vegetables from the cart. We also need to collect dry twigs to light fire to roast them," said Vaishali.

Aniruddha looked at the raw vegetables, green bananas, sweet potatoes and other root vegetables with a little aversion.

"It looks like you have never had roasted vegetables before. But you have to eat them today, you are not going to get your home-cooked curries here," said Vaishali.

Aniruddha collected some dry twigs and prepared a bonfire. Vaishali pulled out two special wood lie pieces from her bag. She rubbed them together to light the fire. Soon the pool of woods erupted in flames. She handed over a sweetcorn to Aniruddha and asked him to roast it slowly over the fire. She started to peel and roast other vegetables.

The smell of freshly roasted vegetables over fire, crackling of sweet corn, warm and mushy sweet potatoes, and the warmth of fire amidst cold breeze Aniruddha felt a new wave of emotions enveloping him. He had never experienced this side of life in the lap of nature. He was simply used to getting cooked food by his servants. He never had even noticed what was being served.

Vaishali sprinkled some salt on a roasted sweet corn and handed it to Aniruddha. "Tell me how does it taste?"

Aniruddha took a mouthful of corns in his mouth and was surprised at how soft they were. With his mouth still full with corn, he said, "Wow, never thought food can be prepared and enjoyed in this way." Some bits popped out of his mouth as he spoke.

Vaishali enjoyed the scene and said, "Your mother never taught you not to speak while eating." As soon as she finished her sentence, she realised what she had said. She looked at Aniruddha's face who was looking sad. Vaishali quickly tried to change the topic. She peeled a roasted sweet potato and stuffed into Aniruddha's mouth and said, "Eat this; this is supposed to be sweet. Just like your smile."

Aniruddha tried to quickly swallow and manage the big potato stuffed in his mouth suddenly. He said, "You should also try this, it's really good." Again a bit came out of his mouth. Aniruddha smirked and said, "See my mother could never have any time to teach me." They both burst into laughter together. They sat there and ate their food and talked casually about everything. After a while, Vaishali got up and walked up to the lake and asked Aniruddha, "Have you ever flicked a stone over water?"

"How can you flick it over water? It will immediately sink."

"I will show you. Give me that pebble."

Aniruddha picked a small pebble lying by his side and handed it over to Vaishali. Vaishali pulled her arms back, swayed down to one side lowering her head, and let go the pebble aiming at just above the surface of the water. The pebble touched the surface but only briefly and wobbled up in the air. "One...two...three...four...five...six...seven... eight...see, you saw that it bounced up eight times," said Vaishali jumping up and down with joy. Aniruddha stood surprised looking at the pebble and Vaishali's antics.

"Now it's your turn," said Vaishali handing another pebble to Aniruddha.

Aniruddha tried to mimic what Vaishali did. As he threw the pebble towards the lake, it flew over the surface, took a couple of bounces and sunk in.

"Ahh don't worry, it's only your first attempt, try again, here you go," said Vaishali.

Aniruddha tried again but the same result. He looked at Vaishali. She was trying to conceal a smile but said, "Keep trying young man until you get to eight bounces while I eat another sweet corn."

Vaishali settled down on the ground by the fire. Aniruddha kept throwing rounded pebbles over the lake.

"Only four, that's all I could manage so far. I can't do better I think," said Aniruddha.

"Only four? Okay don't worry too much. It's enough for the first day. Let's go, we have to go far," said Vaishali. She noticed that Aniruddha's forehead was covered with sweat drops. She wiped that with her scarf and gave a smile looking into his eyes.

Suddenly, they noticed some noise coming from bushes not far away.

"What is this noise? Can you hear it?" Aniruddha asked Vaishali.

"Don't worry...stay put," said Vaishali and pulled a dagger tucked in her waist belt and handed it to Aniruddha.

"What is this? I don't know how to use this."

"You will know what to do with it when you'll have no other option to save your life."

Vaishali quickly rushed to the cart and pulled another dagger and motioned Aniruddha to hide back behind bushes and keep a vigil on what's happening on the other side.

They sat quietly in a hidden spot behind the bushes. Five armed horsemen stood around a loaded horse cart. The occupants of the cart looked flushed with fear.

"Who are they?" asked Aniruddha.

"They are bandits who rob the highway travellers. They are looting that carriage."

"What should we do? Can we do anything at all?"

"We must help the travellers."

"But why should we put our lives in danger for strangers?"

"What if this carriage belongs to your father? If these people are your relatives. What will you do then?"

"When my father doesn't care about me...."

"Then sit here with the anger towards your father and burn in that all your life," said Vaishali.

Suddenly, two young men jumped out of the carriage. They were carrying shining swords.

One of the bandits ordered, "Give up all your possessions and run for your life."

"We get paid to guard the possessions, you expect us to just give it away to you like that," replied one of the two armed guards.

"Then get ready to die." The five bandits jumped off from their horses and pounced upon the two young guards.

Vaishali pulled Aniruddha by tugging at his collar and said, "Come, this is the time to help them."

"I don't know, I am scared," said Aniruddha. He stood motionless behind the bushes.

"When you are ashamed of yourself enough then see if you can muster courage to join me," said Vaishali and drew her scarf from round her neck and tied around her waist tightly. She ran towards the combat zone to help the guards.

Vaishali ran into one of the bandits and stabbed him in his back. At the same time she jumped in the air and kicked another one in his knees. Both fumbled down on the ground. One of them got hold of himself and quickly got on his feet and lunged forward to hit Vaishali with his sword. She swayed to the left and aimed his waist with her dagger. He jumped to one side to save himself and came rushing back again but Vaishali jumped and kicked him with full force. He fell down. She leapt without wasting a moment on his back and slashed his throat before he could react. He stayed there squirming in a pool of blood.

As she realised what he had just done, another bandit was running towards her with pointed sword. Vaishali tackled him with her right leg and he fell down on the ground. But he quickly got up again. As she got up to tackle him another one came from behind and surprised her with a wild slash. She jumped away but the sword hit her right wrist and her dagger tumbled away from her hand. Now she was standing in between two bandits with nothing to defend herself. She quickly turned around to combat the one behind her by jumping in air and kicked him in his groins. He was hit well and he crouched down in acute agony. Vaishali also fell down on her back. The other bandit seized the opportunity and with full force tried to shove his sword in Vaishali's body. Vaishali gave up and was preparing for a certain death. She had closed her eyes when a loud moan and a thud of a body falling woke her up. There stood Aniruddha whose dagger was stuck in that bandit's back.

"Aniruddha...watch out..," shouted Vaishali as one bandit was sneaking up from behind Aniruddha. It was too late. Even though Aniruddha tried to sway away, his arm was sliced slightly by the sword of the bandit. Aniruddha fell to one side clutching his injured arm. Vaishali crawled while still on the ground and tangled the bandit and he fell down on his face. His sword fell away and Vaishali picked up a nearby dagger and stabbed his back.

Vaishali looked at Aniruddha and said, "So you finally got ashamed?"

Aniruddha was visibly embarrassed and blushing. He noticed Vaishali's bare thighs as a result of her saree falling away. He pointed and said, "You better take care of your clothes else you'll be ashamed now."

"Shameless boy, "said Vaishali and quickly adjusted her saree.

The rest of the bandits were taken care of by the guards.

Vaishali's wrist was bleeding. Aniruddha noticed that and said, "You are severely injured." He tore up his bodice cloth and tied it around her wrist to stop the blood flow.

Vaishali also tore up her scarf and tied it around Aniruddha's arm.

Aniruddha looked at her and said, "Promised to live and die together, didn't I?"

"Don't even talk about dying. Seen it from so close just now." Vaishali put her hand on Aniruddha's mouth.

"Arey, Kumar ji, is it you? How come you are here?" asked one of the guards.

Aniruddha identified him now. He was indeed one of his father's staff and so Vaishali's statement came true. The cart belonged to his father after all.

"Yes, don't worry about me just find somebody to treat her as soon as you can," said Aniruddha.

"Yes, there is an ashram of a Swami ji who is also a great *Vaidya*. He will certainly be able to help. Let's go there," said the guard.

□

Chapter 22

Ambrish was sitting in his house resting his head on a large round satin pillow. He was now a middle-aged man with greying hair and sunken cheeks. He was now far slighter than his younger days. His round face now looked bony and angular due to decreasing body mass. This evening his forehead bore clear signs of worry. Aniruddha was his only child. He had been searching him for more than twenty-four hours. All his men had been looking around for his son but to no avail.

Ambrish was getting agitated inside. He was trying to figure out what could have let the young man to leave house like that. Where could he go? Maybe it was his fault. Aniruddh's upbringing in the absence of his mother wasn't sufficient. He could hardly spend enough time with his son.

While he was strolling in the lobby pondering over such distressing thoughts, a servant came running in and said, "Seth ji we have some information about Kumar. He is in a Swami ji's ashram on the Southern way. One of our goods carriage was attacked by bandits there. Kumar Aniruddha fought with the bandits and got injured. He has been taken to the ashram for treatment."

The news brought both happiness and a new anxiety. He got worried to know about the bandit attack and injury to Aniruddha. But he was consoled by the fact that now he knew where his son was. He quickly ordered his men to prepare at once to arrange for him to go to the ashram.

Swami ji's demeanor was compelling. Tall and wide, long beard and dense hair, long and fair face. Vaishali, Aniruddha, and the guards reached his ashram and approached him.

"Swami ji, please see these two people, they have been injured in a fight with the bandits. Can you treat them here?" asked one of the guards.

"Come here my child," Swami ji called Vaishali to come forward. He patted Aniruddha's shoulder as well and asked him to come to him.

The word child touched Vaishali's heart. After a long time she had heard that word. Swami ji took them both in his hut. He applied some herbal medicinal paste from an earthen bowl. He then dressed the wounds with a cotton bandage.

"You will be fine soon. It's almost night so you must have some rest here tonight and leave tomorrow morning. Feel at home dear," said Swami ji.

Swami ji bathed before dawn and he was busy collecting fodder for the cattle. Suddenly, he saw a horse carriage stop in front of the ashram. A middle-aged man came out of the carriage and he looked in a visible urgency. As soon as they both looked at each other, they were pleasantly surprised. A familiar wave of excitement flashed their faces.

Swami ji spoke first, "Ambrish! You here?"

"Damodar! Damodar you are here. God knows I searched for you everywhere," screamed Ambrish and hugged his long-lost friend.

"You bloody liar! You yourself stopped seeing me in those days, don't you remember," said Swami Damodar.

"I am ashamed at that my friend. As soon as I realized my mistake, I started searching you like a madman. Looked for you in every nook and corner but couldn't find you anywhere."

"Let bygone be bygone now my friend. Tell me how are you? Did you eventually get married or still embroiled in merry ways?"

"I got married, yes, but couldn't be loyal to my wife. She was a kind and simple soul. She didn't leave me, as did Shatvari, but couldn't endure my ignorance and left the world out of grief. I am still remorsing and regretting that phase of my life."

Shatvari's name brought many memories in Damodar's conscience. His face sulked.

"I hope Shatvari is happy and well at her father's house," asked Damodar.

Ambrish was surprised to hear this from Damodar. That clearly meant that Damodar didn't know anything about the chain of events that led Shatvari's excommunication from the society.

Ambrish told Damodar everything. Damodar held back tears but eventually gave way and sobbed like a child. He felt as if the sky had suddenly fallen over his head. He thought he was doing penance for his sin by going away from Shatvari but he had committed another sin by doing so. He shuddered to imagine what have Shatvari gone through. He wanted to go and meet her right away but wasn't sure what would she say. He decided that he would go anyway regardless.

"Trust me friend. I tried to help her in every way. I couldn't gather enough courage to go and talk to her but sent my servants to request her for a meeting. But she didn't want to see my face," said Ambrish.

"You don't feel guilty Ambrish. I know who is to blame. Tell me how and why you happened to come here?" asked Damodar.

"My son, Aniruddha, is here in this ashram for treatment."

"Ohh...so he is your son. What a simple boy! Don't worry a bit. He is fine. Sleeping inside."

Ambrish felt relieved. He knew that Aniruddha usually slept till late in the morning just like most of rich family children spoilt by lack of discipline.

Aniruddha woke up when sun was at its full zenith. He walked out of the hut rubbing his eyes and yawning. As soon as he was out, he saw his father waiting for him there.

"Father, you here!"

"How are you my dear? By God's grace you are not hurt much. You don't know how perturbed and worried I was." Ambrish hugged his son in a tight embrace.

Aniruddha was surprised to see such behaviour from his father. He had never seen this aspect of his father's personality. He always thought that his father never cared about him.

"Yes, you can thank God for saving him this time, but you never know about the future," a voice came from behind.

Ambrish looked back at the source of the voice. It was Vaishali. He felt a rush of blood in his eyes. He was furious at Vaishali. On one hand, she had eloped with Aniruddha and now she was preaching him.

"What do you want to say?" asked Ambrish.

"Only this that you cannot leave everything on God. You yourself have to take some responsibilities too."

"What kind of responsibilities?"

"Towards the society. Towards the suppressed, downtrodden, and lower caste sections. Such oppression forces them to become bandits and anti-social."

"But we are God fearing and religious Vaniks. How have we exploited?" asked Ambrish.

"Don't be a simpleton, seth ji. You buy the crop produced by farmers and workers who toil all year round for a pittance. You pay pennies and sell it for a manifold higher price. Is it not their exploitation? Are you upper caste society elitists not responsible for the inhumane conditions of untouchable Chandaals living in the slums of their own society? Slaves and prisoners of wars are treated like animals, why will they not grow into furious revenge seeking monsters? When the oppression goes beyond tolerance, it forces them to pick up weapons in revolt and go against the society. This is what is happening now." Vaishali was visibly animated.

The word untouchable stirred many emotions within Ambrish and Damodar. Shatvari was forced by such atrocities of the society to go to live among the Chandaals. Damodar's own son was now living the life of a Chandaal.

Damodar who had been listening to the conversation quietly also joined in. He said, "Vaishali is right in a way. While we are focusing on making our homes prosperous and comfortable we lose sight of overall social issues. We don't realise that their problems also concern us. We ignore gross injustice done with them. We ignore all the ailments that gradually become part of a society and it can certainly affect us one day. Nobody can remain unaffected from the consequences, be it a Brahmin or a Vanik."

Ambrish and Damodar both were thinking about Shatvari when Damodar spoke those words.

"Now, I understand this my friend. But what do you suggest we should do?" asked Ambrish.

"You can do a lot seth ji," said Vaishali. "Economy has the largest impact on the overall welfare of the society. Those who have the reins of economy can control the whole society."

"But how, exactly."

"Without financial prowess, a state can't be ruled and managed. Even a ruling king is like a beggar if you block all the revenue sources. You must find a way to pressurize the king to let go of his expansive imperialistic ambitions. He must focus on bringing the outcast sections of the community back to the mainstream of society. There should be an austere and non-violent empathic way of living. This is what your Vanik philosophy is supposed to stand for." Vaishali concluded.

The reference to Vanik way of life hit another weak spot on Ambarish's life. The guilt behind losing his wife due to his behaviour had resulted in forcing him to leave the life of luxury and indulgence. He had taken a disciplined and simple life, vowed to follow a life of hard work and dedication. Now was the chance to reach out to others and influence them to adopt the same philosophy.

"You are right Vaishali. I am ready for this but you will have to help me with one thing," Ambrish was an expert negotiator and was going to put down his side of the bargain.

"What is that Seth ji?"

"You have to convince my son to help me in this endeavour. He doesn't listen to me. Maybe you can convince him."

Vaishali smiled and looked at Aniruddha.

"Ohh just that, leave it to me."

□

Chapter 23

King Rudrasen was contemplating upon a scheme to attack Mekal. His chief minister and the chief commander of armed forces were also present.

"Mekal has thrown an open challenge to us by attacking us the way they did at the festival venue. There is only one befitting reply to this aggression." Rudrasen was breathing heavily and thumping his fists on his thighs.

"Your Highness, it's not so easy to attack Mekal now. The tough terrains and valleys that we have to pass through make it an uphill task for our armies. We were taken aback in our last attempt and as it happened we lost our most accomplished commander in the battle," said the chief commander.

"So what do you suggest commander, should we just sit with our sullen faces and allow them to continue guerrilla warfare. This will cost us thousands of lives. We will have to prepare a better strategy and send a bigger army this time to attack them," said the king.

"I beg your pardon your Highness, maybe I didn't make myself clear. All I wanted to say that we need to understand their geographical terrain very precisely. We must know where their military camps are, what the best possible ways to get there are and which the best possible route to reach their capital is. If we prepare our strategy based on all this information, we will be better prepared," said the commander.

"Hmmm...yes you are right. Chalk out a perfect strategy to attack all their important positions simultaneously without giving them a breather," said the king.

"I agree with you, your Highness. We must deploy our spies all over Mekal to gather all this information as soon as we can," said the chief minister.

"I agree with your plan. I think we should make prince Udayan in-charge of this invasion so that he can get experience of such strategic planning," said the king.

"As you command your Highness."

"Call him here; we'll discuss it with him right now."

"Sure, your Highness" bowed the chief minister and went out to order a sentry to fetch the prince.

Udayan got a bit worried by a call from his father. He had been anticipating a discussion about launching an attack on Mekal. He wasn't sure how to express his views on this.

He bowed to his father, commander of armies, and the chief minister as he reached the royal court.

"You're welcome to the court, prince. We have been discussing some strategic planning. His Highness wants you to lead and execute the plan," said the chief minister.

"If his Highness wants me I will readily oblige, but what are we discussing about?" asked the prince.

"We are going to gather all information about Mekal in order to prepare a strategic map for attacking them soon. We need all information on their military strength, their positions, and shortest safer routes to get there," said the chief minister.

"But why attack Mekal in the first place. It's a small hilly state, what will we get out?"

"This is important for our ambition for expansion of our empire. If Mekal is under us it opens the path to get to other Vindhya states," said the commander.

"It's not simply about the expansion of our empire. Do you not remember how they attacked us during the festivities? Do you not want to teach them an apt lesson?" said the king.

"What I am concerned about your Highness is the fate of the people we capture as part of our expansionary strategy. All the Mekal people we imprisoned after capturing their villages have been living a life worse than animals. What do you expect from their countrymen to do in retaliation?" asked the prince.

"This is not the time to discuss on our long-term vision and state policies dear prince. Presently, we called you to help us with the plan to spread our spy network in Mekal to collect essential information," said the king.

Udayan kept quiet. He felt this was indeed not the time or the place to get into an argument with his father. He could talk about this later. For now he would discuss the strategy to deploy the spies. There was still time before they would plan an attack.

The king was a bit worried to hear his son's remark on his policies. He felt an urgent need to discuss what his heir thought about them.

"Your Highness, you called for me," Udayan bowed to his father, entering his chamber.

"Yes, Prince Udayan. I am a bit concerned that you are not in agreement with our policies of state expansion," said the king.

"Your Highness, every state aspires to expand its boundaries. But this should be done within humane ways. Inhuman and oppressive ways of expansionist ambitions eventually result in self-destruction over time."

"Wars must be fought to expand a state. Yes, people do die in wars. What's new in that?"

"War is not always the first resort. We have had ancient tradition of Rajsuya Yagya. There have been other instances of symbolic power struggles."

"Rajsuya Yagya can't ensure there will be no war. Those who will not accept our sovereignty will wage wars against us."

"I beg your pardon your Highness, but I can't somehow agree to kill thousands of people just for the sake of expanding our boundaries."

"You are talking like a weakling, prince. This is the nature's law. Weak must give way to the strong."

"But real strength comes from unity and cooperation. We will lose our strength if we fight against each other."

"You are talking philosophy not the ground realities of life. One must learn to rely upon his arms and strength to fight his way through life. Truth is that power is essentially needed to live a successful life. Mightier you are better for the entire kingdom."

"But where is the genuine spark of life in this? Spending days in duels and nights in warfare planning, you will have to keep fighting all the life to maintain your identity. In that case when do you have time to enjoy the life?"

"Is there any purposeful life beyond this?"

"Maybe you don't understand the realities of life at all your Highness. Life isn't simply breathing one breath after another. Life smiles when there is music in every breath. It's not simply the wayward movement of your limbs. Life must find a tune of its own, a rhythm in its steps to echo with this music, a dream to pull the world in this dance, to sway in a lyrical swirl of oneness."

"These lofty spiritual and sensitive talks do not suit you. A Kshatriya's music is in his horse's hoof and in his bow's twang. His shield and sword are his toys. It's a Kshatriya's duty to fight to finish the enemy. Your talks do not sound like a brave warrior's ardour but that of a defeated soldier's wretchedness. What are you afraid of?"

"I beg your pardon, your Highness. A Kshatriya's duty is not only to fight but to protect his subject. If it requires a war to protect the people then it's fine. Life grows in peace and tranquility and not in crackling of swords and shields. I am scared that life might get lost in the rumblings of battlegrounds. I am scared that motherhood might be stifled and childhood loses its innocence. I am scared that the fabric of our society which is made up of love and trust might get tattered resulting in disintegration of the society."

"You are getting emotional for no reason. Have we not guarded our faith and ethos? Have we not worked hard to embellish our society and culture? Don't we perform Yagnas, cultural festivals, musical events, mantra recitals and the teachings of Vedas?"

"Yes, you are right we have all of those things but that is only half of the story. Real truth is that the jingling of coins in our gambling houses makes more noise than the recital of mantras in our temples. Our pubs pour more wine to our youth than the wisdom from our education centers. Yoga and spirituality is witnessed in *Shamshans* rather than in the valleys of Satpura. Your Highness, you have no idea in which direction your kingdom is drifting. You are so much obsessed with waging wars against neighbouring states that you fail to listen to the groans and cries of your hungry and diseased subject. Dalits are organising themselves for a revolt against our insensitive and ruthless administration. I fear some sort of revolution is simmering all around. Our youth are lost in wine and consumption. Our employees are corrupt and non-efficient. Our servants hate us more than our enemies. Raghuvanshis have planted more spies within our state than you can imagine. They very well know all our weaknesses. They might hit at our roots. I am not sure what makes you think that our culture is progressing in the right direction."

"I beg your Highness to open your eyes and face the bitter truth. We are on our way to a total destruction. Please come out of your illusions to see that we cannot save our identity simply on the strength of armed power. We have to use our conscience rather than our military might. We must create such circumstances where everybody can live in peace respectfully. That is our responsibility as rulers and Kshatriya. We belong to an Aryan culture that propagated *'Vasudhaiv Kutumbkam'* which means the entire world is a family. It's a shame for us to have slaves and untouchables within our society. This is the degradation of our religion and culture. I beg you to peep inward and look at our internal issues rather than focussing on blind ambition to conquer external states."

Udayan's words stirred Rudrasen's heart. Was the prince right in mentioning that the state was going through degradation and a steep downfall? That was a huge matter of concern, especially if the king knew nothing about it.

"Give me some time to ponder over the issues you have touched upon," said the king.

"As you wish, your Highness," said Udayan and bowed to his father before walking out of the royal chamber.

Ranveer's face lit up as he welcomed Neel and Dhananjay.

"Rajan, you are here! We got the information that you were captured by the Yaduvanshis," exclaimed Ranveer.

"Yes, Ranveer. They did capture us but we managed to escape. But how did you find out?" asked Neel.

"Spies of North Kosala's Raghuvanshis are spread all over Shripur. They gave this information to us. They even helped us to rescue you, but the plan could not work out as expected," said Ranveer.

"What are you talking about? Raghuvanshi spies in Shripur? Rescue plan?" asked Neel.

"Rajan, Raghuvanshis planned to attack the festival venue and kidnap the princess Pallavi. We planned to use her as a ransom to rescue you and our other people. But before we could do that somebody else kidnapped her. We still attacked the venue and killed several hundred Yaduvanshis. I am sure, your Highness, would be proud of us."

"Ranveer…what have you done, you ignorant fool! What made you attack and kill innocent people?"

"They had captured you your Highness. We had to do something to rescue you," replied Ranveer.

"Ranveer, we had already escaped when we had participated in the festival. Wait; let me think on all this."

Neel pondered over the whole matter to reach some concrete conclusion.

Ranveer was looking at his young king's face trying to figure out what actually had happened.

"Ranveer, we have been used by your Raghuvanshi friends. They leaked information to Yaduvanshis there and got us captured. Then they used you to attack Shripur during the festival. Thank God you didn't manage to kidnap the princess," said Neel and commanded, "let me talk to Dhananjay for a moment."

Ranveer bowed out of the tent.

"Dhananjay, we have done a grave sin by attacking and killing innocent Yaduvanshis for a wrong reason. No surprise that they are preparing to wage a war against us," said Neel.

"Yes, your Highness. But what can be done now?" asked Dhananjay.

"Apology. We have made a mistake that took many innocent lives. We must convey our apologies."

"Apologies to an enemy state? What are you saying your Highness? I see your point but they won't see it like this. They will certainly think that we are scared and begging to be spared."

"I know you are right but the only right way forward is to express an apology. Otherwise it'll simply make matters worse. Both states will engage in a war planned by a third enemy. I am not afraid of fighting our enemies but only for a right cause. We will send a letter of apology but we will also ensure to make them feel we are not weak. We will ask them to return our captured villages. Otherwise we will fight to get them."

"As you deem right, your Highness."

"Okay, then send an official message to the king of Kosala that we realize our mistake that resulted in the killings of many Kosala soldiers. We would like to apologize for that. Also, we would like to extend our hand for friendship between the two states but not at the expense of our sovereignty and self-respect. We would like to propose that Kosala should return our captured territory and release all our people and we will reciprocate by releasing Kosala's prisoners."

□

Chapter 24

Rudrasen was engrossed in his thoughts when he suddenly realised that Princess Pallavi also had a difficult time recently. How a stranger insulted her in front of the whole gathering. And her kidnapping! She definitely was going through a tough time. He realized he needed to talk to her and console her.

Pallavi was sitting in her chamber going over all that happened. She wondered how her life changed in a day. Firstly, a complete stranger embarrassed her then the same person put his life on stake to save her. Why did he enter the contest in the first place if he didn't want to marry her? Was he too arrogant or was he trying to break her pride and ego? Why wouldn't she be a proud princess, when the whole of Aryavart wanted to get her? Didn't they bet their lives for her that day? One prince almost paid the price. Neel, on the other hand, put his life in grave danger twice because of her but still let her go. And that cruel Kapalika with that woman, who were they? Who was Rishi Vasudev they wanted to know about? What was the Yantra they planned the whole thing for?

While she was busy pondering over the thoughts again and again, she heard a knock and saw her father walking into her chamber. She quickly got hold of her and sat normally.

"How are you my dear child?" asked the king.

"I am fine, your Highness."

"I am very hurt by all that happened with you that day. That Kamboj citizen Shreedutt insulted you publicly. Were it not for our ideals of respecting our guests, I would have had him fed to the dogs."

"Your Highness, neither was he from Kamboj nor is his name Shreedutt."

"What...! Who was he then?"

"King of Mekal—Neel."

"Really! King of Mekal! So they have crossed all the boundaries. Still, the prince is reluctant to attack them. I am not sure why."

"Father, he saved my life by rescuing me from the Kapalika."

"What are you saying? I was in the impression that Prince Udayan rescued you?"

"No, that is not the fact. Maybe he hid the truth to not escalate your worries. Even the prince was captured by them. So much that they wanted to sacrifice the prince for a human sacrificial ritual."

"Human sacrifice in our state! That's atrocious. I will destroy them."

"Father, they are powerful people with mystical powers. Ghouls, ghosts, evil spirits—they can unleash such things at will. You must not infuriate them."

"What are you saying? You want me to forgive Neel and forgive that Kapalika. Are you not feeling the embarrassment?"

"Surely, I felt gravely insulted that day. But when I think of the fact that Neel saved our lives from a certain death, I feel we owe him, we must try and pay back the debt."

"If you think this way then fine. We will find a way to pay the debt. We just need to find out if it's not a political game he is playing."

"Game…?"

"Yes, my dear, these are political things you won't understand."

Rudrasen got up and started to walk out of the chamber.

"Father…"

"Yes dear…"

"Father, who is Rishi Vasudev?"

The name of Rishi Vasudev coming from the princess' mouth surprised Rudrasen.

"Who told you about Rishi Vasudev?"

"Firstly, you tell me if you know him."

"Yes. But he is no more. But why are you asking, tell me?"

"He created a Yantra?"

"I don't know what you are talking about. Who told you about all this?"

"Well...father...if you don't know anything about this then leave it, why bother."

Rudrasen scanned her face and gradually moved out of the room. His forehead was grave with deep furrows of worry.

Pallavi fell back to her train of thoughts. She wanted to find out who Rishi Vasudev was. She was by now certain that her father was hiding some great truth. She felt that she had a connection with Rishi Vasudev and the yantra. But how will she find that out? Who can tell her about that? Not that woman, as she was so full of hatred towards her. Maybe that young man who killed Prahlaad to save the prince's life. She decided to find him.

□

Chapter 25

King Rudrasen was pacing about in his royal chamber. Events of last few days perturbed him. He was a bit surprised to hear from Udayan about the internal state of affairs in his kingdom. He never realized that his policies of expansion had affected his people in such a way. There was a widespread feeling of chaos and instability. Bureaucrats were corrupt and disloyal. They could sell royal secrets for a handful of coins. Slaves and Dalits were preparing to revolt. Princess Pallavi found out about Maharishi Vasudev. Who could tell her that secret? Could they be Raghuvanshis? Udayan believed that the spies of Raghuvanshis knew more about South Kosala than their own ministers. As they couldn't face the South Kosala army front on, they had been up to these sneaky ways. Udayan was right in suggesting that the policy of expansion was not in the interest of the state. It was time to focus upon inclusive development of people. That was the only way to strengthen the state and present a strong front to enemies.

As the king pondered upon these thoughts, one guard knocked on the door to ask for permission to enter. It was a messenger. Rudrasen waved his hand to allow the messenger in.

A twenty-five-year-old man walked in with a small white cloth wrapped around a wooden stick. He bowed to the king and handed over the message. Rudrasen unwrapped the cloth and started to read it.

"Respected king of South Kosala, the attack on the festival venue during the South Kosala's annual fest was carried out in our absence without our inherent permission. It's true that some Mekal soldiers were unwittingly part of that unfortunate incident. We send our apologies and feel ashamed of such an incident. However, it must be reminded that South Kosala has captured several Mekal villages and enslaved our people. This has infuriated the people of our state. There is a situation of revolt. We would like to have friendly relations with South Kosala but it cannot happen at the cost of giving away the freedom of our people. The decision is in your hands. If you are willing to free our people and withdraw from our territory captured by your army, we will gladly free your soldiers. We would like to request you to give a serious thought to this agreement in order for peace to prevail in the region.

Neel"

King Rudrasen looked up after reading the message. He turned around and started to pace his chamber. He found that he was unusually calm after reading the message from the king of an enemy state. He had by now become to realise that Neel had saved the lives of Udayan and Pallavi. It was also true that he was present during the festival that proves that he could not be associated with the attacking party. Now that letter of apology—what could that mean? His large heartedness or weakness! It was also true that if South Kosala rejected the plea to be friendly, Mekal would be exploited by the Raghuvanshis to harm South Kosala in some way. Therefore, there was no harm in meeting Neel.

"Go and inform your king that I would like to meet him to discuss the next course of action," Rudrasen told the messenger.

Mekal's messenger bowed and walked out.

"What brings you here Seth ji?" asked king Rudrasen to Ambrish.

"Your Highness, yesterday one of my carriages was attacked by the bandits. My son Aniruddha was also injured in the attack. Yesterday it was my son, tomorrow it could be anyone. We are heading towards troubled times," meekly said Ambrish.

"We are well aware of the nuisance of bandits and dacoits. We are doing all that is needed. We have enhanced security on the routes most affected by bandit attacks."

"But will that stop the root of the problem, your Highness?"

"What are you trying to say? Speak freely."

"Your Highness, you cannot kill a tree by cutting its branches. We have to unearth its roots."

"We have been trying to do that by sending our soldiers to find and destroy their bases."

"Rajan, their roots are not in the jungles of Dandakaranya. They are right here in our kingdom and in the states that are ruled by us."

"What do you mean?"

"When you snatch a man's self-esteem and pride, he goes to any limits to regain it. Even if that means taking up arms. Violence, robbery, killing and any other thing he can resort to attain his sense of identity. When slavery is unbearable—whether of body or of soul then a slave turns to become a bandit. To eliminate bandits we have to abolish slavery."

"Why have all of you started speaking the same language lately? Yuvraj spoke of the same issues the other day."

"This is not just a language, your Highness. This is the voice of the conscience. If you delve deeper within yourself, you will find the same voice trying to tell you this same thing."

"We are already concerned about this, as I told you earlier. Give us some time and we will find out a solution soon."

"Time is of essence your Highness. Peaceful and ethical solutions are always welcome to us, Vaniks but as you know resorting to violence and cunningness is against our philosophy," said Ambrish and took his leave.

Neel and Dhananjay agreed to visit Shripur on the invitation of king Rudrasen. It was decided that they will meet the king at his palace. Dhananjay was little apprehensive of meeting the king in his own den but Neel asked him to trust the Yaduvanshis this time.

The duo reached the king's palace on time. King Rudrasen came out to welcome the visitors. Neel and Dhananjay bowed with joined hands and the king reciprocated and requested them to be seated.

"We express our agony for the attack on the festival venue. But the truth is that even we didn't know about the attack."

"Yes, I received your letter and I am aware of the fact that when the attack was carried out both of you were hiding in our capital as spies," replied King Rudrasen.

"Yes, your Highness, that's the truth. We have been attacked by your armies in recent times. We needed to strengthen ourselves by gaining more knowledge about your state."

"How do you want me to trust those who hid in our capital in disguise to dig out information to use against us? Could this not be a shrewd political conspiracy?"

"Have we not trusted you by accepting your invite and coming unarmed to your palace?"

"We are Kshatriyas and we do not harm our guests. I am sure you are aware of that."

"And you think that we Nishaads do not have our ideals?"

"It's time you prove it."

"Have we not proved it already? We have saved the lives of your son and daughter."

"How can I be sure that it was not your ploy to get the princess kidnapped first and then save her life to reach us?"

"If you do not have any trust on us then what for you invited us here, your Highness? Without a mutual trust, communication is impossible. We will simply be wasting our time arguing."

"Hmmm...how are your relations with the Raghuvanshis?"

"They are your enemies. If you treat us as foes, then they can possibly become our friends."

"And if you and we become friends?"

"You know the answer. A friend's enemy will be our enemy. I assure you of our loyalty and friendship."

On hearing such words from Neel, King Rudrasen got up from his throne and walked up to them. He offered his hand and said, "From this day onwards we will treat you as friends. We will solve our issues by mutual discussions."

The two kings shook hands and vowed to make Mekal and South Kosala friendly states.

"You had been hiding in Shripur in disguise, now I invite you to stay as our royal guests. Please accept our hospitality. It will be our honour. I am sure Udayan and Pallavi will be equally delighted."

□

Chapter 26

It was a Kapalika den. The new moon night had engulfed the whole surrounding like a Kapalika's black garb. Inside, an enormous idol of Kaali with eight arms stood with one foot over Shiva's chest, who was lying on the ground. There was a small furnace for fire rituals in front of the idol. A strong odour and smoke rose from it and it lightened the mood of the whole area.

Five Kapalikas sat around the furnace. They were dressed in black from top to toe. Their faces were dense and sombre. All of them had garlands of human bones around their neck. They were silently chanting some mantras with their eyes closed. Intermittently, they would open their eyes and offer servings of wine, ghee, and other ingredients into the fire. As soon as they dropped their offerings with the sounds of Swaha, the flames from the furnace would shoot up as if to accept the servings. The faces of the Kapalikas looked devilishly focused in the light of the fire. Not too far away from the furnace sat about two hundred young men. Their fists were clenched and they had strong signs of determination on their faces.

Soon a woman entered the den. It was Shatvari. Her arrival eased the facial tension of the young men sitting there. Shatvari picked up a skull lying by the Kapalikas. It contained wine. She gulped it down in one go and put the empty skull down from where she had picked it up. She sat down by the Kapalikas.

The mantra recital was getting near a crescendo when the sound and the expression got more aggressive and forceful. The offerings to the fire increased and the flame continued to rise and crackle. In a matter of moments, the homa ritual was completed. To complete the ceremony Shatvari invoked Kaali in a raised voice. Everybody, including the Kapalikas and the young men also joined in.

"Mahakali Bhadrakali, give us strength to eliminate all the sins!"

All the young men chorused along.

"Mahakali Bhadrakali, eliminator of sins, give us strength!"

After the invocation, they all joined their hands and silently thanked the Goddess Kaali for the ritual.

"What do we have to do next?" asked one of the Kapalikas.

"Treatment! We have to tend to the poisoned blood in our society that has given birth to the caste system and exploitation of the poor," replied Shatvari.

"But how?"

"Poison can only be treated with poison."

"What's the plan?"

"War! A decisive hurricane of war! So strong and powerful that it will shake the foundations of the system and its weaknesses."

"Do we have the resources for that?"

"I have created an invincible weapon. A chemical weapon. Just a mere touch of the chemical can kill or make a person unconscious. Victory will surely be ours."

"If we have such an unbeatable weapon, what have we been waiting for? Why don't attack without losing a moment?"

"To be able to handle such a dangerous weapon, we must have its antidote just in case we get affected by its vile. I now have created its chemical antidote as well. Our soldiers will drink it and that will shield us from the effects of the weapon."

"Are our soldiers trained to use this weapon?"

"Well trained and daring to go." Shatvari looked back at the young men sitting behind her. She stood up and addressed all, "The time for a decisive battle has finally arrived. We will have to win this even if we have to lay our lives down. The caste system must be destroyed down to the ground. The discrimination based on caste, creed, and race must be eliminated and dumbed faraway from our society. We will build a society where nobody is a Shudra, or, an untouchable. Take a vow!"

"We take a vow that we will not think twice to lay our lives down in order to attain our cause." All the young men roared loudly together.

"Tomorrow night, we will attack Shripur from Brahma entrance. Praise Mahakali! Praise Bhadrakali!" announced Shatvari.

"Jai Mahakali! Jai Bhadrakali!

The darkness and drowsiness of midnight had enveloped the whole of Shripur. Brahma entrance was quiet and peaceful. Guards were alert and wide awake. A group of Chandaals arrived as usual to clean the capital. They were dressed in black, their brooms resting on their shoulders, and a wooden cart to carry away the scum. The guards let open a small door. There was no question of frisking the untouchable Chandaals. As soon as the guards opened the door, the group of Chandaals attacked the guard. A special machine that sprayed the chemical weapon was hid in every Chandaal soldier's clothes. The chemical spread in the air at the push of a wooden lever. The guards started to fall around like amputated tree logs.

Soon, more than five hundred Chandaals, who had been hiding in the nearby forest rushed towards the open door to enter Shripur. They all were equipped with the spraying equipment, swords, and daggers. While entering in the town, they slashed and jabbed the unconscious soldiers lying on the ground. Somehow the guards at the other entrance gate of Shripur found out about the onslaught and they blew the siren hoot. Many units of armed soldiers set about on foot and on horseback to control the sudden assault.

To a layman's eyes, the soldier units of South Kosala dwarfed the Chandaal soldier's might. But the Chandaals had the invincible weapon that the South Kosala soldiers had no idea about. They were not only taken by surprise but also by a weapon that was unheard of.

Panic set within the ranks of South Kosala force. Some soldiers could not fathom the situation and escaped at the sight of their fallen peers. Others who tried to use their swords tried that in vain as the mere spray of that liquid rendered all traditional artillery useless. Even the horses found it hard to run around as they too suffered the wrath of the chemical. Consequently, most royal guards and soldiers either fell down or escaped, leaving a few brave men who too met the same end after trying to avert the inevitable.

The news reached the royal court faster than expected. King Rudrasen was briefed on the events of past couple of hours and he felt blood rushing to his eyes but kept calm and ordered his ministers to convene right away. Neel and Dhananjay who had been staying as royal guests were also called to the meeting. Udayan and Pallavi joined as well.

Rudrasen's face was pallid and tense. Udayan had warned him about the lurking revolt but it all happened this soon took him by surprise.

"We have been told that the chemical weapon they are using cannot be dealt with our tradition ammunition. We have to find a way soon enough," said King Rudrasen addressing the court.

"But how, your Highness? We do not have any idea what this chemical is. By the time we will find out enough about it, most of our soldiers will be dead," said the prime minister of the state.

"Only the Chandaals know about its antidote, I am sure. Only from them we can get it," added Neel.

"How do you suggest we get it from them? Presently, we are even unable to touch them," asked Udayan anxiously.

"One man can help us, I think," said Pallavi.

"Who? Do you know that person? Tell us."

"The same person who saved you from the sword of Prahlaad. I am sure he can help us against the revolt from Chandaals."

"But how will we find him now? We don't even know his name."

"I think if he disagreed with the ways of the Kapalika and saved your life, he will surely come to us to help us," said Neel.

"How can you be so sure of this? We cannot sit here and wait for him to turn up while the Chandaals are making their way to the royal castle," said the prime minister.

"Do you have any other option?" asked Neel.

Just then a guard walked in, bowed to the king and informed him that a young man wanted to meet him. His name was Shatrughan.

"Shatrughan! Yes that's the name of that young boy I told you about," exclaimed Pallavi. Her eyes lit up in excitement.

"Bring the young man in right away," ordered the king.

Shatrughan walked in the court and bowed to everybody and addressed the king, "Your Highness, I have an important information to give to you. The present revolt in your kingdom has been masterminded by my mother."

"Well, that doesn't change anything. Tell us, if you can help us in anyway?" asked the king.

Even before Shatrughan could speak, Neel added, "We need to know more about the chemical weapon that they are using against the soldiers. Do you know where the antidote can be found?"

"I have no information on that, your Highness. But I do not approve of this bloodbath and violent revolution. It destroys both sides," said Shatrughan.

"Is that all you have come to tell us young man?" said Neel.

"No I have come to inform you that maybe I can stop my mother. I am going to do it," said Shatrughan.

Udayan asked, "You know your mother is so full of hatred and her heart beats with revenge. How can you stop her?"

"The time has come to test a mother's affection and a woman's tenderness. Let me see if the love can win over revenge and hatred." Shatrughan bowed and walked out soon as he finished his sentence.

Everybody looked at each other with mixed feelings of hope and disbelief. They discussed what could happen if Shatrughan failed. King Rudrasen was still as flushed as before.

Neel sensed the mood of the court and addressed everybody, "I know we have to rely on the young man who is going to win over his mother with love. It's strange and maybe unfortunate that our fate depends on that clash of love and hatred and we don't know what would happen. But I can feel it that it is going to be a love's victory."

Neel's confident words infused new vigour in the king's eyes and everybody else looked visibly relieved.

Shatvari was intoxicated with the pangs of revenge and a hope for imminent victory. She knew that her soldiers have trapped South Kosala soldiers just like a hunter traps an unsuspecting wild beast. She had killed thousands of men as young as her son. Nothing could deter her from her plan it seemed.

She was taken down from her trance by a sight that she least expected at this hour. It was Shatrughan standing right in front of her, right amidst the battle zone. That too, completely unarmed.

"Shatrughan, don't be a fool, get out of here, fast," shouted Shatvari.

"You are doing a foolish thing by engaging in this mass murder, my dear mother," replied Shatrughan.

"This is not a mass murder. It's a battle, it's a battle for an objective to win back our rights. To demolish this caste system that has enslaved us for generations."

"You are not demolishing a flawed system but the whole civilization out of your madness. System can be improved, changed, but not demolished like this. Look around yourself, what have you achieved. Only piles of dead corpse, getting higher with every passing moment. You are spreading chaos and anarchy."

"Do not preach me Shatrughan. This system has become a devilish atrocity. The people who groom this system have become heinous sinners and they must be punished. That is the dictate of my *dharma*."

"What about these young men you have murdered because they were only performing their *dharma* of protecting their state? Were they not doing their *dharma*? Or have you created your own definition of *dharma*?"

Just then Shatvari shrieked in sheer disbelief as a Chandaal soldier attacked Shatrughan with the spray. Shatrughan collapsed on the spot.

"What have you done, you fool! He is my son." Shatvari ran towards the collapsed Shatrughan picked him up and embraced him in her arms.

"Don't worry my son, nothing will happen to you," Shatvari embraced Shatrughan tightly and asked the soldier standing to go and get her the antidote quickly.

"But we don't have that here. It is in the Chandaal basti, as per your instructions," replied the soldier.

Shatvari remembered that she herself arranged for the antidote to hide in a specific location to keep it in safe custody.

"Don't delay then, let's take Shatrughan back to the basti," ordered Shatvari.

"You want to leave the battle zone? But you are our commander?" asked the soldier.

"You want me to leave my son here to die. Let's go quick."

They picked up Shatrughan and left the battle zone. During their way back, Shatvari felt someone was following them but as she looked back she could not see anyone.

Somewhere in the Northern jungles of Shripur, commander Indrajit was busy discussing next course of action with his soldiers and spies.

"Everything is going in our favour. As soon as the Chandaals will have captured Shripur we would attack South Kosala and recapture the capital from Chandaals. We now know where the chemical antidote has been hidden by them. We must acquire that as soon as possible."

"Yes, commander, but that place is guarded like a fort by the most alert Chandaal soldiers. Not to forget the Kapalikas. We must wait for them to capture Shripur. Then they will be a bit relaxed and may be complacent with joy. That will be the best time to attack to acquire the antidote," said one of the spies.

Just then a spy came running with news.

"What is the matter? You look like you have seen a ghost," asked Indrajit.

"Commander, Shatvari's son Shatrughan has been accidentally attacked by the chemical and they are taking him back to their base to treat him with the antidote," informed the spy.

"So what is there to worry about?"

"The worry is that some South Kosala soldiers have also been spotted following Shatvari. If they manage to find out where the antidote is they might get it before we do and that will sabotage our entire plan."

"Hmmm...that is really a matter to worry. We cannot let anybody to get that antidote before we do. We will have to stop both Shatvari and those South Kosala soldiers at any cost. Delay will lead to death of Shatvari's son and that will devastate her making our goals easier to attain."

"As you wish commander. We will immediately get on their tails and attack at an opportune moment," replied a soldier and moved out with his group.

The party that was following Shatvari comprised Neel, Dhananjay, Udayan and some chosen South Kosala soldiers. It was almost dawn. Slight orange hue appeared on the distant horizon. Neel instructed the unit, "We have to be very careful in this. This is our last hope. If we can get to the antidote, the tables will turn in our favour instantly."

"You don't worry, we are very alert and realize the importance of this opportunity," said Udayan.

Just then they heard loud shrieks ahead. As they looked ahead, they saw that a group of soldiers have jumped from the trees and attacked Shatvari's soldiers. They were taken by surprise and the chemical weapon sprayer dropped from their hands due to panic. Still they held onto their swords and daggers and took to fighting the attackers with full force.

"We will have to go help them. Let's attack," ordered Neel.

"What are you saying? Why save the enemies. Let them die. The attackers are making our work easier," said one of the soldiers.

"Don't be a fool! If they die here like this it will lead to bigger chaos and anarchy. Besides, don't you want to know who these attackers are? We never knew there was a third party interested in all this. We need to find who these people are at any cost," replied Neel.

"But if we went to help them, they will know we have been following them. We might miss our chance to get to the antidote," said Udayan.

"That is a genuine concern, but if Shatvari and her soldiers get killed here we will never reach to the antidote anyway. Let's split in two units. You stay back with your soldiers. I and Dhananjay will go to their aide. In the worst case scenario, you can still follow them to the antidote."

Everyone agreed and the two Mekal warriors jumped ahead to rescue their enemies.

Neel and Dhananjay along with some soldiers pounced upon the attackers from North Kosala. Shatvari and her soldiers saw the help coming that enhanced their vigour. They started to fight with increased zest. Shatrughan was lying on the ground at one side. One of the North Kosala attackers realized an opportunity to attack him. As soon he jumped to stab Shatrughan, Shatvari took the blow on her sword and kicked the assailant with her right foot.

"How dare you touch my son!" She shouted in anger.

As soon as the fallen soldier got on his feet, Shatvari flew towards him like a hungry tigress and pierced her sword through his body. He stood there for a moment clutching the sword with his hand and then fell away on one side.

It was just a matter of time before Neel, Dhananjay, Shatvari and their soldiers killed all North Kosala attackers. Shatvari looked at Neel and tried to recognize him and said, "I am very grateful for your help. But who are you? I am sure I have seen you somewhere before."

"Don't worry about all that, we must think about taking your son to safety right now. Let's take him for treatment as soon as possible," said Neel.

"Yes, that's right. We don't have much time. He must be treated right away," said Dhananjay.

Shatvari looked at Shatrughan and ordered her soldiers to carry him.

One of the Chandaal soldiers waved at another and moved forward to speak to Shatvari. He said, "We cannot take these people with us. We do not know them. They could be enemy spies."

"You have all the right to doubt but as you have just seen that we saved your life. You would have been dead on the ground if we weren't here. We can still be of help to you," said Neel.

"Thus far our trust has been broken hundreds of times. But still I want to trust you people," said Shatvari.

"This is foolishness. We cannot take them with us at any cost. Nobody can be allowed to know about the antidote as you know," the Chandaal youth continued.

"We do not have a choice. It's a matter of my son's life."

"It's also a matter of our vow. It's a matter of our entire plan for victory. Until we have captured the throne of Shripur, we cannot compromise with our plan at any cost," said the young man.

All the Chandaal youth came forward and stood alongside that young man. They looked determined not to allow Shatvari take the outsiders with her.

Shatvari found herself in a great dilemma. On one side was her lifelong devotion to a cause. On the other lay her own son fighting for his life. Affection was battling with the vows of revenge. If Shatrughan would have stood by her side in this battle, she would have gladly sacrificed him. But Shatrughan stood there in her path and got injured by the weapon that she created to destroy her enemies. For now all she wanted was to see her son alive. But was she willing to risk her entire existence and that of her community for the sake of her son's life? Would she trust unknown strangers over her own loyal accomplices in order to save Shatrughan?

Shatvari was lost in the thought for some moments before taking a deep breath. She had made up her mind. She walked towards Shatrughan and said, "I am going to take my son for treatment. Those who are with me can come along. Those who want to stop me show up now."

Two Chandaal soldiers came forward to block her path. Shatvari ran towards them like a roaring lioness, "Nobody can stop me from saving my son's life."

The tussle between Shatvari and the Chandaals commenced and soon Neel's party also joined in to help Shatvari. It was a matter of time before all the Chandaals were killed.

"Don't waste any time now, let's take your son away from here," said Neel while lifting Shatrughan from the ground onto his horse.

Everyone got on their horses and galloped on following Shatvari's lead.

On reaching the Chandaal slum, Shatvari arrived at a rundown cottage. She went in and took out a large earthen vessel with narrow neck. It had the antidote. She poured some in a small cup and brought the cup up to Shatrughan's unconscious lips. She took him in her lap and poured some of the antidote into his mouth drop by drop. He slowly took a few sips, and started to come out from his slumber. In a few moments, he came around fully and looked at his mother. As soon as he opened his eyes, Shatvari embraced him in her arms and kissed his forehead. A torrent of tears appeared from her eyes and soaked Shatrughan's face. He was a bit confused about the whole thing, he asked, "Where am I? What happened?"

"You were attacked at the battle zone. Your mother took you down here to treat you," replied Neel.

Before anybody else could say anything Udayan and his unit of soldiers appeared on the scene. Shatvari stood up alarmed finding Udayan there.

"Prince Udayan here! Is it some cunning conspiracy to trick us?" Asked Shatvari looking at Neel and Dhananjay.

Udayan descended down from his horse and walked in. He said, "There is no conspiracy. I have come here to request you to call off this violent revolt and let us discuss your issues at peace."

"Peace! Issues! Now when your army is down on the ground and you have no options left, you have come to my door talking about peace and solutions. Where was this talk of peace Yuvraj when your king was intoxicated with power and exploited us like beasts? Go away Udayan, your talks of a peaceful solution in the present context reek of fear and cowardice," replied Shatvari.

"You think you are going to achieve a solution by doing this?" interrupted Neel. "The young men you took with you in this revolution refused to support you. The people you want to entrust with the future of this state cannot realize the pain of a mother's weeping heart. You expect those stone-hearted people to build a future for upcoming generations? You still have time Shatvari you can stop this mayhem, else all our coming generations will never forgive you."

Neel's words had an impact upon Shatvari as she stopped in her march towards Udayan. It was true that her own people today wanted her to let her son die. How could she entrust the future of her people to such cold blooded youth she had been associated with?

While she was engrossed in her thoughts Shatrughan rose and started to go and said, "There is no point wasting our time in these talks now. We need to stop the mayhem as soon as we can."

"Stop Shatrughan!" roared Shatvari.

Everybody turned around to look at her.

Shatrughan said, "You can't stop me now dear mother. I can't let this happen anymore."

"I am not stopping you, I am asking you to wait for me to come with you."

Everybody's faces lit up with new found courage and hope.

Chandaal army with the help of this weapon had almost crushed the South Kosala's force. They were inching towards the royal fort and everyone was delighted with the accomplishment. Inside the royal castle, urgent discussions were taking place about escaping from the secret passage.

"Jai Mahakali! Jai Bhadrakali! Let the sinners be crushed!" Chorus of Chandaals deafening roar stupefied one and all.

When it seemed that nothing could stop their decisive victory, suddenly there was silence and the Chandaal wave stalled. It was Shatvari and Shatrughan standing right between them and the royal army.

"Devi, we are at the verge of a historic victory. We are going to fulfil our vow that we took alongside you," said one of the young men.

"Which vow? What victory young man? Strolling over the blood soiled bodies of innocent men, what destination are you heading towards?" asked Shatrughan.

"We aim to bring about the social upliftment of the Dalits and all other downtrodden. We aim to demolish the insensitive supremacy of these upper castes," replied the young man.

"Upliftment or mayhem? What alternative do you propose? Anarchists and disorderly rulers! The people that you have killed today all their dependents are sitting praying for their lives in their homes. They are shell shocked and terrorized by your march to this revolution. What do you plan to tell them?" asked Shatrughan.

"The people of the state have also been part of this rotten system nourished by their upper caste rulers and landlords. They too are equally responsible for our plight and deserve to learn some lessons," replied the young man.

"Punishment is given to those who do not accept, realize and atone for their mistakes. What about those who regret and are willing to observe penance for their follies? A position of strength should also teach how to forgive those who apologise. This is what Lord Rama's lifelong message is and we are the people of the same holy land," said Shatrughan.

"What do you think, they have realized their mistakes? Do you think they are willing to apologize and set entire rotten system right?" asked the young man.

"Why not! This is a land of great sages. I am sure that love and kindness still flows through the veins of people. If we call upon our people with love and compassion then all boundaries can be erased," said Shatrughan.

"If you are so sure of this, why not call upon the people of Shripur and show if they even understand what love is. They only know inequity and discrimination," said the young man.

Shatrughan moved forward and turned towards a section of Shripur's citizens and addressed the crowd.

"I am Shatrughan, an untouchable from the Chandaal community. I call upon the conscience and kind heart of the people of Shripur. If any of you feel that I and the people of my community have been made to lead this animal-like existence which we never deserved, then please come forward and rid us of this custom of untouchability. Remove the entire barrier between you and us. Please come forward and embrace this Chandaal in your arms to prove your love and compassion towards us is genuine."

For a moment, the whole crowd stood quiet. People looked at each other. Some looked down not knowing what to do. Most of them were still in shock due to the events of the day. Suddenly, a young man arose from the crowd and walked forward towards Shatrughan and Shatvari. A wave of excitement went round the crowd and people's gay murmurs could be heard. All the eyeballs in the crowd followed each step of the young man. But what followed surprised not only the crowd but all the Chandaal soldiers and even Shatrughan himself.

The young man came forward and instead of embracing Shatrughan, fell to his feet. Shatrughan held his shoulders and embraced him tightly.

"I don't even deserve to see eye-to-eye with you. I will however, feel it my privilege to touch your feet. You suffered the evil custom of untouchability all your life from our so-called upper caste people and still you come here and not only save our lives but give us a chance to amend our mistakes and absolve us of our sins. You have proved that you cannot be a mere human being but a god incarnate. On behalf of all the people who exploited your community, I fold my hands together and bow in front of you to grant us pardon. I see my whole existence a mere trifle in front of your compassion, your *gyaan*, and your kind heart."

"Don't say such words my friend. You have absolved us of our shackles. This immense favour you have bestowed upon me and my community will be remembered by generations to come. You have embraced a Chandaal and welcomed him back into your society. Now we are one and the same. I urge all of your people to come forward and rid us of our plight. Take us in your arms and free us." Shatrughan hugged the young man and they both were in tears of joy.

Shatrughan hadn't even finished his plea, a herd of people flocked ahead and hugged Chandaal soldiers. Shatvari stood there dumbfounded at the turn of the events. It was no less than a miracle. Her hatred and revenge melted away by the love and compassion of her son. She couldn't control her emotions and burst into tears and plunged ahead to tightly hug her son in her arms. She was extremely proud of her.

"I am proud to be your mother my son. The life you led could have turned you into a monster that we all had become, but instead you have become a saint, a yogi and a Siddha. I have been practicing tantra to gain spiritual supernatural powers to fulfil a revenge but you proved that all powers fall short and seem like tiny dwarfs in front of a heart filled with kindness and forgiveness. I am proud of being your mother."

She turned around to address her people and said, "Our vow has been fulfilled today but not with blood and hatred but with love and forgiveness. These upper caste people are no longer our enemies. We are no longer outsiders and untouchables for them. Look how we stand hand in hand and arms in arms with each other. Let's forgive each other and get back to our homes. Let's all forget the bitter past."

Whole arena erupted with joy and happiness. Gradually, all the Chandaals walked back to their homes with peace and joy in their hearts along with a sense of genuine victory.

□

Chapter 27

"We have a very bad news," said Ranveer while alighting from his horse. He was accompanied by four other horsemen.

"What could be that bad?" asked Neel.

"North Kosala army is preparing to attack South Kosala any moment now. They have full knowledge of the Chandaal attack and how that has left South Kosala in tatters. They want to utilise this opportunity. Attack can come in a matter of days."

"This indeed is a bad news. How can we counter an attack by such a strong army?"

A Chandaal youth came forward and said, "We too will defend our state. Howsoever strong their army is, we still have the chemical weapon with us."

"But our chemical weapon is almost finished," added Shatvari.

"Can we not make any more?" asked Neel.

"Not in such a short time. Some of the rare herbs were collected after years of research and cultivation."

"Then what should we do? We have to find out a way. And fast." Neel's voice was still confident, but his face was buried in sudden worry lines.

Rudrasen was pacing in his chamber from end to end. His head was down and hands at the back. After being defeated and humiliated in such a manner by the Chandaals, he found himself unable to face Shatvari and Shatrughan, who were standing in front of him. They had almost forgiven him for his sins but Rudrasen was unable to see them eye-to-eye. He was pondering over why his kingdom was inundated with problems one after another. As if struck by an unending curse. Suddenly, it struck him that it could indeed be a curse.

He spoke as if driven by a strong inner voice, "Only some supernatural power can save us from these problems now."

"Your Highness, you are losing hope. We have to think rationally to find a solution," said Neel.

"I am thinking only about a solution," Rudrasen's voice was serious.

"Solution, and that too with supernatural powers?" Udayan was a bit shocked.

"Yes, solution. We will invoke divine powers by worshipping this Yantra," said Rudrasen.

The mention of the Yantra alerted Shatvari.

"Are you talking about Maharshi Vasudev's Yantra?"

"Yes, the same."

The name of Maharshi Vasudev and the Yantra also surprised Pallavi.

"So you know Maharishi Vasudev's Yantra as opposed to all that you told me that day father?"

"My dear I lied to you that day. Please forgive me if possibly you can. Maybe I am getting punishments for my sins."

"What sins are you talking about my father?"

"Let me tell you the whole story today in front of everybody. Maharshi Vasudev was a Siddha—a divine saint. After many years of worship, he attained superhuman powers using which he created a Yantra that could provide unlimited powers to its worshipper. When I heard about that Yantra I wanted to have that as soon as I could. But Maharshi, however, found out about my intentions and he hid the Yantra. I continued to search for it and soon discovered where it was."

"So did you get it?" asked Pallavi.

"Yes, I attained the Yantra but incidentally a cardinal sin happened through me. I killed Maharshi accidentally while capturing the Yantra."

"What? You killed a divine saint?"

"Yes, it happened with my own hands and I regretted as soon as it happened. I tried my best to save his life but he passed away. I was engulfed in remorse and guilt. In order to pay penance I took with me Maharshi's only daughter."

"Maharishi's daughter? Where is she?"

"You are the daughter of the great Maharishi Vasudev."

Rudrasen stood with his head bowed down. Everyone went quiet and looked in the direction of Pallavi.

Pallavi was taken aback. The person whom she called father her entire life turned out to be her real father's killer. Everything seemed to shatter apart in front of her. It seemed like an unforgiveable lie. Rudrasen's love was not an unconditional love but was his remorse. It was his way of paying for his guilt. She burst into tears. She tried to stop herself falling apart but she couldn't. She wanted to run out of the chamber, in fact out of the royal palace, far away from Rudrasen. She tried to stop herself falling apart like this but couldn't and she ran out of the chamber. Rudrasen wanted to go after her but a sweet and soft voice stopped him, "You have been mistaken Rajan, I did not die."

All eyes turned in the direction of the voice to find a snow white haired old man standing there.

"Maharshi Vasudev!!" Rudrasen almost screamed with astonishment, "How is this possible? You were certainly dead."

"I was only as dead as you are alive Rajan. You will not understand the intriguing mysteries of life as life never dances in your breath and it never ceases to dance within me even on the cessation of breath" an enigmatic smile appeared on Maharshi Vasudev's face.

Meanwhile Shatvari and Shatrughan were also very surprised to see the old man there. He was the same holy sage who had met them in the cremation ground and had prophesied coming of the Great War.

"He is indeed a realized saint. I was such a fool. I was merely longing for the Yantra made by him when I had the direct access to the great sage himself. This is what they call being under the spell of Maya" thought Shatvari.

Rudrasen felt a little humiliated at saint's remark but by now he had become accustomed to humiliation. He was finding his self-esteem quite insignificant in front of the magnitude of the confounding events unfolding before him.

"But I don't understand that if you were alive then why you let me keep your Yantra and endured separation from your beloved daughter."

"Don't tax your mind trying to understand the cause of every single wave rising in this vast ocean of awareness. Human mind is too small to grasp it. The only possible way is to transcend the limitations of mind and establish a deep connection with the ocean itself. The mystery itself is the doorway to understanding. But as you have asked I will tell you that you were so stone-hearted that realization of a grave sin and presence of a daughter in your life was necessary to soften it to some extent."

"But weren't you afraid that the magical Yantra could be misused?"

"Rajan I always knew that you will not worship the Yantra. No knowledge ever descends until the seeker is prepared. Actually, there are no powers within the Yantra. All powers are within you only. Divine and devil both are within you. The Yantra is merely a tool to help you discover and realize the dormant divine powers within you. But it demands a certain level of preparedness from the worshipper. A certain level of awareness and realization of one's own divinity. So only the worthy person can ever worship and benefit from the Yantra and you were never going to be worthy of this. But time has prepared Shatvari to invoke her dormant divine powers with help of the Yantra."

"But Rajan, were you not ever tempted to worship the Yantra to unleash its powers?" asked Shatvari.

"No because he came to know that the Yantra was cursed." Said the Maharshi.

"Cursed!"

"Yes, cursed to keep it beyond the reach of selfish people. Only those can worship the Yantra who have risen above selfishness and are ready to make sacrifices in the service of humanity. Who are willing to sacrifice their most loved thing or person. This is what I meant by the preparedness."

Shatvari drew back a step and got lost in thoughts. She only had Shatrughan. She couldn't even give her a healthy childhood. All his life he roamed like a Chandaal in *Shamshan* amidst the stench of rotten corpses and flesh picking dogs. Now when his life had a hope and glimmer for betterment how can she think of sacrificing him?

Maharshi Vasudev grasped her internal conflict. He said in a compassionate tone, "I am sorry that I cannot take the curse back. But I can assure you that whatever will happen will be for the ultimate good only."

Shatrughan also came forward and said, "You don't worry about me, mother. I will happily lay down my life to save my motherland any time. It will be a matter of pride and honour for both of us. You have spent your entire life to attain that Yantra for the betterment of our society. Now you have the opportunity. And at what a small cost. Please do not hesitate even for a minute. Observe your *Dharma* and be a *Samarsiddha*!"

Shatvari tightly embraced her son. Her eyes were wet but she held the tears inside lest they should make her look weak. She held him as if this was the last time being spent with him.

"I am ready. Get me the Yantra," Shatvari looked at Rudrasen with a resolute focus.

"Chandaals have made peace with King Rudrasen. Their chief Shatvari is going to worship a Yantra to invoke divine powers," one of the spies informed Indrajit.

"This is an alarming news. This can ruin our plans. We have to stop this from happening at any cost," thundered Indrajit.

"But how, commander?"

"We will attack Shripur as soon as possible. We will rob them of any time to prepare for that Yantra worship. Let's go to Kashi and order our armies to commence to attack."

All men pulled the reins of their horses and galloped away, but they were unaware of two sets of ears listening to their plan. They were Vaishali and Aniruddha.

"Oh...did you hear that Aniruddha?" asked Vaishali.

"Yes, they are going to attack us in a matter of days. We will have to stop them anyhow. But how can we stop an army?" Aniruddha was visibly shocked.

"Wait...let me think...there is a person who can help us."

"Who?"

"Come with me." Vaishali took Aniruddh's hand and walked away.

"How do you expect a recluse like me to stop a giant North Kosala army?" asked Damodar.

"Maybe not yourself directly, but you know a person who surely can," replied Vaishali.

"Who?"

"Amodini."

Just the mention of her name startled Damodar. He looked away deep into the jungle.

"How do you know about Amodini?"

"I heard all the conversation between you and Aniruddha's father, seth Ambrish. After hearing your sad tale I was curious to know more about you and your wife. When I probed further I found out that there was a courtesan named Amodini behind all this. Being a courtesan myself, I wanted to know more about her and I found that after severing bonds with you she went to North Kosala's capital city Kashi. There, too, her beauty's fragrance reached the royal gardens sooner than she had expected. King Prasannjeet fell for her beauty. All these years she has ruled the hearts of not only the king but the lords and mighty knights in Kashi. She garners respect as much as a queen in that kingdom. If she wants, she can stall this war."

"But why would she listen to me after all these years and after all that which happened between us?"

"I hope she still has soft feelings for you. She will definitely help you."

"If you say so, I will try. If I can be of any use in stopping this inhuman war, I will do anything to achieve that."

Amodini's beauty was as amorous as it had been earlier. Fresh and keen buds on a spring morning. She had conquered the effects of age.

"I always knew Acharya ji that you will become a yogi once you go away from me. Welcome to my parlour!" Amodini stood up and walked towards Damodar as soon as he entered her theater.

"Amodini, I am no longer an Acharya or a Yogi today. I have come as a beggar at your doorstep. I have come hoping to get something from you."

"I poured all my youth in your heart, you just could not handle it. Ask for anything that I can give you."

"As you might have come to know Amodini that North Kosala is going to attack South Kosala. Millions of innocent lives will be lost. You can help stop it."

"You have turned a Yogi, I am sure now. I hoped that you'd ask for some share of unspent love finally."

"Amodini this is not the time for your taking things lightly. We have to think about it seriously. I hope you still remember your bonds with South Kosala and Shripur. I am sure you don't want to see it ruined by your present masters."

"That has been the pity; you always thought I am only a non-serious courtesan. Anyway, tell me what I must do to help you in this regard?"

"You will have to persuade your king to stall this war."

"I can try."

"That will be such a great favour Amodini."

"I hope this time you remember to pay it back. You have a bad habit of forgetting."

Damodar and Amodini smiled at each other and for a moment they both forgot the years that had created vast vacuums between them.

"I am pouring one more for you your Highness," asked Amodini while sitting arms in arms with the king, Prasannjeet. He was a middle-aged man tall, of a robust constitution, royal countenance, and a beard cut in sleek fashion.

"You are trying to sedate me with alcohol today. Leave some work left for your eyes," replied the king softly caressing Amodini's face.

"My eyes have long ago stopped intoxicating you Rajan. Else why would I need to serve you wine?"

"Is that so...I will stop drinking wine from now on if you say so." King Prasannjeet moved close enough towards Amodini's face and felt the warmth and moistness of her lips.

"Not possible. I know you...you won't be able to live without wine even for a day."

"If you want, take my word for it. I can make a vow." King pulled Amodini closer towards him.

"Let it be…leave it. What would I get from making you quit wine? Neither am I your wife nor is wine your mistress."

"Then what are you after...ask."

"Will you?"

"'You don't trust a king's words?"

"Have another cup of wine."

"This is what you want?"

"No, but I know what I want you won't be able to grant while remaining sober."

"I have given you my word. Whatever is within my power, I will sacrifice on your feet."

"Don't get excited I am not going to ask for the stars from the sky. Too old for that," said Amodini and cast a playful look at the king and then continued in a sombre tone. "I want from you a promise, your Highness that you will not initiate an attack on South Kosala."

King Prasannjeet leaned back and looked at her with expressions of surprise.

"What are you saying? You shouldn't interfere in political decisions I beg you."

"See this is what I meant. It'll be impossible for you to keep your word."

"Don't play with my emotions like this. Ask anything—unlimited riches, prosperity, and abundance of all kinds. If you want I will win and surrender South Kosala at your feet."

"What would I do with a torn apart and destroyed South Kosala? I have old bonds with South Kosala and Shripur. The city where my anklets echoed in past will turn into a theater of deathly moans and cries. I cannot see the destruction of lives into rotten corpses and empty grounds into cemeteries. Your

Highness I have given you my entire youth, can you not grant me this wish."

Silence prevailed between the two.

"Give me some time to think. Such decisions cannot be taken in hurry and in moments of excitement." His head was bowed low, worry lines emerged on the forehead and he was engrossed in a dilemma.

"Time is of essence my king. Please do remember this."

"Our respected and brave king has lost his mind. That courtesan has played with his good sense," said Indrajit to the chief minister of North Kosala. With clenched fists and acute signs of desperation on his face he added, "We have been preparing and waiting for this opportunity for years. Now when we have a clear path, he is tied in love for a court dancer."

"But it's a royal order and we have to obey it," replied the chief minister.

"Whose order? Our king's or that dancer's?"

"Commander, she is not just a dancer. She garners a lot of respect in the kingdom."

"But her act will not garner any respect from me or any other self-respecting citizen. She is going to destroy us all."

"Then what do you suggest?"

"We cannot stall this attack. What will we tell our army and soldiers—that our king's mistress thinks otherwise? That our king has become a coward in order to win his mistress's love."

"So you are suggesting to not follow the king's command?"

"A weak and coward king fixated only with his emotions of lust and selfishness has no right to command my army. My army is with me. This attack will happen at all cost."

"Think hard and think seriously on it commander. You might have to regret this, if at all you get the chance to do that."

"It would be our king who will be regretting, not me. All I am doing is to correct his mistake. I am going to launch an invasion over South Kosala. If anyone tries to stop the army will revolt."

"My fellow soldiers, that moment of destiny for which we have waited for innumerable years has finally arrived. South Kosala's forces have been battered by the Chandaal revolt. This is the opportunity to break them down and conquer them. Is my army ready for the invasion?" Indrajit asked his army.

"Yes we are," everyone roared in unison.

"What are we waiting for then? Let's proceed and post our victory flags in South Kosala. Victory is ours," Indrajit was pumped up and raring to go.

"Stop. Wait a moment." A female voice came from behind Indrajit. It was Amodini. She came forward and stood between the army and Indrajit.

"Has your commander told you that your king has ordered to stop this attack? I am sure not. Your commander is revolting against your king," said Amodini.

"So our king can't even come and face his army now? He sends a woman to convey his message," said Indrajit.

"I am sure commander you have lost all respect for your king, but please do use a proper language when you are addressing a king of this huge army. His Highness is not well. The news of his most trusted commander going rogue has shocked him deeply."

"This is all because of you. You turned a lion into a coward sheep. But I will not let my soldiers go the same way."

"What you are going to do is not an act of courage. You are going to attack on a weakened army still counting the corpses of its dead soldiers."

"I call upon my army not to pay any attention to sweet talks of this dancer. We all know that there is some difference between a war and job of dancing. She has entrapped our king and making him dance on her tunes. She wants us to do the same and destroy our kingdom."

"Commander, don't be arrogant. You might not be, but North Kosala's army is still loyal to its king."

"Which king—the one whose own loyalty has shifted towards a courtesan from his people?"

"Commander..." Amodini shouted at the top of her voice.

The army was now in a strange dilemma. On one hand, there was their commander asking them to commence and on the other, stood a royal courtesan bearing their king's message to stop the war. The army had prepared for years for this opportunity. Any message that asked them to stall their progression seemed cowardly interference. A large part of the army moved on with Indrajit.

Amodini was left with a small column of loyal soldiers who watched their peers move along with their revolting commander.

The Yantra was made of an unknown metal and it emitted soft divine white light. Shatvari sat in front of the Yantra in *Siddhasana* posture to worship it and invoke her dormant powers. She was slowly reciting some mantras in low voice with her eyes fixed at Yantra. Chandaal army waited outside for her ritual to finish. A small unit headed by Mekal's commander Ranveer was posted at Shripur's Brahma Gate. The remaining South Kosala soldiers guarded other entrances. They all awaited the North Kosala attack with nervousness.

Indrajit's army had already reached the outskirts of Shripur and they gathered outside the Brahma Gate for final strategic instructions. Seated on a white horse, Indrajit turned towards his army and said, "Surround the fort from all around. We will attack all the gates simultaneously. Attack."

The thunderous order to attack rushed North Kosala army into ravenous flurry. They pounced towards the gates and a full-fledged attack was in motion. Mekal and South Kosala soldiers were far too less in numbers to pose any threat to the marching North Kosala invaders. They romped their way through the weak resistance and entered Shripur. Peaceful scenes turned to chaos and brutal madness. People hid in their houses and prayed to their dearest gods. Chandaals still waited for Shatvari's ritual to get over. The attackers were at the top of their confidence and marched on forward towards the royal forte of King Rudrasen.

Suddenly, they were attacked from behind and that took them by surprise. The ray of hope came in the form of the loyal North Kosala soldiers led by Amodini charging on a white elegant horse. Her majestic form and her loyal will to support her king deemed her battalion out of ordinary zeal and confidence. They were being led by an angelic diva and they felt no less than divine soldiers of justice. They baffled their revolting peers. The invading North Kosala army was surrounded from front by the South Kosala soldiers and from behind they confronted the loyal soldiers of their own king. A fierce battle was intensified.

Shatvari's mantra recital grew intense. She felt her body becoming lighter with every mantra. She felt as if floating in the air. Her body infused and absorbed the divine light from the Yantra and started to emit light. Her face was glowing with golden spiritual aura. She bowed down to touch the ground with her head and offered her gratitude to Maharshi Vasudev and the magical Yantra.

As she came out, it was evident that her ritual was successful. A loud deafening roar erupted "Jai Mahakali, Jai Bhadrakali."

Shatvari raised her hand and said, "Today Mahakali is with us. Victory is ours. Jai Mahakali."

The Chandaals, led by Shatvari moved in the direction of the king's fort to destroy the enemies.

Amodini fought with courage and determination. She was not a trained warrior, only a dancer with delicate movements. She saw somebody running with naked sword towards her. It was Indrajit on horseback galloping towards her with the cruelest of intentions. She clutched the reins of her horse tighter with her left hand and held her sword even tighter in her right. Indrajit came closer and made a wild slash at her. She swayed back to save herself. He again attacked and this time she took it on her sword. The clatter of metal on metal thundered her heart but she held on. Indrajit kicked his horse and quickly turned around and made an enormous heave to slash her throat.

Amodini closed her eyes out of fear at the certain death dancing in front of her. She heard the swords clattering and a loud moan of more than one person. As she opened her eyes she saw Indrajit lying on the ground with a sword stuck in his abdomen. She realised that the person who took the deathly blow from Indrajit to save her life was also lying on the ground with a deep gash on his right shoulder. It was Damodar. As she was about to jump off the horse to go to Damodar she saw Indrajit fiercely running towards Damodar carrying a sword.

"Damodar!" She cried at the top of her voice. But it was too late. Indrajit had already hit Damodar with his sword. It was almost certain that the mighty blow would kill Damodar. But with a lightning speed a snow white haired old man jumped in to shield Damodar. He took the fatal blow on his body. He was critically injured. Indrajit had also fallen down to never get up again. Damodar too had sustained some injuries.

Shatvari saw it happening with bewildered eyes. On one side was her old soulmate Damodar. Shatvari had never imagined that she would meet him in the middle of warzone in such a wounded state. On the otherside was the critically wounded old man who had saved Damodar's life. He was no one but Maharshi Vasudev himself. Shatvari rushed towards the Maharshi and touching his feet she said, "You are not only a holy saint. You are an angel. After all why you risked your life to save Damodar."

Maharshi indicated Shatvari to come closer. Shatvari held his head on her lap and heard him saying, "Shatvari do not waste your time trying to understand cause of every odd event. What is more important is to understand the message that it conveys. You must understand that you have always held Damodar dearest to your heart. But your hatred for all was so intense that it shrouded the very love from which it was conceived. And hence you ceased to feel the deep love you have always had for Damodar. Damodar was to become the victim of my curse and I could have saved him only by giving up my own life. This is *Karma*."

He then spread both of his arms towards Damodar and Shatvari. Collecting all his energy draining out fast, he joined their hands and peacefully breathed his last. He had a divine smile on his lifeless face. Both, Damodar and Shatvari bowed their heads at the feet of the pious old man. Tears were flowing from their eyes.

Shatvari took Damodar in her arms and burst into tears. All she could say was utter his name like a mantra. Amodini stood up and took a step back.

"Shatvari...isn't it a poetic justice that we meet again in this battlefield. Please forgive me for all my sins. I realise that all the suffering and humiliation you had to undergo were because of my lust. It was my lust for Amodini's beauty and youthful charms that caused our separation. Now the same Amodini has been instrumental in rejoining us. This is called karmic cycle. We accumulate debt through our *Karma* and pay them back through our *karma*. Life is like this," said Damodar.

Damodar then looked up at Amodini and said, "I hope I have this time paid your debt Amodini. Now you can't say that I forget."

Damodar had never seen Amodini in this state-dressed as a warrior with tear-filled eyes and blood stained badly wounded body.

"Where have you been all this time?" asked Shatvari with moist eyes.

"Shatvari, all of my life I was only searching myself. I had a deep vacuum within me which always made me feel restless. When I found your love it felt like it was all that I was looking for. But soon it didn't feel enough. Then I tried to fill that void with Amodini's beauty and charms. But the void still remained unfilled. It even took away your love from me. Finally, I realised that one has to fill his inner void himself. More we try to fill it with the help of someone else the bigger it becomes, because everyone of us is carrying the same void within. We need to fulfil ourselves by finding our purpose in life and accomplishing it by our own deeds. Shatvari now do not waste your time. Go and accomplish the victory you have been preparing for. You have to win this war, you have to bring a new dawn to this world mired in darkness!"

Shatvari put her moist lips on Damodar's to feel the same magic she had felt years ago. Then she turned around and started to walk towards the middle of the war zone. Damodar and Amodini watched her valiant gait with eyes filled with glimmer and joy.

□□□

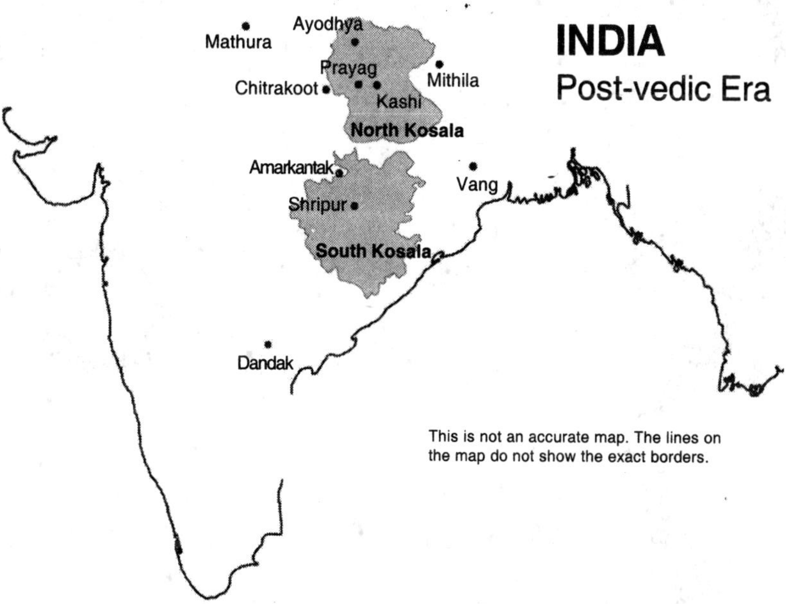

INDIA
Post-vedic Era

This is not an accurate map. The lines on the map do not show the exact borders.